LOOT FOR THE TAKING

INSPIRED BY REAL EVENTS

Don Levers

Tellwell Talent
www.tellwell.ca

ISBN
978-1-77302-715-9 (Hardcover)
978-1-77302-714-2 (Paperback)
978-1-77302-716-6 (eBook)

To my wife, Deb
Thank-you for helping me
to finally get this done.

And to my daughters
Jennifer and Natalie.

CHAPTER 1

April 1987

Carlos Ortega stood on the deck of the *Neptune Pearl*. The ship was a bit of an anomaly, deviating from the normal merchant ship colour scheme of black above the Plimsoll line and rust-coloured paint down to the bottom of the hull. While there were many other colours on ships sailing the seas, the unusual thing about the Pearl was that it was entirely grey in colour, giving it more of a military look. Its high forecastle and squared off stern added to the military illusion. The rust stains that streaked the sides of the hull from the anchors' hawseholes and various other places along the hull stood out against the lighter paint, making the ship look older than she was.

The engines still ran smoothly, burning its fuel cleanly, without leaving a plume of black smoke trailing behind it as it entered the Vancouver Harbour under the Lions Gate Bridge. Carlos marveled at the majestic entrance to the port. They had been at sea six days since their last port of call, and it was a real pleasure to once again smell the aroma of something other than salty air and diesel fumes. He took a deep breath and was sure he could pick out the scent of the fir trees that lined the shores and the thousands of flowers that were blooming on this beautiful spring day.

"It's more beautiful than the captain told us it would be!" Carlos exclaimed to his two companions. The sun's rays were

5

reflecting off the calm waters of Burrard Inlet and the buildings that surrounded it like thousands of tiny diamonds. The freighter was loaded with containers from around the southern hemisphere. The ship's manifest showed that the contents included coffee from the mountains of Colombia, spirits from Argentina and hardwood lumber from the disappearing rainforests of Brazil. The rough-cut lumber was wrapped and banded then stuffed into the containers to protect the high-value product from the elements. To the captain's relief, they had not encountered any environmentalists on this trip.

It is not as easy as it once was to get aboard a ship as part of a crew. Crew sizes are very small and this container ship only carried twenty-six men. Carlos and his companions, Pedro Afonso and Emilio Costa, had joined as deck hands when it arrived in port at Buenaventura, Colombia, some four hundred kilometers south of Medellin. They had spent enough money to ensure that they would be taken on as replacements for three members of the original crew who surprisingly did not show up when the ship was ready to leave port. Prior to this trip, they had never been to sea, but all had quickly learned their respective jobs and after the four-week journey they all felt like old salts.

Finally, there it was, laid out in all its splendour. The mountain peaks to the north known as The Lions seemed to lie there, as if watching their pride to ensure no harm would come to their city. The skyline of Vancouver rivals any of the great cities in the world. Once described as a world within a city because of its diverse ethnic population, it had always been a world class city. A standing that had been reinforced a year earlier, when people of the world descended on the city to see Expo 86, which hosted over twenty-two million people at the fair's False Creek site between May and October. In 1987, Vancouver still boasted the second largest Chinatown in North America, second only to San Francisco.

The ship passed under the Lions Gate suspension bridge. It by no means compared to the Golden Gate Bridge, but then the Golden Gate was not built with private funds like the Lions Gate had been. The vivid colours of all the sailboats reminded the three men of the carnivals in their home town of La Dorada in the high mountains of Colombia. Bright blue buildings, with mountains of yellow sulphur, the red hulls of the many ships anchored in the harbour and the light and dark greens of the trees in the parks beside the shores all added to the kaleidoscope of colours on which they feasted their eyes.

The extra cargo that they had put aboard when the ship was in Colombia would ensure the three of them would be able to retire in comfort here in Vancouver, or almost anywhere else in the world for that matter.

Emilio was standing beside Carlos and began to snap his fingers quietly in an almost compulsive manner. He rocked back and forth on his feet in a nervous state.

"Is everything still okay?" he asked neither of his companions in particular.

"Yes, I checked again this morning to ensure that the seal was still unbroken," said Carlos, shaking his head that, despite having checked their container each day of their voyage, Emilio still had to be reassured two or three times a day.

"And this guy Chang, you are sure that everything will go smoothly with him?" requested Emilio.

"Yes! Yes! Yes! Everything is fine. All I have to do now is call Chang," lied Carlos.

Chang was the most powerful member of the triads that handled most of the heroin that was smuggled onto the west coast of North America. Carlos had gotten his name from a friend of a friend. They were now relying on him for their pot of gold at the end of the rainbow.

Upon docking, Canadian customs officers boarded the ship and scrutinized everyone's papers. Their passports were impeccable fakes. The custom agents said they would be allowed shore leave so long as they were back on board in time to sail, otherwise, a warrant would be issued for their capture. They would then be deported back to their home country at their own expense. This was the third time that Carlos and his friends had gone through this inspection procedure during this trip and it was no longer an unnerving event.

Carlos assigned Emilio the job of keeping track of which aisle their special container ended up in after it was removed from the ship. This was no simple task. Located in the heart of Vancouver, the Vanterm facility is the storage section at one of North America's premier container ports. Using gantry cranes the size of buildings, up to two dozen containers an hour could be removed from ships arriving daily from around the world and set down in a staging area the size of twenty-three football fields and able to store over four thousand containers. Emilio's job was made easier by the fact that the container area was marked with huge grid lines. Each container was placed in a specific sector marked out with grid coordinates. In some places, containers were stacked up to four high and seven wide.

While Emilio left to take care of his task, Carlos said to Pedro, "Can you smell that?"

"Smell what? The rotting bilges and diesel fumes, or the putrid stench of the crap coming from the kitchen exhaust? I sure could go for a home cooked meal."

"No. You know what I smell, my complaining friend? This city was so clean looking as we entered the harbour that I was sure I could smell flowers. But what I smell now is Money. It won't be long now till we breathe in the aroma of the cash we will be getting. That much money has a scent of its very own."

Hours later, darkness had settled on the city, but the wharf area had enough lights to make one think it was still daytime. It was ten o'clock, and the lights of the city, bridges and wharves sparkled on the almost calm surface of the water. Clouds had been rolling onto the mainland since early evening, and the weather report was calling for rain. Showers of sparks from a welder working on another vessel cascaded to the water like sparklers. Emilio and Pedro were standing at the railing on the main deck, absorbing the sights and sounds of the marvelous city laid out before them.

"Vancouver might be even more beautiful at night," said Pedro

The welder on the next ship had finished grinding his welds. Pedro and Emilio just stood in the relative silence listening to the now-familiar noises of the harbour. Waves lapping against the side of the ship, small boats making their way from here to there. Like the waves on the shore, the sounds of a harbour were universal. Only the local language really changes; although, if one listened long and hard enough, they could hear the spoken language of most nations on earth.

Carlos strolled up the stairs, meeting his two friends at the railing. "The container is being moved from where it was set this afternoon. I was able to find out where it will be put before being taken to the customs inspection area. We go over there," he said, pointing to where the container would be moved. "We get into the container, get the bags, then we'll have plenty of time to make our meeting with Chang."

"You got in touch with him okay then?" asked Emilio nervously.

"Smooth as silk. Chang is going to meet us on the causeway right at the entrance to the dock area," answered Carlos.

"I think we should get to the area a little early, before Chang arrives, so that we get a better feel for the area before the drop," suggested Pedro.

"I'll let the captain know we won't be back until just before they start to load the ship the day after tomorrow. I'll also see if he will give us an advance for our shore leave. We might need it." Carlos chuckled as he walked away to find the captain.

Access to the container area was not difficult, as most of the security was at the main gates. They had been given clearance by the customs agents to take shore leave, and it was a long walk across the tarmac to the where the exit gates and building where the customs agents were located. The main thrust of the security was to make sure that all containers were logged in or out as they entered or exited the terminal, and management of the facility had no fear of containers being secretly loaded onto any ship berthed at the wharves. This meant there was no protocol in place to prevent sailors from walking among the canyons of containers. It was not something the Port Authority had ever considered to be an issue.

Pedro and Emilio left the freighter, heading off in search of their container. The container that held the key to their future: two duffle bags, each holding thirty-four kilos of pure, uncut South American cocaine, direct from the fields of Colombia.

CHAPTER 2

It had taken Carlos and Pedro over three years to amass their hoard of cocaine by taking insignificant amounts from hundreds of shipments. The value of cocaine in Vancouver was around twenty-five thousand dollars per kilo. This meant that the bags were worth over eight hundred and fifty thousand dollars each. The total estimated street value of their product would be over three million bucks, not accounting for the fact that the pure cocaine was usually cut with a variety of other substances like baking soda, sugar, vitamin C and lidocaine, which would raise the street yield even higher. The operations on the acres of the container facility were incredible to watch. The huge gantry cranes moved along their tracks, picking up the twenty- or forty-foot containers. Shipping units were shuffled around until the correct container was found, then they were laid onto specially designed terminal trailers called bomb trucks, because they looked like the carts used to load munitions onto bombers. These special dollies were used to move the containers around the terminal. Once delivered to their destinations in the yard, large, rubber-tired, top-picking fork lifts would take them off the bomb carts and either stack them for storage or load them onto road trailers so they could continue on to their final destinations.

When Carlos joined the others, he led them past aisles of containers. The names on the sides conjured up thoughts of ports and countries around the world: American President Lines,

Manchester, Nippon Liner System, Japan Line, and Hyundai Lines from Korea. Scattered among the containers were other large bulk items like parts for the huge ore dump trucks used in the mining industries of British Columbia. The containers were stacked up to four high in some places. There were dozens of aisles, each over four hundred feet long. From the ship to the position of their container was seven hundred feet.

It was 11:20 p.m. when they finally went to the row in which their container had been set. Very soon they would be unable to get at it. The Zee Line container number 1143677 was the top one in a stack of three, it's roof twenty-four feet above ground level. There was a single unit sitting in front of their stack, it's roof eight feet below the access doors to their container. At any time, additional containers could be placed above this one, blocking the doors. Or another could be placed atop their container, eliminating access to its roof. Either scenario would make getting into their unit that much more difficult. "Emilio, you go to the corner. Let us know when the next load is coming."

Emilio headed off to the corner, snapping his fingers nervously as he walked away. "When are you going to tell him, man?" asked Pedro.

"As soon as the deal in finished, he's too nervous as it is. Did you notice that he started with the finger snapping already?" said Carlos, as he boosted Pedro up onto the roof of the single container that had been placed in the line directly ahead of their stack. Pedro then started to scale their stack of containers like a freestyle mountain climber. Now was not the time to take a tumble to the asphalt below. The points that he could get hold of would have made any serious rock climber shudder, but he managed to make his way up to their container without incident. While he balanced on a precarious toehold, he clung to the handles of the container's doors. Removing a pair of pliers from his pocket, he cut the customs seal. By the time the agents discovered it had been cut, they would be long gone.

Pedro unlatched the doors, then continued his climb. He clambered to the top of their unit which had him standing over twenty-four feet off the ground. He laid down and reached over the end of the unit to swing the doors open just wide enough to allow him to swing down inside.

The rain that had been threatening all evening began to fall, making the execution of this task on the water-slicked metal more difficult. It started with a slow steady tapping on the roofs of the metal containers. Pedro lowered himself in front of the opening, then swung inward and dropped onto the floor. He found the bags right where they had been stashed, then tossed the first one down to Carlos. He was set to toss the second one when he heard Emilio's high-pitched whistle of warning.

Carlos had also heard the shrill signal. "Pedro! Pull the doors closed quickly!" Carlos grabbed the first bag and hid between the containers.

As he stood getting soaked in what was now a torrential downpour, he prayed the top loader would not come down his aisle to deposit its load. His prayers for a safe, uneventful evening seemed to be answered; the forklift passed his aisle, going to the far side to unload.

Carlos yelled up to the container, "Pedro ... Pedro, let's go!"

Pedro pushed the door open. Carlos was waiting below for the other bags. The second bag had the rest of the drugs. The third held weapons and extra clothing. The two bags were tossed down, landing with a splash in a newly-formed puddle that was growing by the second as the drenching rain continued to pound down. Pedro managed to pull himself back onto the roof of the container, then pulled the doors closed as tightly as he could.

Pedro began to descend the same way he had climbed up. The rain continued to come down, severely limiting his vision. Water soaked his hair, streaming down his face into his eyes then ran off his chin like a leaky faucet. His fingers were numb with cold, causing him to lose his grip at the same time his foot came off its toe hold. Pedro plunged the last five feet to the roof of the first container. The corrugated design of the roof hampered his landing, and his feet skidded on the wet steel, causing him to lose his balance, fall on his back, and roll over the side of the container. He almost halted his fall, but there was nothing on the roof to grab and he plunged the additional eight feet to the ground. He managed to land feet first and would have been fine, except that one foot landed on a short piece of discarded wood. The four-by-four rolled as he landed on it, and his right ankle bowed then snapped.

The sound of the ankle fracturing was unmistakable. Carlos heard it and winced in sympathy of the pain his friend would feel. Pedro crumpled to the ground, rolled over on his back, cursing the Almighty at this turn of events and crying out in agony. Emilio heard the screams and came running to see what had happened. Pedro was sprawled in a large puddle of water. Clenching both his fists and his teeth, he rocked back and forth, holding his injured ankle.

Emilio looked from Pedro to Carlos.

"He slipped off the roof. Landed his foot on that damn piece of wood," Carlos picked up the four-by-four, hurling it with both hands down the steel valley. It clanged off walls, landing harmlessly twenty-five feet away.

"Come on, Carlos. We can't wait here, there'll be another forklift by any minute. We have to move him," said Emilio.

"Where will we take him?"

"There are some large dump boxes turned upside down just across from where I was. We can take him there to be out of the rain for a few minutes at least."

"Okay you take the bags over to the boxes first, then come give me a hand. We'll move him together."

"Right!" said Emilio. He picked up the bags, putting one over each shoulder then picked up the third bag which held their weapons, heading back to the dry refuge of the dump box.

Emilio came back from the dump box. Huffing and puffing, telling Carlos that they wouldn't be able to get across the yard yet as there was another forklift coming.

"Okay, let's just move down one row, wait for him to finish this stack then we can cross the yard."

The forklift arrived, executing the placement of the final container in the row, then began to head away for another. The lift came to a sudden stop right in front of the gap where the Colombians had taken refuge. The inside cab light switched on and they could see the driver reach to the dash of the cab.

"He's seen us!" Emilio whispered hoarsely. "He's going for his radio."

They watched closely, not sure what they would do now. The driver eased back from the dash holding a pack of cigarettes in his hand. He removed a smoke from the deck, lit it and took a deep drag. He threw the pack back on the dash, switched off the cab light, and then departed back to the main terminal area for yet another container.

They carried Pedro across the driveway, ducking under the open end of the upside-down dump box. The eighty-foot-high lamp standards, complete with six pods of sodium lamps, allowed enough light to filter under the box to see. Their eyes soon became accustomed to the dimness. They were out of the rain, but little rivers of water still ran across the dry pavement under the heavy steel plate. Beneath their steel shelter, unlike in the thin-walled container, there was no sound from the rain, but the slope of the inverted box allowed water to run off the corners in a continuous stream.

"We have lost a lot of time," said Carlos. Were probably four hundred and fifty yards from our destination. "Emilio, get the guns out and check them."

Emilio unzipped one of the bags and removed the extra clothes, which had been wrapped around their weapons. As he unwrapped the guns, he handed dry clothes to Pedro and Carlos.

They all changed and Emilio passed around their weapons. He carried a Heckler and Koch VP pistol, Carlos held an old German Luger he'd taken during a fight in Colombia and Pedro's weapon of choice was a Spanish made Llama. They all checked to ensure that their clips were full. All three weapons used nine-millimetre ammo. Carlos' weapon had an eight-round clip and Pedro and Emilio both had nine rounds in theirs. Emilio also removed a famous Israeli Uzi, which with its wooden stock measured a mere eighteen inches. He inserted a thirty-two-round clip. Two clips were taped together inverse of each other to allow a quick exchange when the magazine was emptied.

Carlos checked the time. "Twelve fifteen."

Pedro and Carlos had discussed how they would handle their rendezvous with Chang. Pedro would now guard their rear while Emilio and Carlos made the exchange.

They left for the drop at twelve thirty.

Pedro could put no weight on the injured foot at all. He wrapped one arm around each of their shoulders while Carlos and Emilio each slung one of the bags of cocaine over their necks. Pedro had the Uzi slung over his. They were in the middle of the roadway when a forklift rounded the corner with yet another container. The three of them shuffled between the rows, waiting impatiently for the driver to finish and move off.

Once the forklift passed, they picked up Pedro and headed off to the main gate area. It was a struggle, but they managed to make it to the causeway without further incident.

CHAPTER 3

The instructions had been to go up the stairs to the causeway. They really didn't expect trouble, but it was decided that Pedro would take a position on one of the benches in an enclosed viewing area that allowed people to see what was taking place in the warehouse below.

After a short wait, they heard footsteps coming from the far end of the causeway. The three Colombians looked around once again. Carlos and Emilio stood and picked up the duffle bags. "Good luck," said Pedro as the other two began to walk toward the centre of the causeway, leaving him to watch their backs. He removed the Uzi's magazine, rechecked it then inserted it back into the weapon.

As the two men proceeded toward the far end of the causeway, they both put their weapons into the waistbands of their pants. The lighting was not very good, with dim bulbs in wire enclosures ten to fifteen feet apart. They could make out the shapes of three men as they approached the middle of the causeway. As they closed the gap they could tell the centre figure was considerably taller than the other two. The closer they got, the more nervous Emilio became. He began to snap his fingers again. With twenty feet separating them, the three men stopped abruptly. Carlos raised his arm to Emilio's chest preventing from advancing any further. There was a tense silence before anyone spoke.

The tallest of the three spoke first: "I believe you have something for me, Mr. Ortega, isn't it?" The man's English was impeccable, with only a very slight accent.

Carlos took one step forward. "Mr. Chang?"

"I am Chang," came the reply.

Now standing less than twenty feet in front of Mr. Chang, Ortega could tell there was something peculiar about the man. He recalled what he had heard about him: he had lost a lot of the pigmentation of his skin. He tried to remember what the very strange name of the condition was, but could not recall the medical term. The condition he suffered from made his skin look like a patchwork quilt. Even though Ortega was only able to see the man's face, it did have a strange effect.

Ortega began, "Señor Chang, please forgive me as my English is not so good."

Chang nodded and began in Spanish. "Not a problem, we can speak in Spanish if you prefer. Besides your beautiful language, I speak seven others, including three dialects of Chinese."

"Thank you, I would prefer Spanish. We have some excellent product for you. Sixty-eight kilos of it, pure and uncut. You have the money for us?"

"First we shall test the product. If it proves to be satisfactory, then we shall pay you the agreed upon one point seven million."

"No problem, señor Chang. You will see we have brought you only the finest product available from the hills of Colombia."

They tossed the bags down. Chang nodded to the man on his left. As he stepped forward, a knife shot out from the man's coat sleeve. Emilio jumped back, reaching behind his back to draw his pistol. Again from what seemed to be nowhere, the man on Chang's right produced a small machine pistol. A Czechoslovakian made Scorpion. The weapon measured just over ten and a half inches long, weighing a little over three pounds with a full twenty-round clip. It was one of the few machine pistols that could be fitted with a sound suppressor.

Emilio had seen these machine pistols in the past and he knew he would never get his HK from his waistband before he was cut down. In the viewing area, Pedro had stood on his good leg. As he looked around the corner from the viewing area, he was having trouble seeing what was going on. All he could make out was five figures standing in the middle of the causeway. "At least everyone's still standing," he said to himself.

Chang broke the silence. "Everyone just calm down. I think we must all be on edge tonight. Put the gun away," he cocked his head slightly to the right. "Tai Yang, it's going to be okay, just do as I say."

The machine pistol Tai Yang was carrying disappeared back up the baggy sleeve of his custom made trench coat. "They have been with me a long time," remarked Chang. "They are very good at what they do. As you can see, they provide me with excellent protection. They are one hundred percent loyal, and are prepared to take a bullet for me if necessary." He glanced at the man with the knife. "Sheng, please check the merchandise before we conclude our transaction with Mr. Ortega."

Sheng was carrying a small briefcase. Once he had set it down, he removed a glass tumbler, a miniature scale, a small spoon as well as a second vial containing simple bleach, which is often used as a testing agent to check the purity of cocaine.

Carlos bent down and opened the duffle bag. Tai Yang stepped forward, reached down the side of the bag and picked two bricks at random, taking them off to the side to test them. He set the bricks on the scale, which showed the weight of each was slightly over a kilogram because of the weight of the wrapping. Using the knife he had produced earlier, he cut through the heavy plastic and dug to the centre of the flakey, almost pure-white substance. Using the spoon to remove a sample, he put it to his nose to smell it. The smell test can vary considerably from different manufacturers, depending on how they cooked the original batch. Sheng seemed satisfied with the product's odour, so he proceeded with the rest of his testing.

He poured bleach from one of the vials of liquid into the glass tumbler. He then dropped a small amount of the powder into the bleach. He watched as the powder very slowly dissolved into the liquid. If the sample had been full of impurities, those impurities would have quickly fallen to the bottom of the glass. Sheng continued to watch as the powder formed mushroom-like white clouds in the bleach. Almost nothing dropped to the bottom of the glass. The haze within the glass was a milky white, almost ghostly looking. When he seemed satisfied with the first sample, he went through the same procedure with the second brick. They would do more testing on the product when they began to cut it prior to distribution. For now though, Sheng seemed more than satisfied with the product they were about to purchase.

Emilio had become more agitated as the minutes ticked on. His snapping began to increase in tempo and small beads of perspiration were now forming on his upper lip and forehead despite the cool weather. He looked at Chang, who seemed to be standing like a statue. The man was dressed in a light grey trench coat over a dark grey suit complemented by a bright red tie. Emilio noticed that Chang's black shoes seemed to gleam in the dim lights of the causeway.

With the inspection of the goods complete, Sheng moved back beside Chang. He bent down once again and counted the bricks in each of the bags and then replaced the first two cocaine bricks back in the duffle bag. With his part of the operation complete, Sheng put his testing equipment back in the briefcase then stood up beside his boss.

Chang did not bother to look at him. He raised his hand, and snapped his fingers.

A fourth man appeared from the shadows. He walked forward and stood next to Chang, holding two large briefcases. The fourth man stared at the Colombians but his peripheral vision picked up his boss' nod. He set the cases on the ground, leaned down and unsnapped the hasps. When the locks popped open he raised the lids, then turned the cases around to show the contents to the Colombians. Emilio's finger snapping stopped abruptly as he stared at the cases that were filled with packets of American money.

"Each of those briefcases contains eighty-five stacks of U.S. one-hundred dollar bills. I'm sure you would like to count it," said Chang.

Carlos, now trying to imitate Chang, just nodded to Emilio and snapped his head toward the cases filled with cash. The briefcases were slid forward and Emilio bent down to take a closer look at the cash. He counted out the stacks in each briefcase. Satisfied that the cases were not just full of some cut up paper, he looked up at Carlos when he completed his count.

"It's good?" asked Carlos.

"Very good," replied Emilio as he closed both cases, then stood up and took his place beside Carlos.

Chang told the fourth man to take the product they had just purchased back to the car. "I think this brings our little transaction to an end," said Chang in fluent Spanish. "I cannot tell you how pleasurable and profitable for me this evening has been. I am sure your bosses will be proud of the way you handled yourselves tonight."

"The pleasure has been all ours, señor," said Carlos.

"Have a pleasant journey home," replied Chang.

Carlos just smiled at Chang. Emilio picked up the briefcases and they began to leave. They had not taken ten steps when Chang spoke again. "Gentlemen, how rude of me. I forgot to mention to you that I spoke to your boss just last night. He told me that I was to give you his regards. He truly hopes that your trip here was enjoyable."

These words brought Carlos to a dead stop. It took Emilio two further steps to realize that his friend was no longer beside him.

"That's right," continued Chang, "I talked to him just last night, Mr. Ortega. He told me how you had decided to go into business for yourself."

Emilio was confused by what he was hearing. He turned back to face Carlos, immediately realizing that something was very wrong. Even in the poor light of the causeway, he could tell that Carlos looked ashen.

"What is it? Carlos, what's wrong?"

"Shit! We screwed up!"

"How? What do you mean we screwed up? We delivered the goods, we have the money, now let's just go."

"Pedro and I screwed up. Not you. Mr. Santoro did not send us here. Me and Pedro, this was gonna be our sale. We wanted you in on it with us."

"Mr. Santoro did not send us here, Carlos?"

"No. We've been skimming little bits of the stuff off the top, putting it away for years."

"Why didn't you tell me?"

"We were going to but we were afraid you would back out on us. We were going to tell you when we split up the money after it was all over."

Chang was still talking behind them. "So you see my friends, unlike the men who work for me, you have not been very loyal. Surely you must have known that such a large shipment of cocaine would be a surprise, especially when it had not been arranged by Mr. Santoro himself. I don't know how you got my name, but right from the start I have been somewhat wary of you, Mr. Ortega. It took me some time, but I was finally able to speak directly with Mr. Santoro last night. A very nice gentleman by the sounds of it. To say he was disappointed by your actions would be an understatement. He felt he had treated you all like sons. He was crushed by your disloyalty and betrayal."

Before Carlos slowly began to turn to face Chang, he whispered to Emilio. "I'm sorry I got you into this, but when I make my move, run like hell—don't stop or turn around for nothing."

Continuing his turn, Carlos took one of the cases from Emilio, set it on the ground then took the other from him with his left hand. At the same time his right moved slowly to the grip of the pistol in his waistband. Carlos sighed as he began to walk forward to where he had stood at the start of the exchange.

"Mr. Chang I'm sure we can work out something. How about we make a deal? You could have yourself some pretty cheap shit. We just give you back half the money. You advise Mr. Santoro that you took care of his little problem. You get a great deal, and we just ... disappear."

"Oh, I'm sorry, Mr. Ortega. I'm afraid that I have already made other arrangements. As for the shipment being cheap, you are correct. They say that a life can be taken as inexpensively as forty-five dollars in your country. Your Mr. Santoro was actually quite generous with you three. You should be flattered; you have a much higher price on your heads. You see, I get to keep both the shipment and the money anyway. So as good as it sounds, Mr. Ortega, your offer is just a bit too late."

Pedro realized that something had gone wrong with the exchange. He slowly hobbled forward, attempting to see or hear what was being said, but the voices were very low and muffled.

"I guess that's it then."

"I'm afraid so, Mr. Ortega. You see, unlike you I am a man of honour. Once I make a commitment, I follow through with it."

As Chang turned to leave, Tai Yang stepped into the void between him and Carlos, protecting his boss from any possible harm. "Goodbye, Mr. Ortega," Chang said very formally.

Tai Yang shook his arm slightly to release his machine pistol from the sleeve of his coat. Seeing the slight movement Carlos screamed "Now, Emilio!"

Emilio began to run. At the same time, Carlos hurled the briefcase toward Tai Yang, then tried to draw his Luger. It was a motion he would never complete. His finger was through the trigger guard, but in his haste to pull out the pistol, his finger snagged on the waistband of his pants.

Tai Yang's Scorpion began firing rounds before his arm was fully extended. The three-round burst sprayed diagonally from left to right. The first two missed Carlos, but the third hit him on the front of his thigh. The first round of the second burst was the kill shot. It struck the centre of Carlos' sternum, sending bullet and bone fragments though vital organs. The fifth shot hit Carlos in the right shoulder, with the next shots missing him entirely.

The force of the impact of the three connecting rounds pushed Carlos backwards, but he remained on his feet. He looked down at the quickly spreading stain on his chest, then without as much as a sigh he collapsed, all life gone from him before hitting the deck of the causeway.

Emilio was now zigging and zagging as he ran down the causeway. He reached to the back of his trousers to get his pistol as he ran. Pedro stood up straight as the shooting started, quite an accomplishment considering the pain he was in. The scene before him seemed to be playing out in stop-action, the muzzle flashes and smoke adding to this illusion. He heard Emilio scream at him but he could not react. Forgetting about his ankle, he tried to step forward and crumpled to the platform.

Tai Yang sprayed two more three-round bursts across the width of the hallway. None found their mark with Emilio. He exchanged clips, and let loose another salvo. This one would have ripped into Emilio if he was still standing, but he had slid in beside Pedro. He heard the whiz of bullets, then the metal twang as they ricocheted off the metal posts of the skywalk.

Emilio rolled onto his stomach, firing his own three-round burst from his Heckler and Koch. It forced Tai Yang to jump to the side of the causeway. Emilio tried to get Pedro to join him.

"Come on man, I'm sure Carlos is dead. We gotta get the hell out of here," he urged.

"I ain't goin' nowhere with this ankle. You get out. Go while you can. I'll try to cover you." Emilio dragged Pedro around the corner into the viewing area. Pedro peeked around the corner. He brought up the Uzi and pointed it down the causeway. "Go now."

Emilio shot another burst down the causeway, then ran back toward the stairwell they had climbed earlier, but instead of taking the stairs down, he continued further down the causeway. Tai Yang fired a full clip in Emilio's direction. The bullets missed him as he continued to run. Pulling out another clip, he hit the release for the empty one and then inserted the fresh one. The whole sequence took less than four seconds.

He fired another short burst. The rounds from this salvo going through the thin walls of the viewing area, shattering the wire-lined safety glass overlooking the warehouse. Another ripped up the fabric on the bench that Pedro had been resting on earlier. In the dim light, Tai Yang still hadn't noticed Pedro lying on the ground. He ran forward, firing as he advanced. One of the bullets pinged off a steel column and hit Pedro in his already damaged leg. The pain stabbed like a red-hot poker in his upper thigh. Pedro managed to block out the pain. He had to give Emilio more time to get away.

Tai Yang closed the gap. To ensure there was no chance of missing, Pedro waited for him to get closer before he opened up with the Uzi. When he judged that Tai Yang was less than twenty feet away, he rolled to his left and pressed his finger to the trigger. Nothing happened. Pedro had committed a deadly error: he had not advanced the safety selector when he last checked his mags. He now attempted to activate the selector switch, but was far too slow.

The smell of cordite filled the air and through the haze gunpowder smoke Tai Yang had seen the movement. Pedro was now laying on his back. Tai Yang stepped forward and kicked Pedro on the side of the head. The pain tore through his head, causing him to almost lose consciousness. This would be the last time he was to suffer any pain. He looked up at the man standing above him who had removed a Mauser pistol from a shoulder holster. Pedro looked directly at the barrel of the Mauser, recalling a night years earlier when he was the one who had his hand on the trigger.

Tai Yang did not give him the opportunity to say a word. He grinned, then fired a single shot directly into Pedro's forehead.

Emilio winced at the sound of the shot but just kept running. Not even two minutes had passed since Carlos had first been shot. It felt like eternity. Finally, he reached a set of double doors at the end of the causeway, but they were locked. Emilio pounded on the doors, screaming for help.

Having previously done work on the causeway, Tai Yang knew he had his prey cornered. But Emilio was not completely trapped; where he was now standing, the causeway only had a half wall that was completely open above. He could see into the yard where there were more aisles of containers. Seeing that he had no alternative, he turned and fired his last three round burst from the H and K down the causeway.

Tai Yang crouched while returning fire at Emilio, who was already up on the pony wall. He leaped over to the roof of a small building that housed the terminal's first aid station. His feet hit the roof, he tucked and rolled like a gymnast, coming back onto his feet as he completed the somersault. The dockyard ambulance was parked outside of the building on which he was now standing. Emilio jumped to the roof of the ambulance then slid down the windshield and over the hood to the ground.

Tai Yang reached the pony wall just as Emilio landed on the pavement.

"Shit," was the only word Emilio could make out. Tai Yang slammed his Scorpion into the wall, continuing to shout four letter expletives in both English and Chinese. Emilio continued to run across the tarmac, then turned but kept running backwards to see if he was still being pursued. His ears were ringing from the gunfire in the corridor

Tai Yang watched as his prey continued to run backwards away from him. The Scorpion would not be effective at this distance. He again withdrew the Mauser. He could at least aim this a little better, but it would still be a very lucky shot at this distance.

Still facing the skywalk to see if the gunman was going to follow him, Emilio continued moving backwards. He wanted to know for sure so that he could decide which way he was going to run. It was probably the ringing in his ears that prevented him from hearing the machine's engine.

The operator of the forty-ton container lifter never saw, or for that matter felt anything when he hit Emilio. He was only travelling four miles per hour. The impact on Emilio was like a fly being hit by a swatter. When the huge wheels on the loader finished rolling over him, the operator noticed a slight bump, thinking it was probably just a piece of dunnage. Emilio was dead before the second set of tires crushed his body further. The coroner would later testify that over forty percent of the bones in his body had been pulverized by the massive weight.

The rain began to fall again, slowly washing streams of blood away from his body, which would not be found till morning.

Chang was waiting in his car. He could tell by the grin on Yang's face that all had gone well. They pulled away as soon as Tai Yang was in his seat. The employee parking lot was quiet as they headed out. The rent-a-cop at the gate had been well paid to ensure they always had unmolested access to this area any time Mr. Chang needed to make a rendezvous at the terminal.

This particular operation had only taken twenty-five minutes in total. Leaving the dockyard, they crossed the rail tracks that led into the port, then onto Clark Drive and turned west onto Hastings street and headed back downtown.

"A most profitable evening was it not, Mr. Chang?" offered Tai Yang.

He handed Chang the two briefcases containing the money intended for the purchase of the cocaine. He had recovered both as he made his way back to the car after watching Emilio being crushed by the huge machine. The first case was still laying where Carlos had left it prior to telling Emilio to run. The other that Carlos had hurled at him as a distraction had landed close to where the evening's events had begun.

"Very profitable indeed, very profitable indeed," he murmured in return. "Tomorrow we have a very large deposit to make."

The following morning Chang made his deposit. His deposit box could easily hold five million dollars. The total weight of that much money would be more than that of the average twelve-year-old boy. The box before him today had a little over three-and-half million, including the one point seven from last evening's endeavors, along with an additional half million dollars recently collected from various other enterprises. Too bad today's extra was Canadian currency he thought. Calculating the day's exchange, he worked it out to a ballpark figure of four hundred thousand worth of US dollars.

Most offshore purchases were made with American cash, however they did have off-the-books payroll commitments they paid in Canadian currency. This money would slowly be filtered back into the system to legitimate businesses operated by the triad. By the time it came out the other side it would be clean enough to deposit directly into any Canadian bank.

He then filled two of the other deposit boxes with the sixty-eight kilos of cocaine that had found its way into his possession compliments of Mr. Santoro. With their banking completed, Chang, Chow and Yang left their depository.

CHAPTER 4

As the sun began to creep through the venetian blinds, I woke up, rolled over and squinted at the radio alarm clock. Through bleary eyes I saw what I saw every weekday morning: 4:48 a.m. I never knew exactly why, just that my system seemed to be wired to awake at that time. On days when I didn't have to get up for an early morning trip, I would usually fall back to sleep for several more hours. Waking up without the alarm let my wife have some more uninterrupted sleep, although it wasn't that restful because no matter how quiet I was, she instinctively knew I was out of bed. So much for the early morning REM sleep they said was so important to a good night's rest.

I rolled myself out of our waterbed; no one really jumps out of one of those. I couldn't do that when I was a spry twenty-five and it was even tougher for me now that I was considered by my oldest daughter to be middle-aged. I would never have thought that being in my early thirties meant that I was now middle-aged. I guess if I only live to sixty-five like some of my uncles, then yes, I could be officially considered middle-aged. Burning the candle at both ends did seem to be getting the better of me. I often felt I was getting closer to forty than thirty-three, a milestone some of my friends have already seen come and go.

Once my feet hit the floor everything started to improve. Glancing out the window at the imminent sunrise told me it would be another hot, sunny day in the Okanagan Valley of

British Columbia. Habit had me peeking through the blinds every morning, rain or shine. In the winter, it let me know if the clouds would prevent a good day of skiing on Big White Mountain. In the spring or summer, I could estimate how the tourist traffic would be on the narrow roads that stretched between Penticton and Vernon. At least in my mind I imagined I could tell. If my neighbour was standing naked on her pool deck I would probably never have noticed, as at this point my eyes were never fully open.

I closed the ensuite door to keep down the noise from my morning ritual. Before my eyes had fully adjusted to the light, I was running the shaver over my face. As I stared at the reflection in the mirror, I often thought the credits of my life would begin rolling down the reflective surface. Today's episode brought to you by Chris Porter, written and directed by Fate. Executive producer great-grandfather Porter, producers Gerry and Barb Porter, soundtrack available on radio.

It's just as well that doesn't happen every day—nobody watches the credits anyway. Shave done, teeth clean, it's time for the shower. A quick scrub of the body then onto the hair, which seemed to be going greyer faster than it was going down the drain each time I washed it. I sometimes tried the 007 routine by turning the water from a nice body-warming stream to a bone-chilling blast of straight cold. They call it a Scottish shower. I never did understand what James Bond got out of this ritual. I had hoped that the cold would seal my pores, stopping the loss of so much hair. It didn't seem to do anything for the hair follicles, but sure did make other parts shrink in a hurry.

Out of the shower, a quick stroke of deodorant, a splash of cologne, quick brush of the ever-thinning hair, and I was ready to set the world on fire. Then again, for a six-foot-tall guy weighing in at one hundred and ninety pounds, without poster boy looks how big a fire could I really get going? If the cops wanted to do a suspect line up with garden-variety guys, I would be the one in the middle that no one noticed, except for my great moustache.

In the bedroom, Trish seemed to be sound asleep. She looked great in the light of the sun trickling through the blinds. I was tempted to just crawl back in bed and stay there for the day. Regretting that I couldn't do that, I quickly got into my sales uniform. Slacks, dress shirt, plain tie and sports jacket. I grabbed my overnight case containing a change of clothes and shaving kit, which Trish had faithfully packed for me the night before, as she always did when I went out of town. I leaned over, gave her a kiss on the forehead then pulled the covers over her shoulders. I should have known I wouldn't make it out of the room without waking her. All I heard as I closed the door was, "Drive carefully." I walked down the hall, stopping at each of my daughter's rooms. I pulled up their covers, kissing them on their foreheads as well. They, however, did stay asleep.

Down the hall to the kitchen where the coffee had already finished brewing. Having timers on most things did make life simpler. I let the dog out of the garage where he spent his nights. Patches scampered past me without so much as a "Good morning, how did you sleep?" Before I got to my coffee, he would be in lying in my place beside Trish.

I poured coffee into my Tim Hortons traveling mug and snapped the lid down so that when I drove I could hold the mug in my right hand and sip it through the supposedly drip proof hole, even though spots on my ties and shirts were proof that these spouts were not as good as advertised. I grabbed my wallet and all the loose change from the kitchen table, turned off the lights then let myself out the front door.

The dog got the garage, while my 1986 Caprice Classic standard-issue company car sat outside on the driveway. I lived in an area where you didn't have to lock your doors, although things were not quite as country-like as they had been before they put up all the street lights. I had the advantages of subdivision living, good neighbours, nice yards, but also had a peaceful country drive to begin the day or mellow out on the way home.

I began backing down the drive before the car had reached its full idling speed. Opening the window, I stretched my arm out, tapping around the roof until I found my coffee cup, which I had yet again left on the roof when I got in the car. I took one more look at the house before heading off for several days. It was the same trip I had made every two weeks for the past seven years. I looked back at the house and there in the window of her bedroom was my youngest, Lana, waving at me as I left. I stopped and we blew kisses to each other before I put the car in drive and headed off. I left hoping she would let Trish sleep a little longer.

I glanced at the clock on the dash: 5:30. Just over forty minutes. A song by Trooper called "Quiet Desperation" from 1979 was just finishing. A song about starting the day at 5:30 in the morning while still half asleep. I sang along with the last lines as the song ended. I could usually find a song or lyric to fit any situation. A small quirk, I thought to myself, although I know a lot of people consider my quirk to be more like an annoying habit.

The early morning news followed the song: Vancouver recorded its 36th, 37th and 38th murders of the year last night, in what police sources were saying could be gang related violence. "It might have been a drug deal gone badly. The bodies were discovered early this morning in the Vancouver dockyard area. Details are sketchy at this point but we have confirmed that automatic weapons were used. At this time police have no suspects. The names of the victims have not been released, pending notification of the next of kin. We will have more details as they become available. In sports, last night the Blue Jays ..."

I'm not really a baseball fan so I popped in a cassette and cranked up the volume. I can sing along with the best of them, if I do say so myself. Trish and the girls would strongly disagree with me, but Simon and Garfunkel, Phil Collins, Paul McCartney, Men at Work, all seemed happy to have me join them in their recording sessions.

I was in high demand from producers everywhere. Robert Lamm of the band Chicago called to have me take over lead vocals because of the departure of Peter Cetera. Chicago was one of my all-time favourite bands. I loved the way they added the trumpets and other brass instruments to the music. I couldn't play at all but I sure could purse my lips, helping them to belt out the tunes. I pounded out the beat on the steering wheel, smashing the imaginary cymbals that were strategically located above the passenger seat.

Travelling the roads through the interior of British Columbia can be an experience like no other for people who have never been here. Taking the same route every two weeks for the past seven years took some of the splendour off it. One of the things that I could do was tell anyone who might be travelling with me the exact time we would be at any given point on this stretch of road based on the time that we left town. Today was no exception. I knew that I would begin to see the kids getting out and ready for the school bus at the ends of the driveways of the farms and ranches I passed. I knew it would be 6:49 when I passed the little closed down gas station in Westwold and it would be 7:02 when I went by the cut-off to the Monty Lake sawmills.

I also knew that if I saw the police car in the back of the Falkland RCMP building that I would not have any trouble with radar traps along the way. It was when he wasn't there that you could never be sure where he'd be hiding. I saw the back end of the patrol car right where it should be. "My radar detector should stay quiet today," I said to myself.

I was starting through an isolated section of road with twists and turns, where the highway was marked with a solid yellow line to prevent anyone from passing on the curves. I have two golden rules when driving: never pass on the solid, with a caveat that it was okay if the driver was an old guy from out of province wearing a hat. The other one was never, ever pass on the curves.

I always trusted what I considered my driver's sixth sense, which had kept me out of more accidents than I care to remember. It would kick in when I was about to turn or pass someone at a spot where most people would think it was safe. I would check both mirrors, take another look, then just before I was about to make my move I would change my mind. That's when another car would come off a side road most drivers would be unaware of, or a car would come over a rise from an unseen dip in the road.

I was rocking my way along the highway in my own little world, driving on autopilot. I didn't notice the logging truck in my rear-view mirror until it was right on my bumper. I stepped on the gas, the logging truck kept pace with my increase in speed. The truck got closer, so that I could only see the grill. All I could tell from looking in the mirror was that a Kenworth was on my ass.

I continued to increase my speed. The highway along this section had been blasted out of the rock, leaving no place to pull to the side to let anyone pass. The logging trucks on this stretch of highway were notorious for their aggressive driving as they raced to get in as many runs per day as they could manage. Continuing to accelerate, I lifted my left foot up and tapped the brake pedal to flash the lights. The trucker sounded his air horn, continuing to get closer to my bumper.

I might be an everyday guy, but I know what I'm doing behind the wheel. I have driven over six-hundred thousand accident free miles over the years and I didn't intend to ruin that record. I have traveled many of my routes in times much faster than the auto club's suggested driving times. I once made the Castlegar to Kelowna run in slightly more than three hours—a trip that should take four hours by the books. Even so, my pulse quickened as the huge logging truck inched ever-closer as both vehicles neared double the posted speed limit.

Finally, the Kenworth saw his opening and began to pass me. I continued to press further down on the gas pedal, but he was still coming on strong and pulled up beside my driver's side door. My heart was racing as we rounded a blind bend in the highway side-by-side at breakneck speed.

CHAPTER 5

The next stage of the drive became a blur. The two vehicles were neck and neck as we rounded the curve, and suddenly right in front of me was the back end of the familiar yellow-and-black school bus.

"Right on time!"

Coming from the other direction was another vehicle that I could have set my watch by: the Loomis Armoured Truck, making its Tuesday morning run to the Okanagan Valley from their regional base in Kamloops.

I slammed on the brakes as the Kenworth continued speeding past, planning to pass the school bus as well. The Loomis truck and the Kenworth were closing on each other at fifty miles an hour each. I couldn't see exactly where the two trucks were in relation to each other, but on this part of the road I knew there wasn't a lot of room for the Kenworth to pass the bus. At the speed these two were going, they would be closing the gap at around one hundred and ten miles an hour, meaning a collision could occur in less than eight seconds. Even if the Loomis Truck tried to slow down, the Kenworth was increasing speed as he passed by me, now travelling well over sixty miles an hour.

The Loomis driver didn't know what to do. He had three choices: run straight into the Kenworth that was hauling a trailer full of logs. He could swerve to miss the truck, which meant a head-on collision with a school bus loaded with kids—the

Loomis and bus drivers normally waved to each other as they passed each other on their morning routes. The third option was to head off the side of the road in one of the worst spots of the entire road between Kelowna and Kamloops. The road here dropped quickly, at least twenty feet down a forty-five-degree slope into a hay field. It would be impossible to hold the truck upright if it went over the side.

In the two to three heartbeats it took to make the decision—a heartbeat that panic had jumped to over one hundred and twenty beats per minute—the driver probably didn't even have time to warn the man riding in the back with the money. In a heroic gesture, the Loomis driver with over fifteen years of armoured car experience went for the side of the road rather than crashing into the bus. He rammed his foot hard onto the brake pedal, leaving a trail of smoking rubber on the pavement. It was a wonder the force of his foot didn't break the pedal completely off. The truck fishtailed, then straightened just as the front wheel went onto the shoulder of the road. The trajectory of the truck took it right over the side of the embankment.

The driver steered further to the right, trying to follow the bank down to the hayfield. If he had hit the gas after he went over the side, he might have been able to pull off the manoeuvre. But as the rear tires went over the side, the truck toppled onto its side, slid down the hill a little further, turned onto its roof, and then completed its roll by falling onto the driver side as it came to a stop in the field below.

The engine was still running and a cloud of dust swirled around the overturned vehicle. The heavy truck had gouged out a trough of dirt as it plowed down the embankment. Dust hung in the air like fog, slowly settling back to the ground.

The Kenworth had left a hundred-foot streak of vulcanized rubber on the road as it came to a screeching halt. The school bus pulled over to the side of the road, then backed up to where the armoured car had gone over the side.

There was no other traffic coming from either direction. I eased as far as I could to the side, then put on my hazard lights and shut off the car. The only sound I could hear was the ticking of my overheated engine. Otherwise, there was nothing but an eerie silence. The armoured truck's engine had shut down and was now silent as well. Though the windows on the school bus were all closed, anyone witnessing this scene would have expected to be hearing screams from the kids on the bus. There wasn't a sound, and I was well aware of the reason for that silence.

The school bus driver got out and headed for the embankment. The driver of the Kenworth casually stepped from his rig. Neither of them seemed to notice that I had pulled onto the narrow shoulder. Both drivers had on black coveralls, with balaclavas over their heads.

I undid my seat belt, reached into the back seat and grabbed my briefcase. I dropped it onto the passenger seat and tried to pop it open. It was one of the Samsonite's that won't open if it's upside down. I flipped it right side up then flicked open the clasps. Lifting the lid, I reached in and removed a .38 Smith and Wesson revolver. It was the same model I had trained with while I was with the Vancouver Police Reserves. I could still put six shots centre mass in a standard police target at thirty feet.

Maybe I wasn't such an ordinary guy after all. Unlike our American cousins, we Canadians didn't normally drive around with handguns in our cars. In fact, the only time I was supposed to have it in the car at all was when going back and forth to a registered shooting range.

I took a deep breath, summoned my courage and then prepared to get out of the car. I pulled my sunglasses down from the visor and calmly put them on, then with the .38 calibre in my hand settling my nerves, I grabbed the door handle, pulled the lever and gave the door a kick so that it swung out past the stops, staying completely open. There was still no traffic.

With my right arm dangling at my side, and the pistol gripped in my hand, I headed toward the passenger side of the bus. There was still an acrid smoke from the tires of the Kenworth hanging in the air. I could no longer see either of the drivers. The reason for the absence of terrified, screaming kids was very simple: there were no kids on the bus. Just a bunch of the stuffed dummies that fire departments use for evacuation and resuscitation practise.

I moved cautiously toward the front of the bus, trying not to let my shoes scuff the dirt as I put one foot in front of the other, I peered around the front of the bus. The two men were standing at the top of the embankment, staring down at the wreck below.

They were engrossed in an animated discussion, using wild hand gestures in what I imagined was a discussion of how the Loomis truck had ended up driving over the embankment. The Kenworth driver was the shorter of the two, I pegged him around five ten, probably one seventy-five. The bus driver was taller. He looked like he might be in shape under the coveralls. The two men were still deeply engrossed in conversation as I stepped up behind them.

"Seems to have gone according to plan wouldn't you say. As our friend Hannibal Smith from the *A Team* likes to say, I love it when a plan comes together," I remarked as the two men began turning in my direction.

Even though they were expecting me, I had still managed to startle them. "Jesus Christ!" gasped the one driving the bus as his eyes widened and he put his hand on his chest. You scared the crap out of me, I hate when you do stealth shit," he yelled.

"You need to pay a little more attention to your surroundings my friend, I was anything but stealthy," I said. "And you had better look in his shorts to check his diaper, because I think he might have just filled them," I laughed as I pointed my revolver to the taller of the two men. A stunt that would have had me banished from any range I'd ever fired on.

"You said that once we started this there would be no talking," he chided.

"Correct as always, isn't he?" I whispered to the shorter one. "My fault." I glanced at my watch, rocked my head back and forth as I calculated the time used up to this point.

"Just give me my stuff. We'll get this thing done without another peep. We have exactly twelve minutes left to get that thing open, clean it out, then get the hell out of here." I reached into my sports jacket pocket, removed my own balaclava, and pulled it over my head. No other conversation took place during the next twelve minutes.

The Kenworth driver reached down to the sports bag that was sitting at his feet, pulled out a third set of coveralls and tossed them to me. I passed the revolver to Kenworth, then climbed into the disposable nylon garment. From the bag, a pair of black overboots identical to what the other two were already wearing were also passed to me. I tucked the legs of the coveralls into the tops of the boots and zipped them closed. Next was a pair of black rubber gloves and lastly, Kenworth handed me back my revolver, then picked up the sports bag.

The three of us did a quick inspection of each other's clothing to ensure that nothing was out of place, with no signs of hair colour or faces showing through the balaclavas. I again looked at my watch then showed the others that we now had ten of our pre-allotted fifteen minutes left since the truck passed the check point. I pointed down the hill and we hopped down the embankment toward the overturned Loomis truck.

When we reached the truck, Kenworth removed a pair of bolt cutters from the sports bag and snipped off the truck's antennas. The armoured car did not really seem in bad shape, considering the crash it had suffered. The paint that covered the half-inch steel plate was scraped on the side and roof but the integrity of the unit was intact. The mirrors had snapped off and there was dirt jammed into every crevice.

I looked in on the driver. He had a large gash on his forehead, and he appeared to be unconscious in his seat. He had been held in place by his seat belt. I could tell he was alive as I watched his chest slowly rise and fall.

Kenworth was looking into the back, checking to make sure the guard was alive and conscious. He was alive but definitely shaken up. He had not been strapped in at the time of the crash. He had a lot of scrapes on his face, and would probably have many bruises showing up in the hours to come. He spat out some blood, then rubbed his fingers over the jagged edge where two of his teeth used to be.

Bus Driver was wearing a backpack. He wiggled out of it and set it on the ground. Removing a cassette player from the bag, he took up a position by the roof's air vent. He turned on the player, then looked over at Kenworth, who was now watching for a signal from me. We had changed places. I was now the one peering through the rear window at the guard inside. Kenworth had moved back so that he had a view of both the back and side of the truck.

I watched the surprised expression of the face of the guard in the back as the tape began to play. I gave a single nod to Bus Driver, indicating that I was sure the guard was hearing our tape. I had produced the clip by recording bits and pieces of dialogue from various movie and TV shows—*Rambo, Sleuth, Star Wars V, 2001 A Space Odyssey, The Shining*, among others. The dialogue from these movies had been dubbed together into a short explanation of what the guard was expected to do. It also explained the consequences of noncompliance. Putting the tape together took more hours than I cared to think of. I did have a lot of fun doing it. I told everyone I was making a new trivia game. The edited tape sounded like this:

"You have one minute—Please open the door—If you don't comply, that's your choice—We'll smoke you out—As soon as you come out the door—Just keep going, straight ahead—You will take ten paces—Get on your knees—Keep your face down—You can leave the keys in the van—Do you smell that?—It's quite harmless—Only for a moment—If you don't cooperate, we're gonna be put off—Can you say nerve gas?—The choice is yours—After all, it's fully insured—There is no escape, don't make me destroy you—Now drop your gun.—I can see you're really upset by this—Empty your pockets, buddy—No second chances—Fifteen seconds and counting."

While the tape was playing, Bus Driver had sprayed an aerosol air freshener toward the top vent. It was one of those disgusting floral scents used in gas station washrooms. The guard did not have to be told twice. He complied precisely with the tape's instructions. It had been drilled into all employees that they were to always comply with the demands of anyone trying to rob them. He was not willing to lose his life to protect money that belonged to the banks. Especially since he was only making around ten bucks an hour

I watched through the back window as the guard followed the instructions, including placing his gun belt and keys at his feet. The guard came to the back to open the rear door. Fortunately, the way the truck had tipped allowed the overlapping door to just drop to the ground. It would have been much more difficult had it landed on the other side. Then we would have had to lift the heavy steel door upwards.

Kenworth and I stood to the side, watching as the guard exited the vehicle. He walked his ten paces then got on his knees. Bus Driver approached the kneeling guard, then removed a hypodermic needle from his pack. If this had been a movie, he would have just brought out a fifty-calibre dart gun and shot the man in the back with it. Darts could actually take a lot of time to take effect. Bus Driver had the guard put his feet together and place his hands behind his back. He then wrapped the man's legs and wrists with Velcro straps. With the man's wrists behind him, he injected his wrist with a fast-acting anesthesia.

I had the keys for the front of the truck in my hands before Bus Driver had trussed up the first guard. We extracted the driver from the front of the truck. It took a little bit to pull the unconscious man out of the passenger side. This was quite a chore because the truck was laying on its side, which put the passenger door seven feet in the air and the driver wasn't a small man. As I was pulling him up, the sleeve of my coveralls snagged on a screw which held down the fire extinguisher. The fabric ripped through, also putting a tear in the sport coat underneath. It pissed me off, but I made sure there were no fibres from either piece of clothing left behind on the tip of the screw.

We dropped the driver beside the now unconscious guard. Bus Driver duplicated his actions from the first man, using a separate needle on the driver. When he was done, he put both needles into the backpack, then joined us at the back of the truck.

The operation to this point was right on schedule. I looked at my watch yet again, then held up five fingers, showing the other two how much the time we had left. Our timetable was based on how long we believed the armoured truck's radio checks with the regional base could go unanswered. This part of the valley had a lot of zones with less than ideal radio coverage, and FM signals tended to fade in the area. We figured that Loomis' communications used a UHF signal, which would be affected to an even greater degree in the valleys as they travelled to Kelowna. We had more like twenty minutes before anyone really missed the truck, but when it was missed, alerts would be sent to all police units along the truck's route.

We wanted to be well on our way before any alerts were issued. Apart from me scaring the crap out of the other two at the top of the embankment after the initial crash, the entire operation had taken place without a single word being uttered by any of us. We had practised every action many times, and now proceeded with the precision of a highly-trained military operation.

I ducked into the back of the truck. There were bags of money scattered everywhere. The Loomis Company used shelves when they were transporting bags of money. Brinks used compartments, which would have kept all the bags in place but would probably have required a lot of extra time to unload.

I began tossing out the bags that contained only what I presumed were bills, as the ones with the coin would be too heavy to just toss around. Kenworth was positioned outside the truck. As the bags came through the doors he heaved them to Bus Driver, who in turn threw them to the top of the bank. We emptied twenty bags from the back of the truck. There were another twenty or so that appeared to be full of coin when I kicked at them. It had taken only forty-five seconds to empty the truck.

Back outside, I did one last walk around to ensure we hadn't left anything behind. I picked up the tape recorder and placed it in Bus Driver's backpack. While checking on the guards to ensure they were both still breathing, I removed my gloves, leaned over, checking each of the men's radial pulses. The driver's head was still bleeding quite badly. I put my gloves back on, removed a bandage from the pack, placed it over the wound and grabbed some tape. It was tough to get the tape started off the roll with the gloves on but I was finally rewarded for my persistence. I taped the bandage down then replaced both items in the pack. "Take nothing but pictures, leave nothing but footprints," I whispered to myself.

Footprints shouldn't be a problem, as the boots we had chosen to wear were available everywhere. Each of the pairs had been bought with cash at a different store. Convinced that both Loomis employees were still alive and that there was no evidence left behind, I joined the others at the top of the embankment.

The other two had opened the rear emergency door of the bus and were tossing the money bags into a compartment concealed beneath the floor. I set the backpack beside the duffle bag, which had been brought up by Kenworth. The last two sacks of money were put into the compartment, then Kenworth and I handed Bus Driver the black bags. Laying them on the floor, we removed the balaclavas gloves, coveralls and boots, placing the items in the duffle. I handed over the revolver and it was also put into the bag.

The bags of cash would be stored until later. None of the money would be going back into circulation for some time. The coveralls, boots, tape recorder and balaclavas would all be burned. Bus Driver pulled the cover over the compartment, securing it in place.

Looking again at my watch, I gave them the two-minute warning then pointed my finger in the air, twirled it around as a signal to get under way. I grabbed a garden rake that was lying on the bus floor. Bus Driver climbed inside, closed the emergency door tightly, and then headed down the aisle to start up the bus and leave.

There still had not been one vehicle drive past us during the robbery. The bus pulled out onto the asphalt surface, turned around, and headed back in the direction it had come from when I first encountered it. I gave him a thumbs-up as he passed, getting a huge smile in return. Kenworth then jumped into his rig, starting it as soon as he was settled in the seat. When the air pressure reached its minimum level, he flipped off the park lever, releasing the air brakes. The truck slowly started to pick up speed. As he shifted gears, black diesel smoke spewed like smoke signals from the chrome stacks. Kenworth pulled onto the road, heading off in the same direction he had been travelling fifteen minutes earlier. He glanced out the huge side mirror, seeing me giving him a thumbs-up as well.

I grabbed the rake, quickly pulled it around the area where the bus had been parked hoping to destroy any evidence of tire patterns. I walked to my car, got in, leaving the door open, with my left foot hanging over the door sill. I turned on the car, pulling forward onto the highway. I jammed the car into park, jumped out and used the rake again to clean up the area where my car had been stopped. Mission accomplished, I popped open the trunk and put the rake inside. Back in the car, I put on my seat belt, closed the door, put the car in gear and headed off for my first sales call of the morning.

As Kenworth left our position he grabbed his CB radio microphone, giving the talk button two quick clicks, then two long ones. At either end of the isolated valley, flag ladies had been in position since 6:30 a.m., waiting for all the vehicles involved in the heist to pass their checkpoints. Once the armoured truck passed the prescribed point, the flag lady on the west end of the valley had exited her car to set up orange cones as well as Road Construction Ahead signs and had alerted the Kenworth and bus driver that the target vehicle had just passed. This signal would allow the Kenworth driver to get up to the speed required to be at the precise place where the visibility of the Loomis truck was restricted coming around the curve. When the armoured truck emerged from the blind curve, his options to avoid the crash would be reduced to the three that we had planned for. It had been a hell of a game of chicken, but it had been worth it. On the east end of the valley, the flag lady had set up her barriers as soon as the Kenworth had gone by her position.

The flag girls had stopped traffic and apologized to the drivers, explaining to the first few in line that there would be a ten to fifteen-minute delay. The flaggers had stood in the middle of the road in bright orange jump suits and hardhats, holding reversing six-foot-high signs with "Stop" on one side, "Slow" on the other. Each of the flag ladies also wore heavy work boots and both carried two-way radios. They wore tinted safety glasses, and not that anyone at the opposite end of the road closure would know, they each had long, wavy red hair that flowed out from under their orange hard hats.

After the first vehicles had stopped, with a line forming behind, the ladies moved slightly ahead of the lead vehicles. They stood with their stop signs facing the traffic and gave updates to each other over the radios. The radio on the Kenworth had been able to receive the radio chatter. While our heist was unfolding, we had listened to Kenworth's radio. Occasionally, the flaggers would turn toward the front driver, give him a big smile, then indicate how much longer they might be stuck there. If a patrol car had come along, they would have asked each other over the radio if they had seen, *Who's the Boss*, on TV last night. They would have repeated the question numerous times to each other. If anyone had the same frequency as our flag ladies, they might have thought they had poor reception. Hearing "Who's the boss?" three or four times would be our signal to abandon ship, leave everything and get back on the road. Fortunately, they hadn't had to ask about last night's sitcom.

Both flag ladies had been waiting for the signal from the Kenworth. When they heard the two short, two long clicks, they twirled their signs around to the slow side, giving all the delayed drivers big smiles as they waved them onward.

My assumption was that after a fifteen-minute delay, most people at that time of the morning would now be running late. The only thing they might be considering was calling the highways department to give them an earful for the lengthy delay. The frustrated drivers might not pay attention to the fact that there wasn't anyone working on the roads as they drove the next handful of miles.

The exact location for the "accident" had been chosen because it met all the requirements to pull off the heist: No side roads coming onto the highway for miles. The number of curves in the road. The fact that the roadway had been carved out of the side of the mountain, meaning that there was only one way the Loomis truck could go when faced with an imminent head on collision. Very poor radio reception. Finally, an embankment that dropped off the side of the road, which would make it very difficult for drivers to see the bottom of as they later drove past.

The flag ladies gathered up their equipment, then headed to their cars. There is never a great deal of traffic on this part of Highway 97, and by the time they got underway the last of the traffic that had been stopped was passing where the original lineup had started. With their cones, and signs loaded, each flag lady retrieved their own rear licence plate from the trunk, quickly exchanging it for the ones that had been temporarily installed. The lead drivers had been sitting there so long they could have the licence plates subconsciously etched into their brains.

Each of the ladies turned their cars around, taking the first gravel roads that led them on circuitous routes to Armstrong, then head back to the Okanagan Valley to an old farmer's shed, that had been rented on the premise of rebuilding the school bus into a motor home.

I proceeded slowly and waited for the first of the traffic heading my way to get closer. As I saw them coming around a bend in my rear-view mirror I increased my speed, continuing my journey to Kamloops as though nothing had happened.

CHAPTER 6

While I drove, Steve Miller's "Jet Airliner" was blasting from the speakers. I wasn't at the controls of a 707 airplane, but I was flying down the road.

I drive over sixty-thousand miles a year, and I tended to let hours of time pass without any notice. Over the years, I had ended up travelling through entire towns on a kind of automatic pilot. My mind often wandered; I might think about my last sales call or maybe the next one, I might drift off to thoughts of my marriage, friends, or last week's golf game where I three-putted the eleventh. The next thing I'd know, I would be in the next town, having travelled the past thirty miles in la-la land, unable to remember for sure if I had stopped for the only stop sign or traffic light in the last town.

I glanced at the clock. 7:29 a.m., just in time for the news on NL radio in Kamloops. I ejected the tape and pushed the preprogrammed button for the Kamloops station. The killings in Vancouver topped the news on this station as well. The announcer continued on to the regular small town stories. There were hockey scores from the playoffs, stories about upcoming football training camps, predictions about the baseball pennant races that would not conclude for another five months.

"Best time of the year for these sportscasters. Never have a chance to run out of things to whine about," I said to myself, looking at the clock yet again then back to the highway and thought it should be around the next corner. Just before the Bar M Ranch.

The Caprice was on cruise control. I was still irate about the damn Kenworth that had passed both me and the school bus. I couldn't believe the son of a bitch had done it. He could have killed us all. My car was now following the corners as if it was on a slot car track. And there it was, right on schedule as usual: the Loomis truck approaching me in the opposite direction. I steered the car with practised ease and watched. Every time I came this way I could tell exactly where that truck would be based on the time I got to a specific spot. I could set my clock by it. The same time every Tuesday for the past seven years. Not that there are a lot of other routes you can take to get to the Okanagan, but I thought they might at least change up the travel times.

Could it really be done? I wondered what was really inside of that truck. Lots of cash and coin for all the retail outlets, maybe cash to fill up the ATM's that had sprung up everywhere? Why would they keep such a predictable routine all these years?

I just shook my head as I pondered the possibilities. What would I do if it was full of money, which was suddenly all mine? The next twenty-four minutes of driving were spent with my mind watching the setting sun on the beaches of Hawaii, hitting the blackjack tables in Vegas, where I would play five dollar slots instead of the nickel ones we had played on our first trip there, looking out at the sights of New York City while standing atop the Empire State Building, then heading home to a penthouse suite at some luxury hotel. I thought I could handle that kind of a life.

At 7:55, I reached the shop of my first customer of the day. Right on time as usual. He would have his order ready for me. He knew my schedule, and always had it prepared ahead before my sales calls every second Tuesday. He could have called the order in to the branch office, but liked the personal attention I gave him. I got out, waving to Jake, who was just opening the oversize, roll-up style door to his shop. "Want me to go back to Tim's for some coffee and donuts while you get the day underway?"

"That would be great. Thanks Chris, my treat next time."

"It had better be more than coffee. You still owe me lunch from when I sold you that winning ticket on the Super Bowl lottery from our charity group last January. Two cream and two sugar, right?"

"You know it. You get the coffee and donuts, then we'll arm wrestle for lunch."

Not a chance in hell, I thought. Jake must have been at least two hundred and fifty pounds, and at six-foot four, he would probably give Hulk Hogan a go in an arm wrestle.

CHAPTER 7

There is an obscure Paul McCartney tune called "Average Person" from his *Pipes of Peace* album about coming across average people and finding out what they really thought about. I figured that I was that person. No one would pay a lot of attention to me in a movie line, nobody was really interested in what I did for a living because it was basically ordinary. Of course, I thought that I had smarter, prettier kids, and a beautiful wife. I spent a fair amount of time in the yard, mowing the lawn after picking up the dog crap that I hoped wasn't too soggy. For the most part, my friends and I were all regular guys that played a game of golf that was run of the mill.

At the last class reunion, I heard of old classmates that got heavily into the drug scene, some of them selling, some of them dying from overdoses. Others had become very successful in business. My current friends and I, however, were just regular guys, doing the routine things that most mainstream people do. We dreamed about having all the money we needed to live the lifestyle we all felt we deserved.

When we got together for drinks we had a ritual. We didn't have swords like the three musketeers, so we would just raise our glasses, clink them together, then pronounce: "To life! Our way!"

Another ritual was our Sunday morning golf game. Almost every Sunday during the spring and summer, we would be the first ones off the tee at the Kelowna Golf and Country Club, rain or shine. The earlier the sun would come up, the earlier we would be on the first tee, allowing us to finish early so we could get on with our days with the families.

Depending on the time of year, Saturdays were reserved for coaching one of the kids' sports teams, taking them to piano recitals, mowing the lawn, or going on hikes with the dog. We had managed to join the club when membership had not cost an entire year's salary just to get on the waiting list. We weren't great golfers—at best, we could be considered intermediate. This Sunday was no exception. Bob Tarleton, Dan Kramer, Harry Bentley and I had teed off just after 6:00 a.m. The sun had just eased over the cliffs that partially surrounded the lush green grasses of the beautifully landscaped course.

We really enjoyed each other's company, friendship and camaraderie; the game was secondary. There were times that it got a little tedious, and I was never the most gracious loser. Some people, including my wife and kids, said I could be more insufferable when I won. As we headed to the tenth tee box, there was an announcement over the PA system that there was a call for me. I headed to the pro shop, listening to the sarcastic banter from my friends behind me.

"Don't forget to pick up a loaf of bread and quart of milk on your way home, honey bunch," offered Dan in a high, mocking voice. I could hear the other two snickering as I entered the pro shop.

The new pro at the club had been the pro at my dad's course when I first learned to golf, back when I was ten. When Sean Metcalfe had taken over at the Kelowna club, I had walked up to him and asked if he remembered me. He of course had no idea until I explained that I was the son of Gerry Porter, and that I had met him when he had been working at the Quilchena Club in Richmond, where my dad had been a member for decades.

"Morning, Chris," said Sean.

"Morning, Sean. Which line is my call on? Probably some customer who wants me to re-rush his rush job that I rushed for him last week only to find out that it has already been delivered."

"Actually, I think its Trish. Probably needs you to pick up eggs and a loaf of bread, when you're done with the game."

"Great! Not you too."

"You can take the call in my office. It's on line one."

"Thanks," I said as I headed in. His desk was cluttered with tournament notices and pro shop invoices. A box of courtesy score card pencils was laying right in the middle of the desk. I reached over the box, picked the handset out of its cradle and punched the flashing button for line one.

"Yes dear, what do you need? I've already been told milk, eggs and bread." I paused, waiting for Trish's response to my sarcasm. I already knew it was a little more serious than that or she would never have bothered me on the course, but I was not ready for the bombshell she was about to drop on me.

When Trish started to speak, her voice began to crack. I had been sitting on the edge of the desk when I took the call. Now I stood up, then slowly slipped into the chair at Sean's desk.

"What is it—what's the matter? Trish ... honey ... talk to me!"

A chill ran up my spine as I heard Trish take a deep breath. "It's your mom and dad. Chris, they have been in a car crash. According to your brother, it appears your dad had a heart attack while he was driving. He ran a red light and was broadsided by a truck coming off the freeway. Your mom's still alive, but they don't think she'll make it much longer. Your brother says it was a miracle she survived the crash. They had to use the Jaws of Life to get her out. Vic's not sure she'll make it through the night." Trish again broke down into a series of moaning sobs.

The realization of what she had just told me sent the chill in my spine throughout my entire body. My hands had become a little cold when I first started to talk to Trish, now they were downright frozen, even though Sean's office was over seventy-five degrees. A hundred questions attacked my brain at the same time, but now was not the time to ask them.

It was my turn for a deep breath. I closed my eyes, gathering my thoughts. "I'll be right home. Could you get a bag packed for me? Check on when I can get the next flight to Vancouver. Get back in touch with Vic. See if he can pick me up at the airport. Let him know what flight I'll be on. I'll be home in fifteen to twenty minutes." Without waiting for a reply, I just hung up the phone.

I felt like I was glued to the chair. I slowly worked up the strength, got up, and headed back into the pro shop. Sean was helping to get the next foursome ready to tee off. He glanced over, and must have sensed that something bad had happened. My face felt as if all the blood had drained from it, I knew I was visibly shaking. Sean excused himself from the other golfers. "Is everything okay? You look like hell."

I looked up at him, positive that I did look like shit. "There's been an accident, Sean. It seems dad had a heart attack while driving. My mom might not live to see tomorrow," I said, my voice raspy.

"Christ! I'm sorry. That doesn't seem like enough to say right now. Is there anything I can do?"

"Yeah. Could you please arrange to get my clubs into the storage room? I have to get my keys out of my bag, then head straight out."

"Sure, don't worry about a thing. Say, can I get someone to give you a ride home? You don't look like you should be driving right now."

"I'll be fine. Thanks anyway."

I headed back outside to see the rest of my foursome. They had all met my folks over the years. They had also met my brother Vic. The three of them were standing on the tenth tee waiting for me. Dan was annoyed at the delay, starting in on me as soon as I got within earshot. "Come on for crying out loud. What the hell took so long? We had to let two foursomes go ahead. They're so damned slow it'll take us at least two and half hours to finish the back nine."

"Sorry to hold you up guys. I have to go. Right now. My folks have been in a car crash in Vancouver."

Dan was the first to react, "Oh man, I'm so sorry. Here I am worrying about being a little late and you ..."

Bob quickly cut in. "In Vancouver? How are they?"

I looked down at the ground, trying to hold my emotions in check. "I don't have all the details yet, but my dad didn't survive. He might have had another heart attack prior to the crash. Probably never felt a thing. Mom was banged up pretty bad; they don't think she'll make it that long. Listen, I have to get going. Trish is looking into flights. I have to get to the coast; will you guys make sure that Sean gets my clubs into storage?"

"God. Man, I am so sorry. Is there anything I can do for you or Trish?" asked Dan.

"No, I don't think so. Maybe just have Rita give Trish a call later. I'm going to catch the first flight out of here. I'll try to see Mom before it's too late." My friends watched as I raised my fisted hand, closed my eyes then rubbed the bridge of my nose. There was an awkward silence as the three of them observed me in my grief. Standing there, stunned into silence, not knowing if I should break down in tears or scream at the world. I have been known to be a screamer at times.

"Damn him! Damn him! He never gave me a chance to say goodbye," I shouted at the top of my lungs. People turned and stared at the bunch of us after my outburst.

"It's okay, Chris. There are a lot of people who never get that chance. Get going so that you get to see your mom," suggested Bob, using his most compassionate and comforting voice. It had taken him years to develop the tone and style that had helped so many families get through what I was now enduring. He was respected by his colleagues, adored by his staff, and his patients revered him. Bob had a reputation for having one of the best beside manners of any doctor in the region.

I reached into the golf bag and grabbed my keys, wallet and watch. I didn't take the time to go back to the clubhouse to change out of my golf shoes. I figured I could drive with them on. I had driven many times with a cast on my foot, so this should be a piece of cake.

It seemed the golf day was finished for us all. Harry and Dan gathered up the carts, then began to wheel them back to the clubhouse. Bob escorted me back to the car. "What hospital is your mom at?"

"I didn't think to ask Trish when she called. I just told her to get me on the next flight to the coast. I'll meet my brother down there. He'll know where we have to go. Trish and the girls can drive down when we know more."

"Listen, if there is anything—I mean anything—that you need, don't hesitate to call at any time, day or night," he offered.

"Thanks, Bob. That means a lot."

When we reached the car, I fumbled with my keys, but finally managed to open the door. I got in, closed the door and opened the window. Bob reached through and shook my hand. It wasn't a "nice to see you" shake, more of a comforting, "I'm sorry" kind of one. A shake, I'm sure he had been required to share with many families over the years. Bob's warmth, friendship and compassion radiated through that grip.

I tried to speak, but the words caught in my throat. The tears finally came, and looking up at Bob, all I could utter was a feeble, "Thanks." Then I headed out of the parking lot while Bob just stood and watched.

My emotions were intense, and all I could think about was the fact that I'd never really told my dad that I loved him. It just wasn't something we ever did. Now it was too late.

I wasn't there when he died, but I would sure as hell try to be there for my mom if it was at all possible.

CHAPTER 8

The tires squealed as I turned into my driveway, then screeched to a halt before I hit the garage door. I jumped out of the car, and if it hadn't been for the scraping of the metal cleats on my golf shoes, I probably would have marched right in the door onto the new hardwood floor in the entry way.

"That would have been just fricking lovely," I muttered as I sat down on the front steps to take them off.

Before I was down to my socks Lana and Rebecca were by my side giving me the comforting hugs that I so badly needed. The tears began to flow freely down my face as they came around to sit my lap. I couldn't stop the flow, feeling very silly sitting there on the porch.

"Come on, let's get in the house."

Rebecca, our oldest daughter, a tall, gangly eight-year-old, came around to jump onto my back, and Lana, our mischievous six-year-old, grabbed me around the neck, then and wrapped her legs around my waist. Carrying them upstairs like this had been much easier in previous years. Trish was waiting for us at the top of the stairs. As the girls climbed off I gave her a long loving hug. The dog then joined in, wanting his share of love.

Lana piped up, "Let's have a happy family."

"Not just this minute," said Trish.

"I think now would be the perfect time," I suggested.

This family ritual had started when the girls were small. We would all get together in a circle, put our arms around one another like a football huddle. We would bring our heads to the centre of the circle, giving each other hugs and kisses. The dog usually managed to wriggle his way to the centre of the circle. He would stand on his hind legs, trying to give everyone a wet, slobbery kiss of his own. This usually brought the family hug to an end because Lana would act just like Lucy in the peanuts cartoon whenever Snoopy gave her a kiss. I always hoped that she would act the same way the first time a boy tried to kiss her.

We finished our hug without the dog being a part of it. Trish told the girls to take my bag to the car. I headed down the hall to change, with Trish close on my heels. She told me she'd booked a flight to Vancouver, which was leaving at 9:45 and it was now just after 9:00 a.m. Luckily, we lived close to the airport. She had also contacted my branch manager and explained the situation and he had told her that I could take all the time I needed. My brother was all set to pick me up from the airport and get me to the hospital. "Said he would get you there with lights and siren."

My brother, Vic, was a sergeant in Vancouver Police Force's homicide squad, and had told Trish that he had been on night shift, investigating a triple homicide that had taken place earlier in the week. He had heard about an accident involving a white Plymouth Barracuda. Having a gut feeling about the accident, he had headed off to investigate it. He told Trish that mom was at Vancouver General Hospital on life support. He would fill in the details when I arrived at around 10:20.

"You call and let me know what else you need when you're down there and I'll bring it when I drive down with the girls. I made you a drink, thought you might need one," she said, heading into the kitchen, and returning with a tumbler filled to the brim.

I took the glass, tasted it and my meager eyebrows arched. "Double rum and Coke," she said.

"Thanks, I think I do need this. And after all, it is past noon in Newfoundland." I lowered the glass, then raised it back up high in the air. "Here's to you, Dad. I'm going to miss you." I lowered the glass to my lips, drinking the contents down in a continuous swallow.

The girls were in the car when we got to the driveway. I took the suit bag off Rebecca's lap and put it in the trunk. At the airport there wasn't a lot of time before my flight. I had to have the ticket made up at the counter. The cost was shockingly high, but they told me I could apply for the partial refund for people flying on compassionate grounds. I advised the passenger agent that I only had one carry-on. He told me the flight was getting ready for boarding, and that I could go right through to security.

The girls had run over to watch a plane arriving. They were staring through the large plate glass window, calling for Trish and me to come and see the planes. They loved coming to the terminal when Granma and Grampa arrived in town for their quarterly visits and would stand with their noses pressed against the glass, watching for them as the passengers came down the stairs of the plane.

"Airport's cleaning bill should drop now. They won't have to clean the windows from their little noses," I commented to Trish as we joined the girls. She didn't reply, just took hold of my hand, giving it a big squeeze. I could tell she was way too emotional to say anything right now.

The final boarding call for my flight to Vancouver came over the speaker system. "Give Gramma a big hug for us. Give her this. We made it for her," said the girls in unison. I took the folded construction paper that Lana handed me and put it my jacket pocket.

"I'll give to her as soon as I see her," I promised. We all hugged one more time. Trish was having trouble staying composed, so I broke off the hug, then headed off to the plane without looking back. The girls insisted that they stay to watch the plane take off, not heading home until they could no longer see it.

CHAPTER 9

When I flew to the coast, it was usually on business. Under normal circumstances, I would start up conversations with just about anyone I sat beside. Today, I just wanted to be alone with my thoughts and stare out the window, trying to pick out landmarks as we flew over. The landscape looked like the big relief map that used to be on display at the Pacific National Exhibition when I was a kid. The clear-cut areas, the small lakes that dotted the mountains around Kelowna, the big open pit mine by Peachland all took on a different perspective from up here. It was the end of April, there was still snow left on a lot of the mountains. Hell, one year it had even snowed at the Big White ski hill on July first.

It seemed that the 737 hadn't even reached cruising altitude when we began our descent into Vancouver. The pitch of the engines changed and the nose dipped ever so slightly. Though I had grown up in Vancouver, it always amazed me at how big it had grown. It now started well into the Fraser Valley. From my seat, I could pick out places I used to go: Burnaby Mountain, Central Park, I could see all the high rises downtown, I saw the home stadium of the CFL's BC Lions, and Pacific Coliseum, where the NHL's Canucks played.

We touched down, taxied to the terminal, and then came to a complete stop in the scheduled time of fifty-five minutes from terminal to terminal. I emerged into the passenger waiting area, seeing my older brother Vic immediately. Just like with our dad, there was never any big show of emotion between us when we got together. Vic walked up and stuck out his hand. There were no big hugs, just a handshake as though we were business associates.

Vic probably outweighed me by a good twenty to thirty pounds and all his two hundred and twenty pounds were firm and well-proportioned. He had inherited our dad's barrel chest. He always needed to get his suits and sports coats custom tailored to fit properly. The funny thing was that dad had only been five-foot five. I was six feet, with Vic coming in around six-foot two. I had never known either of them, but both my grandfathers had also been six feet tall or better.

Vic grabbed my overnighter and we headed off toward the parking area, where he had left his unmarked police cruiser in a police-only zone. Anyone looking at the two of us would probably think we were both in the force. More than once when I had been in a bar people had mistaken me for a cop.

As he started the engine, Vic said, "Put on your seat belt, grab the 'oh shit' handle and hang on. We is going to get you to the hospital in record time." Vic put the car in gear, put the flashing light on the dash and cranked on the siren. He left a twenty-foot patch of rubber beside the curb as we raced away from the terminal, and we were reaching speeds over sixty miles per hour as we passed the Canadian Airlines hanger before we were halfway down Grant McConachie Way. We carried on, weaving our way past cars on our left, then right. Many of the cars ahead of us were pulling over as they heard the siren or noticed the flashing lights. I'm sure people who saw us flash by were wondering what kind of emergency we could be heading to. We raced over the Arthur Laing Bridge getting close to seventy-five miles an hour.

"What the hell are you trying to do? Wipe out the entire family in one morning?" I shrieked above the sounds of the siren and screaming engine.

"Just want to take your mind off your troubles, little brother. Just sit back and relax."

"Relax my ass. I would like to get there in one piece, thank you very much."

"I hope we don't hit any radar traps heading into town," he replied as he took the Marine Drive exit so fast I was sure we were only on two wheels.

A big dip in the transition between the bridge and Marine Drive caused the rear end to scrape on the pavement. If it had been dark out, people behind us would have seen sparks flying. "Got to get the shop to check the suspension next time it's in."

The normal driving time for the nine miles from the airport to VGH is around twenty-five minutes, maybe twenty without traffic, for any sane, law abiding citizen. We were already close to halfway there and only five minutes had passed. Vic changed the pitch on the siren as we ran a red light that took us off Marine Drive into a long-radius one hundred and eighty degree turn that led us onto Oak Street.

In my mind, the minutes were reduced to seconds. Weaving in and out of traffic as the volume increased, Vic's foot appeared to never touch the brake pedal. We sped through intersections from 71st all the way to 41st, changing lanes as required. At times, my foot was pressing on an imaginary brake pedal so hard I thought it would penetrate the floor boards, turning his cruiser into a Flintstone car with my feet scraping on the pavement below. I was pressing my back so hard against the seat that I was afraid I might break it and leave us both staring at the dome light as we careened down the road.

Vic called off the streets like a transit driver. When he did have to slow down, the tires would chirp, and then he would shift his foot back to the gas so hard that I felt like a fighter pilot pulling high G-forces. We shot through amber lights and I saw my life flash before my eyes when we were nearly broadsided by a concrete truck at 41st Street. Our speed didn't decrease any but we made it through the next intersections without further mayhem. As we passed the Canadian Blood Services building, I piped up: "Being as our AB positive blood type is so rare, I hope they have some of it in there, because if we crash this thing, neither of us will have any blood left to give the other."

"Approaching sixteenth," was the next thing I heard him say after another twenty-five blocks passed in a blur. As we crossed 16th, the road chicaned to the right, then ran straight all the way to 12th Avenue, where Vic slammed on the brakes. The front of the car dipped toward the pavement as the back wheels locked and smoke poured from protesting tires and brakes. Vic's high-speed pursuit training allowed him to keep from losing command of the car. He cranked the wheel hard to the right, taking the turn in complete control. He shut down the emergency equipment as we proceeded east on 12th. We drove down the street like normal citizens, pulling into a parking area right in front of the emergency ward, and Vic parked in a spot reserved for the police.

"Thanks, I owe you one."

"You're welcome," came Vic's reply.

"Not you, Him!" I said as I pointed to the heavens.

"Oh."

I slowly opened the door and stood up on shaky legs. My back was drenched in sweat. The ride from the airport to the hospital had taken under ten minutes. Vic was way ahead of me, already walking across the parking lot toward the automatic doors. He was pressing buttons at the bank of elevators by the time I got inside. I caught up to him just as the doors opened. There were other people ready to join us in the elevator, but Vic pulled his badge out and showed it to those waiting to board the elevator.

"Sorry folks, would you mind catching the next car? Police business." As I stepped past the waiting passengers, I noticed dirty looks, and was also able to read lips as the door closed. The consensus was that my brother was an asshole.

I looked over at Vic. "This sergeant shit has really gone to your head, hasn't it? You are starting to act like those assholes on TV. It was guys like you that convinced me not to join the regular force when I was on the reserve force. Didn't you get a chance to look death in the eye while you were in Vietnam? You were the stupid Canuck who ran off and joined the Marines, so that he could be a Real Soldier, just like his dad."

"Rangers," came Vic's response.

"What?"

"Rangers. I joined up as a Ranger," said Vic.

"Whatever. When I was in the reserves, I was on patrol with a bunch of jerks that let the cop crap go to their heads. Tried to be like some bad ass cop on *Police Story*. There were just as many crazies on the job as there were on the streets."

I continued with my rant, "And what about the fact that back then, there was a higher chance of getting divorced than getting shot at. For all the jokes about salesmen and the farmer's daughter, I can assure you that sales people get a lot less stray stuff than any cop who really wants it. You know, a little quickie down by the Fraser River instead of issuing the cute blonde a speeding ticket. That's why I went into sales."

"Your drive here just proved that you probably do need a screw loose to be on the job. Next time you contemplate suicide, don't bother taking me along for the ride." Finally finished with my tirade, I just stood and looked at him. The doors began to open for the fifth floor. Vic reached over, smashed his thumb onto the door close button. He pushed me against the wall with his right hand, while continuing to hold his left thumb on the button.

"Just who do you think you are? Just who the hell do you think you are to criticize me? Where the hell have you been the last ten years? While I've been down here taking care of them. When they needed someone to do something, who did they call? Me. When they wanted someone to complain to? Me again," he spat out as he removed his hand from my chest and started pounding it against the elevator wall.

"Granted, it wasn't often, but who the hell do you think they called when they were mad at one another? It was me that got the earful." I still hadn't had a chance to say a word in reply. "Who was the one that had to go down to the God damn morgue at six o'clock this morning and identify the body? Me! That's who! You self-righteous son of a bitch. Don't you dare criticize me with your holier-than-thou sanctimonious attitude."

"I was also there at the accident scene, forced to stand to the side while the fire department tore the side of the car off. The car you learned to drive in. I had to watch while they dragged our mother out, then use a defibrillator on her twice to get her heart going, with enough electric current to power a cordless drill for a month. And where the hell were you this morning? I waited to call you at a reasonable time, and when I do I find out you're at the fucking golf course. I was the one who had to tell our mother that Dad was gone when she woke up for a bit right after the emergency surgery, just before she went for more x-ray's and CAT scans. Try doing all that before breakfast someday little brother, then we'll see just what you're made of. When you do that, you tell me how your attitude is. Mister I'm always positive no matter what happens."

Vic's eyes seemed totally unfocused as he finished ripping into me. He had stopped hammering the wall and had now hit his chest so many times I wouldn't be surprised if he had bruised himself. He drew his hand back, making a fist. I was sure he was going to slug me in the head. His closed fist flew past me pummeling against the elevator wall again. The alarm bell for the door started to chime, so Vic released it and the doors opened. We stepped out to the fifth floor, where the ICU was located. Fortunately, no one had come to check out the alarm.

"I had no idea. I am so sorry. I guess I have gotten off pretty easy," I offered as an apology.

"Not your fault. I just felt so helpless standing there. I knew those guys were fighting a losing battle as soon as I got there. I've seen that look on faces in the past. In Nam, even though the medics would be working their asses off to save someone, you knew when it was a forgone conclusion that their efforts would be futile. We knew that once the injured were taken away we would never see them again," he said as he finally broke down and began to sob. "I knew, Chris. I just knew."

For only the second time in my life, I watched as my brother continued to cry. I reached around him with both arms, pulling him tight to my chest, letting him cry out his grief. "It's okay," I said, "I'm sure Mom knows that you were there. You would have done more if you could." I released my grip on him as the doors of another elevator car opened.

We turned toward the ICU ward, walking slowly toward the nurse's station. As we walked, Vic explained that he had not had a lot of time to spend at the hospital prior to picking me up. At the morgue, they had explained that preliminary indications were that it probably wasn't the crash that had killed Dad. "More likely a heart attack. They won't know for sure until after the autopsy," he said. "According to witnesses at the scene, the car just seemed to suddenly lose control then ran a red light. The car was broadsided in the intersection by a transport truck."

We stopped at the nurse's station. Vic asked to speak to the head nurse, whom he had met earlier. "By the way, just what the hell were they doing on the road that early in the morning?" I asked.

"Didn't you know?"

"Know what?"

"They were heading up to see you guys. I thought you knew. They had planned this trip for weeks. You know Mom, she doesn't do anything spontaneously. I just assumed that you knew they were coming."

"He knew I didn't want him driving that far by himself any longer. I told him that if he ever wanted to come by car, I would come down here and drive them back. It doesn't take long to get up or down the Coquihalla. I end up in Merritt at least once a month. It's only a three-hour drive from there. Christ, he still has all those free flights from when he retired."

Vic nodded, "I know. He told me he had cleared it with the heart specialist he was seeing. He said that if they stopped every hour and a half to get out and walk around it should be fine."

"I can't believe that. Hell, he never even got out of town when he had the attack."

"It could have been a lot worse, little brother," said Vic, "there could have been a lot more traffic on the road. That accident might have killed a lot of people."

"How is the driver of the truck?" I asked.

"Just fine considering. The truck wasn't going very fast but he still managed to destroy the entire side of the Barracuda. You know that car still only had sixty-eight thousand miles on it. Show room condition, as always. It will just head off to be crushed now though."

The Head Nurse returned to the ICU central station. She was probably in her early fifties, around five-foot six in height. You could tell she was keeping her hair blonde with the help of something out of a box. I noticed the grey roots at her scalp. She was wearing a set of scrubs that appeared to be a little too tight. Her face didn't look like she was wearing any makeup, and one of her most attractive features was the smile on both her face and eyes. She recognized Vic from earlier in her shift.

"How are you, Sergeant Porter?"

"Please just call me Vic. I'm not on the job right now. Susan this is my brother, Chris. He just flew in from Kelowna. If he tells you he also flew from the airport to here don't believe him."

I shook hands with Susan. We exchanged the usual, "Nice to meet you," pleasantries.

Vic asked Susan to fill me in on everything that had taken place to this point.

"Your mom is back here in ICU after a battery of tests. She's sedated and on oxygen. She has a fractured pelvis, right femur, humerus and clavicle. She has a cervical spine injury from the lateral force of the impact, as well as a subdural hematoma. She also suffered fractured ribs which caused lacerations to her liver as well as bruised kidneys. The ER doctors got the bleeding stopped but she is in critical condition. As you might be aware, she had to be resuscitated twice on scene."

Not good, not good, I thought, outwardly just nodding dumbly as she continued. Was that really the only reaction my mind could muster as I heard the fate of my parents laid out so clinically?

"She's in and out of consciousness. Her long-term prospects are not good. She was awake for a bit when I checked on her. It could be hard on her if you both go in, so maybe only one at a time. Room 512 on the left side."

Vic indicated that it should be me who went down there first. I had been in intensive care rooms many times, especially when Dad had his triple bypass in the early seventies when it was still a relatively new procedure in Vancouver. Once inside the room, I saw that her face had bruises that were already a bright purple. There were small cuts and scrapes on her face and her right eye was swollen shut. Over her face was a clear oxygen mask that looked like something a fighter pilot might wear. The various leads attached to her body were monitoring her vitals: pulse rate, oxygen levels, blood pressure, and one that I discovered later was measuring the pressure on her brain.

An intravenous tube in her arm was hooked into saline and morphine sulphate bags hanging on a cart beside the bed. She appeared to be sleeping, so I pulled a chair close to her bed. The scraping noise startled her awake. I leaned over, giving her a kiss on the cheek. I couldn't bring myself to look right at her. I had to close my eyes, avoiding having to look directly into her good eye.

"Hi," she whispered hoarsely from under the mask.

"Hi to you to. How are you feeling?" As soon as the words left my lips, I knew that was a stupid question to ask. She probably felt like shit and looked worse. She would never say she felt like shit because I don't think I had heard her swear in her entire life. "I have something from the girls for you." I pulled out the folded piece of construction paper and showed it to her. It was a basic stick picture I figured was my mom holding hands with the girls, they had printed "Get well soon Granma" on the top.

Her good eye appeared to light up a little. The cervical collar prevented her from rolling her head but, I could see through the clear mask that she was trying to wet her lips so that she could speak.

A feeble, "Water," was all I could make out.

"Just hold on a second," I said, holding up a finger, as I got out of the chair and went to find a nurse. The nurse came in to assess the situation, looking at the monitors, and then poured Mom a glass of water and put in a straw, removed her mask then allowed her a small sip. Taking another look at the vitals, she informed me she shouldn't have her oxygen mask off for too long. She left the room and we were alone again.

Mom looked up at me and began to speak very slowly, "I'm dying," she stated quietly.

"No, you're going to be fine. They think the worst is over. You'll be on the road to recovery," I lied.

"You don't understand. I know. It's okay. A person just knows," she hesitated, trying to take a bigger breath of air before she continued, "There are things I have to tell you before I go. Get Victor, then we'll talk." She had always call my brother Victor when we were in trouble or about to get a lecture. It was Christopher for me.

"You just rest. Get stronger, then we can talk about anything you want."

"No. We have to do this now. But before you do get him, I want you to promise me that you two won't fight. No matter what happens throughout your lives, you have to remember that he is your only brother."

"I'll get him in a second. I just want to tell you that I love you, and Dad too. I never really got the chance to tell him how I felt. It wasn't that way between us. Now I feel sick that I never said the words."

"Don't worry about the words, he knew you did. He never said the words either, but he was very proud of both of you. So am I. Just promise me you won't fight with your brother."

I reached over and grasped her hand lightly, she in turn gave me a feeble squeeze.

"Could you rub my legs please? They are so sore and tired from shopping all day."

"Sure, Mom, I can do that." Her eyes slowly closed as I rubbed her legs though the blankets. I watched the monitor, noticing her heart rate slowly decrease as she drifted back to sleep.

I stopped rubbing her legs, got up and gently put the oxygen mask back on her face. I left the room to search for Vic. The nurse at the desk told me he had headed outside for a smoke and gave me directions.

I found him just outside one of the hospital entrances; there was absolutely no smoking anywhere inside the hospital itself. In the area around this side entrance was an odd mix of visitors and patients. There were patients in wheelchairs, some of whom had brought out their portable IV stands, alongside nurses and orderlies dressed in colourful scrubs. Patients dressed in faded blue bathrobes were sitting on the benches. All of them were there for the same purpose, however, to have their nicotine cravings satisfied.

Vic was just finishing his smoke. He butted it out in the huge ash can and we headed back up to Mom's room. I explained what had gone on while I was with her, telling him everything she had to say.

"Funny thing is, when I saw her just before she went into surgery, she said that she had to see you. Said she had something to tell us both. All she kept on about was, 'Don't blow it all.' I couldn't tell what she was talking about. I figured she was still more or less out of it," Vic explained.

"She's still out of it. Thinks she was shopping all day. She said she knows that she's dying."

"She probably does," Vic agreed.

She was still sleeping when we got back to her room, but she must have felt our presence, because she opened her good eye. We stood at the foot of the bed, allowing her to see us both without having to turn her head. I reached down and squeezed her foot. "We're both here, Mom. What did you want to tell us?"

Vic stepped up to remove the oxygen mask. After giving her a small sip of water, he joined me at the foot of the bed. "Who's that with you? Is that another doctor?" she asked.

We both looked behind us at the same time. There was no one there. "It's only Vic and I."

"The man behind you, the one over there," she said as she lifted her hand slightly off the bed and pointed to the corner. "That man there. The one with the beard, is he another doctor?" she asked again.

Shivers ran up my spine while a chill again enveloped my whole body. "Oh. No, he's just an orderly," I lied.

"Well he should get rid of that beard if he's going to be working around here. I never did like it when you had that beard of yours, Christopher," she chided.

"I always thought you liked it."

"No, I must say that I really didn't. It was always scruffy looking."

"What did you want to tell us Mom," I asked.

"You both have to promise me never to fight with one another Christopher, and Victor just make sure you don't blow it all," she demanded weakly.

Vic broke in. "Why don't you just rest? We can come up and see you later when you get a little stronger."

"Both of you promise me now," she insisted.

We looked at each other, nodded our heads in agreement and then both of answered in unison. "We promise."

"Thank-you," came her sleepy reply.

"Would you like me to sit with you a while longer?" I asked.

"That would be nice." She drifted back to sleep before we left of the room.

I joined Vic in the hall. "That was really weird. The guy with the beard and all. It gave me the heebie-jeebies."

"Me too," Vic said, as I watched a shudder roll over him as well.

"Why don't you head off home, get cleaned up, see Helen and the kids, get yourself something to eat, then come relieve me? No sense in both of us sitting here the whole time. I'll call you if things change."

Vic headed off and I re-entered the room. She was still asleep. A sleep that would slip to a coma, from which she would never regain consciousness. In reality, she died before the two of us had left the room; however, they wouldn't pronounce her dead for at least fifty more hours. She had done her duty. She'd seen her two boys together again, holding on until she had a chance to ensure everything would be all right, getting promises, that in future years might prove very difficult to keep.

That first night, I was sitting by her side when one of the evening nurses came in. She told me that people in comas needed to be spoken to. They had to be reassured that everything was alright. When they feel that everything is right with their world, they can let go and slip away in peace. I told her about her seeing the bearded man. She said, "I've seen and heard many strange stories," from what she termed the death watch.

One story she shared was about having an elevator door open on a floor where someone had just passed away. Not unusual, except that elevator was empty. There was no one getting off, and no one waiting to get on. "We couldn't tell if the car was going up or going down. It's not like it only happened once, but often enough to make you wonder."

I then watched as the nurse did a very strange thing. Removing a watch that was pinned to her breast pocket, she held it by the fragile chain above my mom's body, letting it swing back and forth. I observed as it went in small circles then stopped, and swung back and forth two times. She told me that over the years it was amazing how accurately she had been able to predict the ultimate time of death. "Two o'clock in the morning," she stated.

Two o'clock in the morning came and went. The machines were keeping her alive. She was still in the coma, her life support system still beeping, lights on the monitors blinking showing her feeble heartbeat.

I got a hotel room on Broadway so I could get some sleep. Vic and I took turns keeping vigil by her bed. We spoke reassuringly to her, telling her that everything would be all right. We promised we would keep our word about not fighting or blowing it all, still not really knowing exactly what she had been talking about.

It was close to midnight on my shift. I decided to go out and get something to eat. She had been in the coma for forty-eight hours, so I headed down to the Day and Knight Restaurant, needing something other than hospital cafeteria food. I finished my huge omelette, toast, and a container of coffee, then took a long walk back to the hospital. It was a nice warm, pre-summer night and there wasn't anyone else out walking. I was halfway back when I got the strangest feeling. Like Obi Wan Kenobi when the death star destroyed Alderaan, it felt like a disturbance in my universe. I picked up my pace, running all the way back to the hospital. As the doors opened on the fifth floor, I knew what the disturbance had been.

Rushing down the hallway past the empty nurse's station to her room, I found it was filled with nurses, an orderly and a doctor. The doctor held Mom's chart, asking one of the nurses the actual time of death. The one who told me what the time would be, looked at the same watch she had been wearing that night. "2:04 was the time the monitor stopped, doctor."

"Time of death 2:04," he repeated, noting the time on the chart then handing it to the nurse to witness the time. Turning around and seeing me for the first time, he extended his hand, telling me how sorry he was about the loss of my mom. There was no real warmth in his voice, I thought, but then he probably had to do this all the time. *How does Bob do it?* I wondered as the nurses offered their sympathies. Then the orderly began to get her ready for the trip to the morgue.

That's it. That's all there is. One minute we're here the next we're on a cold slab in the basement. I went to find a phone to give Vic a call. As I walked down the corridors, I began to hum Peggy Lee's "Is That All There Is?"

CHAPTER 10

We had a memorial service. Big and fancy wasn't something our parents were into. Their bodies would be cremated, then be interred under some big maple trees at a funeral park in Surrey. With their usual propensity for making sure that they had no debts, they had bought and paid for their eternal resting place years earlier.

It seemed surreal that only a year ago, both Vic and I and our families had surprised Mom and Dad with a family photo shoot for their fortieth wedding anniversary. Now here we were exactly one year later having a funeral service on what would have been their forty-first anniversary.

Back at the house, we had a small reception for the people who had been at the service. An aunt and uncle, some friends of Vic's from the force, old friends of me and Trish who we had stayed in touch with since high school. There were some of Dad's co-workers from where he worked prior to his early retirement due to a heart condition.

Everyone had thought he was in great shape and would be fine for years to come. Seventy-five doesn't seem that old any more, I thought. People offered their opinions of how unfair it seemed that the heart failure had also caused an early demise for Mom, who was seven years younger than him.

Partway through the reception I slipped out to the garage, wandering around the empty space where his beloved Barracuda used to rest, just looking at old tools. I had been out there alone for about twenty minutes when Vic joined me. "People are getting ready to leave. You should come in to say your goodbyes."

"It sure doesn't make sense, big brother."

"What doesn't?"

"Well, it's like the Billy Joel Song 'Only the Good Die Young.' He was right. Dad was the model of a good citizen. Did his duty during the war, didn't beat us. He was no Fred McMurray from *My Three Sons*, and certainly no Ward Cleaver, although there were many times I felt like the Beaver when I was getting in trouble, but all things considered I think we did pretty well with the parents we were born with."

"I still think I'm starting to agree with Joel, though. We should be laughing with the sinners. I'm tired of crying with the saints. It seems that sinners always have more fun. You probably have a slightly altered viewpoint considering your profession," I said. "It's just that I think there has to be a lot more to life than picking up the doggy doo, cutting the lawn and being Mr. Nice Guy all the time."

"You haven't seen the shit and carnage on the streets, or the cretins I have to deal with all the time. That case I told you I was on when you arrived, it had as many bodies lying around as a Dirty Harry movie. Not a pretty sight. One guy was crushed by a huge fork lift," was Vic's reply.

"What's the difference anyway?" he continued. "You're a nice guy, just like Dad was. You've got two great kids, a super wife, and a well-paying job. What more do you want? There are guys out there who would kill for half of what you've got."

"That's just it. I'm struggling with so many emotions right now, I don't know what I want."

"Just let it go, little brother. Things will get back to normal in the weeks to come and you'll forget all about it. Let's go in and say goodbye to everyone."

Vic grabbed me by the shoulder, giving me a brotherly squeeze. We locked up the garage, then began to head back to the house. "Race ya!" I shouted as I took off to the house, taking the back steps three at a time. I was in the house before he reached the bottom of the stairs, and was holding the door open for him. "I sure hope you can chase the bad guys faster than you chase me!"

"You cheated, you bugger!"

"So do the guys you're chasing, I presume?"

People didn't stay long after the first few left. When the last of them were gone, we locked up the house. Vic, his wife and their kids headed home. Trish, the girls and I all headed back to stay at Trish's parents' home.

I told Trish they should get on back to Kelowna so the kids could get back to school and she could get back to work while I stayed in Vancouver to take care of all the paperwork. It was going to be a full-time job for the next week. I arranged with my boss for another week of vacation time so that I could get it all done. I would stay at the house, giving me more time to look through their personal effects.

The next morning, I had the car all packed up for my family to head out by nine. The girls gave Grammie and Poppy, their only remaining grandparents, hugs and kisses. Lana had been extra quiet all morning. Despite Grammie trying to coax her off my leg, she just wouldn't let go. "What's the matter, sweetie?" I asked.

At six years old, she had not yet really grasped the concept of death, still thinking that Granma and Grampa would be back some day. When they were much younger, their cat had been run over. To this day, Lana kept waiting for it to return. Whenever the back-screen door would rattle in the wind, she would get all excited, run to the door calling out the cat's name, "Frisky ... Frisky."

Unlike the bedtime story we used to read to her, the cat was not coming back the very next day. No matter how many times we told her she refused to believe it. Now that Granma and Grampa are gone like Frisky, she said she was afraid that it would be Trish or I that went away next. "It's okay Pimkin, I'll be home as soon as I can. We'll still have Granma and Grampa with us in our hearts, just like Frisky. Remember when we went to Stanley Park last year?" I continued, "We spent the day with them, and took all those pictures. We still have that video tape of them from Uncle Vic's camcorder."

An almost inaudible, "Yes," was all I got.

"When you get home you guys look at all the pictures. It will be like they're right there with you. Just like when you really miss Frisky, you can pull out those pictures. Remember how they make you laugh when you see him in the paper bag or up on the valence, or hanging on the screen door."

"Uh huh, sort of."

"Well there are no pictures of Grampa up on the valence, but remember the train ride at the Stanley Park Zoo? We can go on that ride with them anytime you want. All we have to do is use our 'maginations and watch the video."

The girls asked Trish if they could watch the video and look at pictures when they got home. Tears were flowing down Trish's cheeks and her voice seemed raw. "We sure can," she assured them. With that settled, I hugged Trish, reached inside the car and fastened their seat belts, giving them each a kiss and telling them I would be home soon.

CHAPTER 11

Vic had loaned me one of his personal vehicles. One of the perks of being with the homicide squad was being able to take his unmarked police car home with him, because he never knew what ungodly hour he might get called out. While he was technically on compassionate leave, he could still be called back in at any time.

Returning to my childhood home, I began going through my parents' stuff. It would take time to figure out even where to begin. I was saved from that decision when Vic showed up.

Using Mom's old Underwood manual typewriter, we sent off numerous requests to any of the companies with whom Mom or Dad had credit cards, as well as sending inquiries to insurance companies regarding a variety of old policies and mutual funds. It took us a pot of coffee, a lot of white out, and most of the day to get the letters typed.

"Need a new coffee maker?" I asked.

"What?"

"We gave them this one for Christmas last year. Our old one is just about shot. If you don't want it, I'll take it home." The discussion of various possessions ran on for a while. We finally agreed to leave everything in the house for the time being, and each make of list of anything we thought we would like to have.

The day before the funeral, we had found some very poor thermal paper copies of their wills. One of the only things we could make out on the faded paper was that the two of us were the sole heirs of anything in their estate. After a day of taking care of the estate business, we were both mentally exhausted, so we headed to the Keg for a hearty dinner. A nice bottle of wine had lightened our spirits. "It's too bad that it has taken something like this for you and me to spend some extra time together," Vic lamented, as he drove me back to the house.

Too wound up to sleep, I decided to look through some more paperwork, as well as stuff from the hall closet. A large box on the top shelf caught my eye, so I climbed up on an old steamer trunk, grabbed the box and brought it back to the living room, setting it down on the coffee table.

All it held were old pictures, little ornamental figurines, and a letter opener from some insurance company that probably didn't exist anymore, a small glass fishbowl that must have come from the PNE—a prize for popping balloons with darts. The bowl still had the little porcelain house in it that the fish used to swim though. There was a pair of bronzed baby shoes as well—basically, a bunch of junk.

All that was left in the box was a dull black metal box with a small hasp and tiny lock. I shook the box. There was definitely something inside. I checked the now empty cardboard box to see if there was a key. No such luck. Mom had always kept a bunch of the miscellaneous keys in a catch-all drawer in the kitchen. Heading in there to check, I decided it was probably a good time for a stiff rum and Coke, which I promptly drank down, and ended up pouring myself a second. I didn't find any keys, but I did find a small screwdriver that might work. The other place it could have been was one of the jewelry boxes in the bedroom, so I headed there to investigate.

I felt like a thief, skulking through the house looking through things. "Alexander Mundy. *It Takes a Thief*, starring Robert Wagner, Tuesday nights on ABC," I pronounced, using my best announcer's voice.

It felt strange to be looking through my parents' things. The last time I did this was the year I got my Strombecker road race set for Christmas. Found it in the bedroom closet and ended up spoiling Christmas for myself. I always wondered if they knew I had found it, or if I had done a good enough job of acting surprised on Christmas morning.

I started looking for the key in Dad's dresser caddy. Finding nothing there, I tried Mom's jewel case. I lifted the case out of the drawer and sat on the bed with it on my lap. I knew it certainly wasn't full of diamonds or gold. A family ring, a lot of junk costume jewelry, a nice pearl pendant that had belonged to a great aunt who passed away years ago. Nothing else of any consequence, there were some small suitcase keys but nothing to fit the small black box.

I then noticed a small piece of cardboard sticking up at the back of the case. Just the corner of a tag of some sort. As I pulled on it, the entire bottom section of the jewellery case also lifted. The piece of cardboard had an elastic band attached to a key.

It was not the key I was searching for, but it was intriguing. There was no mistaking that the shape of the key had to be for a safety deposit box. I held up the tag for a closer examination. The card looked old, and was stamped on one side with the location of where the key had come from: Vancouver Safety Deposit Vaults. - 402 West Pender. On the reverse, in Dad's precise penmanship, was the box number.

"I'll be a son of a bitch," I declared, and then looked up at the heavens. "Sorry, Mom. How long have you guys had this thing lying around? I don't remember anything about a private deposit box. Come to think of it, there should be a safety deposit box up at the corner at the Bank of Commerce."

I grasped the key and returned to the living room. As I sat down on the couch, the screwdriver in my back pocket jabbed me, reminding me that my original intention had been to open the black box. I used the screwdriver to pry it open the small lock. There were four of the medals my dad had received after World War Two. They were still in the original boxes. I was sure he never wore them.

I thought about calling Vic to tell him about my find. Checking the clock on the wall and realizing it was now 11:30, I decided it could wait until he came in the morning.

The very bottom of the box had a lot of papers all neatly stacked and stapled together. They were all original documents from the purchase of my dad's beloved 1967 four-barrel carb, 273-cubic-inch Barracuda, including the original build sheet and invoice from Kingsway Plymouth Chrysler.

Thinking again about the safety deposit key, I grabbed the phone book from under the telephone in the kitchen and stretched out on the couch to see if the depository was still around. I flipped through the white pages and sure enough, there it was—Vancouver Safety Deposit Vaults. 402 West Pender, 555-7654. I set the phone book on the coffee table, picked up the tag with the key attached again and examined it. The number on the tag was unmistakably written by my dad. Number 383. There were four small numbers engraved on the key but no identifying marks to say that it had come from the same place as the tag.

The Tonight Show with Johnny Carson had just started. I didn't really hear his monologue or see his guest, George C. Scott. All I heard was good old Ed McMahon giving his trademark "Heeeere's Johnny." I must have drifted before he finished his set.

The pounding in my head wouldn't go away. I lay still, trying to get my bearings before rising, my neck stiff from being propped on the armrest all night. The pounding continued. I swung my feet onto the floor and rolled my neck in large circles, which produced distinctly satisfying clicks from my neck. I finally understood the pounding was coming from the door, not my head. Most, but not all of it. "I'm coming, I'm coming. Hold onto your shorts," I yelled.

The TV was still on, now broadcasting the morning news. Taking the remote from beside the bronze baby shoes, I turned it off as I went to open the door. Vic was standing there with a smoke dangling from his lips, looking bright-eyed and bushy-tailed. I, on the other hand, must have looked like hell, and felt worse.

"Why the hell didn't you use your keys?" I asked.

"They're on the key ring I gave you. You look like hell this morning."

"Yeah, well it might have been the extra rum and Coke's I had after you dropped me off."

"You know what your problem is, don't you?"

"No, but I have the feeling you're going to tell me anyway."

"Too much blood in your alcohol system."

I just looked at him and shook my head, rubbing a hand over my stubbly face and thinning hair.

"What time is it anyway?" I asked.

"Well, you just missed the eight o'clock news."

I vigorously rubbed my face and head again, then headed down the hall to the bathroom.

"Let me look after the four S's and brush my teeth. Then I might be able to carry on an intelligent conversation with you."

"That would be a nice change," laughed Vic.

"Screw you! Besides if you're not nice to me I won't tell you what I found last night." I left him with that cliff hanger, heading off to shower, shave, etcetera.

Vic had made coffee and put bread in the toaster. I felt somewhat human again. A cold shower did have a positive effect at certain times. He was sitting at the kitchen table looking through an old picture album. "Remember this?" he asked. It was a picture of the two of us, standing with our mom under the Rogers Pass Monument.

"Yeah, I do. That's when I found out that you'd been able to start smoking when you were sixteen."

"I was framed. In that picture, I was just holding Dad's smoke while he took the picture. You tried to get me with that same line when they caught you smoking behind the boy's club when you were ten."

"I was sure you would have quit when your lung collapsed years ago," I said.

"The day I got out of that ambush in Nam, the one where I was the only one of my squad to make it back, I decided that if the communists couldn't kill me, then I wouldn't worry about the Surgeon General's warning about a little tar and nicotine."

"A little. With the amount you smoke? Your lungs probably have enough crap in them to re-tar the roof on this house."

"Whatever," he drew out another smoke and lit up, blowing a cloud of smoke right at me.

"Now, what's this big secret, little brother?"

I poured us both a coffee, buttered some toast and then sat at the table with him. I reached into my shirt pocket, pulled out the key, holding the card while the key bounced and twirled around on the elastic, and then tossed it onto his toast.

"Feast your eyes on that, big brother."

Vic looked at the key sitting on his toast. "So? It's a key to their safety deposit box."

"Very astute, sir. But where do you think they would have said box?"

"Up in the Canadian Imperial at 54th and Victoria of course."

"That would be the logical spot. But your assumption would be wrong. Take a closer look."

Vic looked at the key, examining the card that was attached to it. He looked at me then back to the card. "What the hell. When did they get a box down there? I never knew anything about this, did you?"

"Never had a clue."

Vic looked at the tag again. "I know this place. It's been around for years. Heard some talk around work that there are probably a lot of people using this place for less than legal purposes. Why the hell would they have had a box in a private vault? That's not their style. It's just not like them at all."

"I suggest we go up to the corner bank with a copy of the death certificate. We can find out if they had a box there as well. Then we'll head down to see just what's in this mystery box 383."

CHAPTER 12

Although I was apprehensive, I got into Vic's unmarked police car again. Before he closed the door, he made sure that his seat belt was fastened.

"Take it nice and easy this time please. I'm down to my last pair of underwear."

"Relax little brother, just a little ride up to the bank, then we can head to town."

"Downtown," I sang off key. "Petula Clark, 1965. Dad had that tape when we got that first Ampex tape recorder."

"Oh man, are you still doing that song trivia crap? I thought you gave up that annoying habit years ago. It really *is* annoying."

"Well, now that I know how much it bothers you, I'll make sure I do it twice as much," I joked.

"It will be me who gets the last laugh, little brother," he snarled as he pushed the accelerator hard to the floor, sending us down one of the narrow streets in Fraserview. Cars parked on either side of the street left only enough room to get one vehicle down the centre. The street ended at a T-intersection at the bottom of the hill, giving the driver no choice but to turn left or right. The other option would result in flying over the curb, across the sidewalk, becoming airborne over the rock wall, culminating with a sudden stop inside someone's front room.

It was amazing that in all the years we'd lived on this block that it had never happened. Especially in winter when the drivers of Vancouver thought about getting snow tires three hours after the first snow fall of the year. Vic reached the end of the block, skidded the car expertly around the corner then sped up again.

"Okay, okay. Dammit, slow down. You win."

Vic practically stood the car on its nose as he came to a complete stop. The sudden deceleration threw me against the shoulder strap, bouncing me hard against the seat.

Vic was roaring with laughter at my expense. "Gotcha." The rest of drive to the bank and the subsequent drive to the downtown core was quite subdued compared to my first two rides with him.

We had a short wait, but were soon meeting with the local manager of the Canadian Imperial Bank of Commerce. After showing him our identification and a copy of the will, the manager explained that Mom had taken out all her contents and returned her key because she thought the rates were too high.

"By the way, Mr. Harder, would you be able to give us the current bank balances? We haven't found their bank books yet," said Vic.

Harder left to get the up to date account balances while we waited in his office. "Do you remember walking up here when we were kids?" Vic asked. "I recall it being such a long trek, but it's probably less than a mile."

"Ah, yes. But through the eyes and imagination of a kid, it would take so long that we could probably cover two miles in the same time today. It's sort of like the kids in *Family Circus*, going around in circles, poking a head in here, jumping over a can there, and then changing the time on your watch to show that you had indeed arrived at home on time."

We both sat silently, then we spoke about days gone by, when there had been a lot of bush and raw land in the neighbourhood. Vic was six years older than me. His friends had been the older brothers of my friends. As baby boomers after the war, there were always bunches of kids in every neighbourhood. In our imaginations, we fought Nazi's and bandits, had sword fights with the Three Musketeers. Once, we were sure we had discovered a sack of real hidden pirate treasure. In truth, it was just an old sack of rusty washers, still we were positive they must have been Spanish doubloons. The sacking material had mostly rotted away, but it was the best treasure any of the kids had ever found. We buried it again and had made a treasure map of where it was. As I sat there reminiscing, I wondered if it had ever been discovered again.

Harder came back to his office, breaking up our trip down memory lane. He handed us each a photocopy of the updated bank statements.

"Holy shit!" Vic whispered

"Son of a bitch," I cried aloud.

We both looked at the manager in disbelief. "Are you sure these are the accounts of Gerry and Barbara Porter?" asked Vic in a state of disbelief.

"Absolutely, and unequivocally," assured Harder.

"I had absolutely no idea," I gasped

We thanked the manager for his help, and headed downtown. As we drove I continued to look at the bank statements, "If my addition is right, the total in these accounts adds up to one hundred and thirty thousand dollars," I uttered as Vic drove, "Add this to the house, which is probably worth at least one seventy-five, and we're sitting on over three hundred grand."

"Where the hell did it all come from?" queried Vic.

"Remember when they used to buy all the savings bonds? I'd forgotten about it, but they were still buying bonds in the late seventies and early eighties. I bet there wasn't an interest rate of less that twelve percent in those days."

"Well, let's go see what other surprises they might have left for us."

"Four-Oh-Two West Pender please, driver, and step on it," I chirped.

"Your wish is my command, sire," Vic pronounced as he stomped on the gas pedal again.

"Just kidding about the stepping on it," I growled as I was again thrown against the seat back. "Just get us there alive."

"Right! Alive! Yes, master."

We didn't speak for the rest of the trip to town, passing buildings that wouldn't be landmarks on any tourist map. Crossing the Georgia Viaduct to downtown proper, we could see the North Shore Mountains even though there were thirty-story towers looming in the foreground. On Beatty Street, the tank was still on display outside of the old armories, home to the British Columbia Regiment. Once on Pender, we drove right past the building that was home to the Vancouver Safety Deposit Vaults Company.

CHAPTER 13

We found street parking on Seymour, then walked back to the building. "Kind of a plain looking place isn't it?" I commented.

Vic looked up at the building, then gave me a backhand smack on the shoulder. "It may be plain on the outside, but check that out," he said as he pointed toward the upper floors. On the side of the building were letters that looked to be three feet high. They were painted right on the brickwork, a style of signage that must have been the standard when it was built. The writing on the wall high above advertised one of the building's outstanding features:

VANCOUVER SAFETY DEPOSIT VAULTS
SAFEST ARMOUR STEEL VAULTS IN THE WEST
BURGLAR AND FIRE - PROOF

I realized that mom had always been a stickler for keeping things safe and sound. I guess she had found just the spot.

The rest of Pender Street is old but plain. There was a used book store, across the street was the Niagara Hotel and the Montgomery Apartment Hotel. The side of the street we were on was cool in the early morning shade. We walked under a sign with a huge happy face advertising the Smile restaurant. An iconic electric bus passed by with its long trolley arms reaching up to the overhead wires.

"Can't imagine trying to manoeuver one of those suckers around all day," I said.

"Did I ever tell you about the crazy guy in a jacked-up muscle car that I ended up chasing down in one of those? Had to run him off the road, right at the corner where the Birks building is. The car took out the old Birks Clock, going right into their showroom. Made one hell of a mess of their crystal display." I had started to buy into the story. Then he started to smirk and I knew I'd been had.

"Bullshit! You really had me going there. That's the trouble with us sales types, we always like to believe what people are telling us."

"You wouldn't make it out here then. We don't believe anyone," he said as we reached the front of the building. The awnings over the front entrance had newer green canvas. The structure had granite columns with decorative inlays and the stonework was very clean looking, as though it had been recently scrubbed. There were two beautiful brass and glass doors at the top of the stairs leading to the main lobby. Inside, there was a lot of other brass, including a highly-polished old mail drop box emblazoned with the post office's coat of arms.

The rest of the lobby was done up with marble panels on both the floors and walls. Marble plant stands stuffed with a variety of greenery were spaced around the lobby. The plants managed to give some colour to what was otherwise a rather sterile environment. "Trish could probably name each of these plants," I told Vic.

We found the wall directory. I read off the names of some of the tenants who made this address home. "There it is. Vancouver Safety Deposit Vaults is in the basement," I said, as I pointed to the white block letters of the directory.

The gleaming stainless elevator doors behind us opened as Vic was turning toward them. Seeing a group of men exiting the elevator, he abruptly turned back to me. At the same time, he spun me back toward the directory.

He whispered in my ear. "Don't turn around, just keep looking at the directory. Don't ask any questions, I'll tell you why later."

The group that had emerged from the elevator passed behind us, then headed out through the brass and glass doors and down the steps toward Pender Street. I glanced over my shoulder, trying to see who they were, but all I could tell from where I stood was that there were three of them, with the one in the centre being taller by a head than the other two.

"Who were those guys?"

"The correct question is. 'Who are those guys?' *Butch Cassidy and the Sundance Kid*, directed by George Roy Hill, 1969."

"What?"

"Gotcha," he said "Annoying isn't it. You wonder what the hell the other person is talking about when you throw a trivia answer into the middle of a conversation. You asked who were those guys. Well Butch and Sundance kept asking. 'Who are those guys?' throughout the movie."

I nodded in submission. "You're right, you got me. Now, will you please tell me who the hell those guys were that you didn't want me to see?"

"Are. Who are those guys? The big tall one is Chang. You probably didn't get a chance to see his face, but it looks like a patchwork quilt. He has a skin condition—I think it's called vitiligo. He is quite the high roller in this town. Very influential—lots of property holdings, champion for the Chinese community on the east side. He does lots of charity work to give him an air of respectability. That's his public persona."

"The smart money down at headquarters is that he's also the head of one of the largest triads on the West Coast. Supposed to have connections from Hong Kong to LA. The only problem is, no one can prove a thing. Not a damn thing. I don't think he's ever had a parking ticket."

"What is he doing here?"

"Like I told you when you showed me the key, I've heard this place mentioned in some joint task force meetings. The task force says people like him are frequently coming and going from here. Anyway, enough of the shop talk. Let's go check out what we have behind the doors down in the basement."

We took the half-spiral stairs down to the basement. The basement flooring was plain compared to the main lobby, twelve-inch square white tiles with a black one here and there for contrast. There was marble on the walls here as well, but it only came partway up. Above the marble wainscoting there was a bank of windows covered with tightly closed venetian blinds for what appeared to be the office.

The wood around the windows down the rest of the hall was a darkly-stained mahogany, typical of the decorating style of years gone by. The ceiling was at least ten feet high, but the most impressive sight of all was the line of steel bars, thicker than barbells, that stood between us and the vault. Each bar had a pointed tip that came to within a couple inches of the high ceiling.

The round bars were held together by cross members of steel that looked to be at least one inch thick by four inches wide. The entire barred wall was a dull steel grey colour. "Those bars are thicker than the ones in the holding cells at the station," Vic pronounced.

"I've been in bank vaults before, but this is impressive," I replied as I glanced back up at the ceiling. "Good choice, Mom."

We proceeded down the hall toward a Dutch door that was closed on the bottom. There was a couple I figured must be in their eighties conversing with each other in front of the door. The man was nicely dressed in a fashion right out of the sixties, including a cardigan sweater and a driving cap. The lady wore a flowery mid-calf dress and a plain white button-up sweater. Her ensemble was completed by a pillbox hat like my mom had also worn in the sixties.

"I sure would hate to be driving behind this guy. You know you're in trouble when the guy in front of you is wearing a hat like that," I whispered.

We heard whoever was on the other side of the door finish a phone call, then acknowledge the couple waiting at the counter. "Good morning, Mr. and Mrs. Penny, how are you two today?" We couldn't see who the elderly folks were speaking to but, continued to listen to the conversation.

"You amaze us, Mr. Unger. The way you're always able to remember our names. I am so impressed," stated Mrs. Penny.

"That's right, Mr. Unger. You are quite remarkable. A good memory is a real gift. These days I have trouble remembering my own name, let alone all the people who must come down here," offered Mr. Penny. "Just how many people do you see down here every day?"

"Not that many. Maybe twenty on a busy day," was the reply.

"Just how many customers are there in total?" inquired the older gentleman.

"Well, I'm not really sure how many active customers we have. A lot of them haven't been here for years. So far as the total, I've never bothered counting them up. We have around five thousand individual boxes of various sizes, but there are a lot of customers who have more than one box. As for my memory, it's a game I play to try and relieve the boredom. Not only do I try to remember names, but I try to put the name to a box number."

"Do you remember ours?" inquired Mrs. Penny.

Vic and I stepped up behind the Pennys. The guard was still seated, seeing us before answering them. "Be with you fellows in a minute"

"No problem," we replied in unison.

He looked back at the Pennys. "Five Six Eight?"

"That is quite amazing. Right on the nose. Here is our key, could we please get into our box?" Mr. Penny asked as he handed Unger the key.

"Yes, sir. I'll get you right in there."

He stood up from his desk and both Vic and I were taken aback when he rose to his full height of at least six-foot six. He came through the Dutch door, closing it behind him. "Please sign the register," he said as he turned the book around for them. The book was resting on a large shelf built on the top of the lower section of door. Mrs. Penny took the pen from its marble holder and signed them in.

Unger had a large key ring that looked like something out of an old western movie. The ring was packed with keys, but he flipped to the exact one on the first try, then he proceeded to open the steel gate that stood between us and the vault area. He allowed the Pennys to enter first, then followed behind them, closed and locked the gate. "I'll just open up their box, then I'll be back to help you two."

"Thanks. No big hurry," said Vic.

The Pennys had already gone into the open vault area. We backed away from the guard's door, peering down the hall toward the vault. The door that separated the barred-off section of individual safety deposit boxes was huge, at least eight feet high and five feet wide. It had ten large bolts that would insert into the side wall of the vault when it was closed. The door appeared to be at least four to five inches thick, with massive hinges. The front of the door had two wheels on it, one the size of a steering wheel and the other looked like an oversize vintage faucet handle with four spokes. Through the open door, we could see another barred door behind it.

Shortly after they had gone inside, the three of them came back out. We noticed Mr. Penny carrying a regular-looking safety deposit box. The couple headed down the hall toward some cubicles that were obviously there for the privacy of the clients. The guard came back, let himself out of the gated area, locking it behind himself, then nodded to us as he re-entered his station behind the Dutch door.

"Let me do the talking. Just go with me on this," Vic quietly instructed.

Vic reached his hand across the top of the door, offering it to the guard. "Good morning. Mr. Unger, is it? My name is Vic Porter, this is my brother, Chris." Unger shook hands with both of us.

"I'm afraid we have a slight problem, sir." Vic reached into his sports jacket, brought out his police credentials, showing them to Unger, who instantly looked concerned.

"Just what kind of a problem are we talking about?"

Unger was probably around fifty-five, dressed in a generic style of uniform, and though we were inside, he was wearing his white cap with a bright shiny peak, reminding me of the hat I used to wear when I was in the police reserves doing traffic duty at the PNE.

Unger was a big man, appearing overweight even for his height. I'm sure this was caused from sitting in his little cubicle all day, getting no exercise other than escorting customers back and forth to the vault area. His face was pale, probably because he didn't get out to walk around the block on his lunch breaks to soak up any sun.

"Relax, Mr. Unger, I'm not here in any official capacity. I just wanted to show you my creds, hoping it will help with what we need to do." I watched as the guard's features seemed to relax. His shoulders eased down and the creases around his eyes seemed to soften. I was sure he wasn't paid enough to get involved in police business.

Vic continued. "We have a key for one of the safety boxes here that belonged to our parents. Their names were Gerry and Barbara Porter. Perhaps you knew them?"

"The name rings a bell, I'm usually better at putting names to faces rather than faces to names," he stated, as he turned around to grab a book from a row of ten on the desk behind him. The black ledger book appeared quite old. The letter P was stamped on both the cover and spine, he opened it up then started to skim through the names on the pages.

I looked down at the big dog-eared ledger book, observing that the names on the first pages suggested they had been written with a straight pen and inkwell. I could see little blobs of ink where the pen had stopped at the end of a name. The penmanship was impressive, and the names seemed to flow across the pages. My grade school teachers would have given whoever had put pen to paper an "A" for sure. If it had been my scribbles, no one would ever have been able to decipher it.

"That book looks extremely old, Mr. Unger," I commented.

"Yes indeed, it goes right back to our first customers when the building and vaults opened in 1912. We have a lot of safety boxes in here, but over the years we have not had a lot of customer turnover. A lot of these boxes have just been handed down from one generation to the next. Oh, sure we get a hundred or so new customers every year, but for the most part our clientele has been the same for decades."

"You haven't put all this information on computers?" I asked incredulously.

"Why bother? We don't need computers any more than we need an alarm system. The names don't change often enough. Accounts are paid each year in advance, and in some cases, five or ten years ahead for a slightly better rate."

"You said you don't have an alarm system?" Vic asked, his voice rising in amazement.

"Just another big waste of money as far as management is concerned. Just look at this place. That door is over four inches thick," he said as he pointed to the door. "Armour-plated steel. Probably weighs close to ten thousand pounds." He then pointed down the hall. "The walls of the vault are over thirty-four inches thick, made with the best concrete available in its day. Those walls have four inches of steel plating embedded in them as well."

As he spoke, Unger had been running his finger down columns of names. I could almost see a history of writing styles along with the various writing instruments that had been used over the years. I noticed six or seven writing styles made by the various clerks of different generations. I could tell when the ink well and blotter had changed to the ballpoint pen. A lot of the newer names looked as though they were written with one of the fine-tip markers that were becoming more prevalent.

"Here they are, Gerry and Barbara Porter. What did you say their address was?"

"I didn't give you an address," said Vic, smiling at the crafty old bugger. "Their address is 1700 Upland Drive, Vancouver."

"Right you are, Mr. Porter. Now that we have established that, perhaps you would like to tell me what the problem is that you mentioned earlier."

Just before Vic began to tell him about our situation, the Pennys emerged from the hallway where the cubicles were. They called out to Unger, telling him that they were all done.

"Be with you in minute," he called back.

"You can go ahead and finish with them, we've got time," I said.

"I appreciate that," he said as he emerged from behind the door, proceeding with his ritual of letting the customers return their boxes to the proper place. While they were all in there, Vic stole a quick glance at the register, pointing to the last entry prior to the Pennys'. The name confirmed that David Chang had been down here just prior to our arrival.

"Interesting," he said as he tapped his finger on Chang's signature.

The three of them emerged, and Unger escorted them out through the barred gate to the counter. He asked them if they had everything they needed today.

"Oh, yes indeed. Thank you, Mr. Unger. As a matter of fact, we took out a little extra," Mr. Penny lowered his voice in a conspiratorial way. "Took some out to go to the races with this weekend. It's our anniversary on Saturday, so the Mrs. and I will go to Exhibition Park in the afternoon then go do some dining and dancing." He gave Vic and me a little wink.

"Well, you folks have fun and behave yourselves, just don't blow it all on some nag," suggested Unger.

"Having fun and behaving yourself don't go together, Mr. Unger," laughed Mrs. Penny.

"Okay then. Just have fun, and by the way, happy anniversary." They thanked him again then headed over to the elevators.

Looking back to us, he said "Alright let's get you two taken care of. Where were we?"

Vic explained about the accident and our situation, showing him the poor copy of the will we had. "The thing is, this is just a copy. We believe the original is in their safety deposit box, and we wondered if we could get in to see if it's there."

"In circumstances like this you're supposed to make an appointment with the manager, who then has his secretary accompany you while the box is inspected, and she documents its contents. The problem is, the manager is on holidays and his secretary is off with the flu."

"Look, Mr. Unger, I'm from out of town. I don't have a lot of time left to spend here. The sudden passing of our folks has made all this very difficult and I have to head back to the interior to work. Unfortunately, as you're probably aware we need the original to get a lot of the paperwork started. Is there any way we can speed up the process or do I need to keep coming down here? Are you open on weekends?"

"No, I'm afraid we close down on Friday at 5:00. We open again at 9:00 on Monday mornings. That's one of the good things about working here: nine to five, Monday to Friday."

Unger paused to evaluate our dilemma. "Okay, I guess I can do it for you. What with you being with the police and all." He lowered his voice and whispered to Vic, "Just don't tell anyone I let you in there please."

"That would be great. I'll give you my card. If you ever happen to have any trouble with the local constabulary, show them this card and ask them to call me."

"That's very kind of you. Now, where is that key you said you had? You know the numbers on the keys don't match those on the box. It's one of the security measures we do have."

"Well our dad obviously wasn't thinking about security, because he wrote the box number on the tag," Vic said as he handed the key to Unger.

Unger looked at the tag, comparing it to the ledger, "Well, we do have a match, box 383. Okay, let's do this before I change my mind. Again, please don't tell anyone I did this for you guys," he pleaded as he handed Vic back the key.

"You have our word," promised Vic.

We again shook hands with him as he escorted us.

CHAPTER 14

We were not prepared for what we saw when we entered the vault. If my life was a movie, a thousand choir voices would have been belting out a chorus of "Hallelujah" or Mozart's "1812 Overture" would be reaching its crescendo. The inside of the vault was amazing: the ceilings were ten feet high and the walls were lined by the five thousand individual boxes. Thousands of small brass hinges protruded from brilliant chrome doors, row upon row. There were numerous boxes of at least twelve inches square. The fluorescent tube lighting was not overly bright, but the polished chrome doors still reflected it like sunshine on a smooth lake.

Like other safety deposit boxes I had seen in the past, each of the five thousand doors required two keys to open. One would be the master or guard key, carried by whoever escorted you to the room, the other would be your own personal key that only worked with your box. I wondered if, with so many boxes, there might actually be two keys exactly the same.

After leading us to our box, Unger placed his key in one slot, unlocked it, then he got Vic to put ours in the second slot and turn it as well. We heard the audible click of the latch and he eased the door open. Unger twisted his key back to the locked position, then removed it. "My side is already locked. When you're done, you can just replace the box and lock your side. Older folks like the Pennys prefer me to assist them when they put theirs back, but it really isn't necessary. There are some cubicles down the hall you can use for privacy. Lock yourselves in and stay as long as you want."

Vic pulled out the twenty-four-inch-long drawer, then we headed down to the cubicles to see what surprises were in store for us. We both offered our thanks as the guard let himself out to the vestibule in front of his office.

The hallway was lighted by a row of eight-foot fluorescent tubes. The ballasts appeared to be failing, because I could hear an annoying hum coming from above, and many of the tubes also appeared close to burning out, having the telltale black smudge on both ends. We proceeded to the third cubicle, stepped in, turned on the light, then closed and locked the door. Vic placed the box on a wooden table as we sat down on a small wooden bench that looked like it had also been down here since 1912.

I opened the clasp and swung up the lid. The box was full to the top. "We'll take turns like we used to at Christmas. You open one, then I will," Vic suggested.

I brought out the top envelope. It was emblazoned with an old Pacific Western Airlines logo. This one held a lot of personal papers like birth certificates and baptismal records. But it also included the original copy of their last will and testament just as we had hoped. I put the will aside, then began to stuff the other papers back in the envelope. "Wait a sec, there's one more paper here." I brought it out and unfolded it.

"It's a hand-written letter from Mom," I remarked. "This is freaky. It's dated February 12, 1987."

"Well, read it for crying out loud."

Dear Boys

I am sorry that we were not here to talk to you in person. Since you are reading this, something has probably happened to both your father and me. We want you both to know that we loved you very much. We were always very proud of everything you did. Well mostly.

Vic, you made your dad extremely proud when you went off to join the Rangers, and Christopher, he was impressed with the man you became after your stint of training at the Outward Bound Program.

Just so you know, Victor, we knew it was you who damaged the side of the car, not some hit and run when it was parked. And Christopher, we knew you had found out about your Road Racing present that year. You see we really did know everything.

We hope that when you read this letter that the things we have left for you will still have some value. Maybe not the BRIC shares, but your father was very proud of himself, and of the excellent job we did of investing.

As you will see in our will, everything has been left to the two of you.

So, when you are done here, have a drink at the house on us, and don't forget Dad's Christmas stash down in the crawl space.

One last thing: DON'T BLOW IT ALL!

Love,

Mum.

"God damn. She managed to get the last word in after she died," laughed Vic. "I had forgotten about the liquor stash in the crawl space. I guess we really didn't get away with all we thought we did."

"Well let's see what else she was referring to in her letter," I suggested. "Your turn." I handed him the next envelope from the box. It contained fifty brand new 1967 Canadian Centennial Dollar bills. They had no serial numbers. Instead they had 1867 – 1967 printed where those numbers would normally be. There was also five thousand dollars of US currency in the envelope.

Next was a manila envelope, folded up to fit into the narrow box. I removed and examined the papers, which included savings bonds, certificates for some very profitable blue chip stocks, as well as insurance company guaranteed investment certificates showing interest rates of twelve percent. Without calculating for interest we realized that these stocks, and bonds added up to over one-hundred thousand dollars.

"Son of a bitch. Jeeesssus H Keyyyrrsst! Will you look at this stuff!" Vic exclaimed as he passed me the papers.

I began a stuttering laugh as I looked at them. "Ho ho, ha ha ha...holy shit! I don't believe it."

There were other papers and more stock certificates. Vic said, "Dad and I bought some of these right after I graduated. They were only penny stocks, but I felt like J. Paul Getty when I bought them. Not worth wiping your bum with them now though."

There were hundreds of the BRIC shares the BC government had issued back in 1979 that Mom had mentioned in her letter. When the government first brought them out, they were valued between six and nine dollars apiece. "Not worth a hell of a lot today," I said. "A lot of people took a bath on these when they started to drop back in eighty-four. Might be good enough to line the bird cage with."

I gave Vic the last envelope from the bottom of the box. I could tell there was something hard inside as I handed it to him. He removed the contents, showing me eight plastic holders, each one holding a single Troy ounce gold wafer. Tucked inside one of the plastic covers was an original sales slip showing they had paid over six hundred dollars per ounce in July of 1980. Gold had started out over eight hundred an ounce in early 1980 right after Russia invaded Afghanistan.

"I think I've heard on the stock quotes during the morning news the last little while that gold's currently trading around four hundred an ounce," I said to Vic. "I remember when they were going off the Gold Standard in seventy-one. Dad told me I should buy a bunch at thirty-five dollars an ounce. Yeah right. If I was lucky I might have been able to put together a whole three ounces. This envelope is worth a lot less now than it was back in 1980."

"That's it," I said as I checked under the last part of the box behind the hinge section.

"Let's make a list of everything and put it back in the box," said Vic as he brought out a pad of paper and pen.

We made a detailed inventory of the contents, then closed the box. Vic headed back to the gate to get Unger to open it for us, while I took the drawer back inside. When the box was securely locked up, I stopped and looked around again in amazement. My overactive imagination began to spiral, wondering what kind of treasures might be hidden behind the shiny doors. My folks had never seemed that well off, yet they had amassed a small fortune. What might be in the boxes of people whose families were wealthy? It could be absolutely staggering. And, what's lurking behind the doors of those who use this place to store their less than legal holdings—what incredible secrets might those boxes hold?

"Mom and Dad were by no means rich, but they had managed to garner a small fortune. Adding up a mortgage-free home, cash in the bank, the various bonds and stock certificates and we are probably looking at close to half a million bucks," I said out loud.

I heard Vic calling me, so I left the interior of the vault, joining him just as Mr. Unger was unlocking the gate. Locking it up behind us, we once again thanked him for his help, then showed him the original copy of the will and assured him yet again that his assistance would be just between us. Vic told him to make sure he used his card if he ever needed it.

When we got back to the car, we just sat for a minute before I started to vent. "It's bullshit, utter bullshit. They had all that money sitting there and never really did anything with it. The trips they could have taken. They could have redecorated the house, bought new furniture any time. But no, they always said they couldn't afford it. I know Dad loved that Barracuda, but he was always looking at new cars. Hell, he could have kept the Barracuda, and bought himself another new car regularly.

He could have doubled the size of the garage to keep them both inside."

"Take it easy, Chris. There's nothing we can do about it now," said Vic as he started up the car. We drove back to our parents' home in silence.

CHAPTER 15

It took us a few more days to straighten out all of Mom and Dad's affairs. The paperwork was relentless. We contacted the insurance companies, including the government-run car insurance company to get a settlement on the car. Despite the low mileage, the Barracuda was still five years away from being considered a classic, so book value on it was not high. We set up a joint account at the place where Mom and Dad had banked, arranging for either of us to write cheques for costs that we might incur in the next little while. We paid off and cancelled their credit cards. We arranged the usual newspaper announcements in case there were any other creditors lurking in the shadows.

We had just finished our third day of being on the go since 8:00 in the morning. Vic had gone home around 4:30. I had watched the local news for a while then made my daily call home. Afterwards, I decided to listen to some of the old records at the house. At 8:00, I realized I was famished and headed to the kitchen to make some supper. I fixed myself some classic—broiled open-faced cheese sandwiches just like Mom used to make, complete with her homemade mayonnaise that I found in the fridge.

I sat down at the table, waiting for the toaster oven to do its magic. On the table were two items cut out from *The Province* newspaper. One was the obituary we had placed and the other was a single-column article about the crash, complete with a picture of the Barracuda taken right after the passenger door had been pried open by the Jaws of Life.

"That's it then. That's all we get. Us mere mortals who are just routine people. No bouquets of flowers on the front steps or at the crash site left by adoring fans, no lowering of the flag to half mast, no recognition by heads of state, no documentaries," I said to myself as I shook my head in sadness. It dawned on me that I spent a lot of time talking out loud to myself when I was alone.

I got up from the table to check on my sandwiches. "Damnit. It would cook a lot quicker if I had turned the damned thing on." With the broiler activated, I stood waiting for the cheese to bubble to just the right colour. On the counter in front of the oven was the safety deposit key, which I examined again. I had been doing the same thing so many times, I was sure the patina was wearing off. The key did look like the brass was getting brighter. I ran it through my fingers, feeling the contours of the teeth that were cut deeply into the thin brass. I stared at the key for so long I didn't keep my eye on the boiler. It wasn't until the pungent aroma of burning cheese and toast attacked my nostrils that I came back to reality and remembered why I was standing here in the kitchen.

I tossed the charred mass of my ruined dinner into the garbage. "Should I just head down to the Mickey D's on Marine?" I wondered out loud. It was now 8:30 p.m. and I knew that a gut bomb at this time of night was not a great idea. I used to be able to eat crap like that into the wee hours of the morning with no ill effects.

"Screw it. Just a night cap." I made myself another rum and Coke. Vic and I had already finished off one the old forty pounders of Lambs Navy since we had been here.

Taking my drink, I went to lay on the couch, setting the glass on the coffee table which I had made for them when I was still in high school. "A fine piece of furniture if I do say so myself."

I opened my hand, which had been clenching the key. Staring at it again, an idea began to form. The more I thought about it, the more I excited I became. I lay on the couch, creating small specific details to fill in gaps of what was becoming a full-fledged plan. My hands became cold as ice, as they did whenever I was excited or worried about something. My stomach began to twitch as though a swarm of butterflies was dive bombing my innards. I finally fell asleep. Thoughts of the plan I was constructing even penetrated my dreams.

When I awoke early the next morning, my neck was stiff from having slept with it on the armrest again. The drink I had made was full except for the one sip I had taken before going into imagination lockdown.

Vic and I had decided the day before that we had done all we could for the time being. One of the last things to take care of was cleaning out the fridge and freezer and all the food in the house, as well as getting all the liquor into Vic's car for him to take home, and finally to get the house transferred into our names. This was going to be a little tricky for us to handle on our own, so we got in touch with Vic's lawyer. He was arranging everything for us, including looking after all the probate requirements. The house would go into both our names in joint tenancy so that if something happened to either one of us it would automatically go into the other's name without the need of a probate court. The legal documents allowed for the surviving spouse to then be placed on title.

Vic had arranged to meet the lawyer at 11:00. I had just enough time to get to town and back. Thirty minutes later, I had showered, put on a jacket and tie, and was standing in the back alley of 402 West Pender. I was there to get a better feeling for the place. The first thing that struck me was how clean the alley was. There were no piles of trash or flying papers churned up by the winds that swirled around these box canyons. Like most multi-story buildings from the turn of the century, there was a large black metal fire escape with stairs and ladders. Waste bins sat along the lane that divided it from a similar four story structure to the south.

A door just below and to the right of the fire escape opened. I watched as what appeared to be a custodian emerged, taking garbage bags over to the trash bins. I took a chance and approached the man.

I have always been amazed at how much people will tell you when you engage them in pleasant conversation. A customer had once told me how he had entered the yard of the Western Star truck plant in Kelowna. Putting on a hard hat and carrying a clip board in one hand and a stop watch in the other, he wandered throughout the plant, talking to employees for most of a day. Not one person approached him to find out what he was doing.

His belief was that if you acted like you belonged, then usually no one will notice you. "It's hiding in plain sight. You just have to blend in." I was about to put that hypothesis to the test.

By the time I left, I knew that the custodian had been working in the building for three years, as well as hearing the incredible story of how he got there. He had arrived in Vancouver from Poland by ship. While the vessel was loading wheat at the Cascadia Terminal, he and two of his friends had literally jumped ship. Plunging from a lower deck into the frigid waters of Burrard Inlet, the three of them swam the two hundred metres to shore at New Brighton Park. They then found the first police officer they could and requested asylum in Canada.

I complimented his accented but easily-understandable English, telling him I thought stories like his only happened in the movies. He assured me that it was all true, and that while it had taken some time, he was now on his way to getting Canadian citizenship.

I explained about my parents' safety deposit box, and how I was checking out the neighborhood, asking him if there had ever been any problems that he was aware of. He assured me that he had never heard anything but good things from tenants in the building, going on to say that he was the only custodian, and like Unger he only worked five days a week.

Taking me to the back door I had seen earlier, he showed me where the old boiler room was, pointing down a set of winding metal stairs toward the room below. Adjacent to the stairs I noted an old chain hoist. He explained that it had been used in the early years of the building to help remove the coal ashes from the boilers.

"I'm sorry," I finally said, "I was so caught up in your story that I forgot to introduce myself. I'm ..." I still don't know why I suddenly blurted out a fake name, but it just happened, "Eric House." I reached out and shook his hand. "And you are?"

"Jakub Stankowski," came my new friend's reply as we vigorously shook hands.

Once again, he pointed downstairs. "Your deposit box is right down there, on the other side of that wall, right behind the boiler room. It will be very safe to keep your things there." He then confirmed what Unger had told us: "Nobody's going to get through the thirty-four inches of concrete and steel."

"Thirty-four inches, that's amazing," I said, giving a small whistle and trying to sound surprised. "Wow. I think you're right, Jakub. Things will be very safe in there. Listen, I have to go to see a lawyer about my mom's estate, but it has been a pleasure speaking with you. Can I bring you a coffee next time I come to the vaults? I would love to hear some more of your amazing story."

"I would like to talk to you again, Eric. It helps me with my English. Next time, we go down the street to the Smile Café, and we drink tea together."

"I look forward to that, Jakub," I said as I left him in the alley.

Jakub was a nice guy. I wondered if I ever would see him again. If he'd had any idea that he had been used to get some very valuable information, which I would probably never use, he would likely have been very disappointed.

I once had someone jab a big beefy finger into my chest and call me a "devious bastard." The guy had been pretty liquored up. We were supposed to be business associates. To this day, I swear that if he had jabbed me one more time with that pudgy finger I would have grabbed it, then twisted like Chuck Norris and dropped the bastard right to the ground. As I walked back to my car, I thought about how I had bullshitted Jakub. I started to wonder if maybe the guy was right that day. "I am a devious bastard," I said as I laughed out loud.

I wasn't in the house more than ten minutes when Vic pulled up to the curb out front. We decided to just rent out the house, complete with the existing furniture, then decide later what we wanted to do with it. Property values were still rising, so it might be a good investment. At the lawyer's, we set up a numbered company to handle all the transactions for the property. Our company would also pay for a storage locker where we would keep Mom and Dad's personal effects for the time being.

With the last of the paperwork out of the way, Vic offered to buy lunch at the Waldorf Hotel before he took me to the airport. He knew a lot about the colourful history of the Waldorf—a Vancouver landmark since 1948—telling me stories about the place as we waited for our server in the iconic Tiki Bar.

"The guy who built the place had been a U.S. Marine. *Semper Fi and Oorah,*" he said jokingly. "I always liked the sound of their motto better than our Ranger one *Sua Spnonte,* our motto was fitting for me though. Its Latin meaning is, 'of their own accord.' I certainly went off on my own accord."

"Our other motto comes from D-Day. The commander of our 5th Battalion on Omaha beach was asked by a general what our unit was. Someone yelled out '5th Rangers,' to which this General Cota replied, 'Well then Goddammit, Rangers lead the way!' And that's how we ended up with our second motto."

Vic carried on with his history lesson about the Waldorf. It was quite the place in the fifties and sixties. He told stories of health inspectors of the day getting paid off with Lions tickets, and another story about how bookies had tried to set up shop here.

Our server came to the table and Vic suggested we get one of their famous Manhattan cocktails. Then we gorged ourselves on a meal of huge stir fried garlic prawns on beds of rice, completing our meal with dessert, but passing on wine because Vic had to drive me to the airport.

"This is a great place. Merci, mon frère," I mocked in a terrible French accent.

"Well, I think we have everything pretty well in order. Now we can let the future come our way," we clinked glasses together as he pronounced. "To the future."

"To life. Our way," I added.

Vic requested the bill, and as our waitress left, I noticed the hostess seating the Chinese man that Vic had seen our first day in the building on Pender Street. "Vic, I think the hostess is seating the guy we saw at the vaults the other day. What was his name? Chow, or Chin?"

Vic glanced over his shoulder. Chang was being seated a few tables away. One of the men with him made sure his boss was seated comfortably, then took a seat at another table with a second man, leaving Chang to sit on his own.

"You're right. His name is Chang. How'd you recognize him?"

"You told me about his skin condition. He does stick out in a crowd. He's tall, and the mottled skin reminds me of a male stripper the girls told us they had seen one time. Called himself 'Patches.' I wonder if that's why Trish named the dog that. Anyway, his whole body was like that according to the girls. I do mean his whole body, if you catch my drift."

"Well, there are a lot of people who refer to him as that, but I'm sure no one has ever said it to his face, and I doubt he has ever been a stripper."

I was looking past Vic, noticing that the two men who had accompanied Chang were sitting at a booth against the wall, with their heads constantly twisting, taking in the surroundings just like the men in the Secret Service who protected the US President.

Chang was sitting alone at his table. I watched the other two taking note of each group of people being brought into the room. The noon rush had come to an end and the hostess seemed be keeping an invisible line of empty tables around Mr. Chang.

"Let's get out of here before I regret having stayed too long. I have to get back to work tomorrow. I can get caught up on Chang's activities from the intelligence boys when I go in. I'll tell them about seeing him down at the vaults. Although they might already be aware of his activity there. They have a pretty good pulse on what goes on in this city," Vic continued.

"According to some of my guys in homicide, we think that he or some of his people might have been involved in those shootings down at the docks last week."

Vic paid for our lunch and we headed past Chang and his associates who appeared more interested in who was coming in than heading out. We were parked in the Hotel lot and once there, we noticed a car with decals on it from the Ministry of Municipal Affairs, recognizing the Minster from television. Accompanying him were men and women who might have been deputy ministers or aides.

"I'll bet you dollars to donuts that they'll be joining Chang for lunch. I read that Chang wanted to build some more affordable housing on the east side of Vancouver. Good optics for him, especially if he gets the government to kick in more than their fair share," offered Vic. "But let's not worry about things we have no control over. You have a plane to catch, so let's get going."

"Promise no code three. I have plenty of time to get there," I pleaded.

Vic made the promise and kept it. We said our goodbyes at the curb. Grabbing my bag from the trunk, I headed inside, where it took me almost as long to get through security, walk to the departure gate, and waste time in the pre-boarding area as it took to fly to Kelowna. For the entire flight, I kept going over the farfetched idea that had been evolving in my mind since last night.

Trish and the girls were there to pick me up. I could see Lana and Rebecca with their noses pressed against the glass as I descended the mobile ramp stairs. The girls started to jump up and down and wave as I stepped onto the tarmac. When I came through the motion activated sliding doors, both girls came bounding over and leaped into my arms. I managed hug to them both, momentarily hanging on before I had to set them down.

"Easy does it, ladies. You almost knocked me right over." They both gave me another big hug, telling me how much they had missed me.

"Come on girls, let's go get Dad's bag and head home," suggested Trish. She gave me a big hug while the girls ran over to the baggage area to watch for my bag. She finished her hug off with a nibble on my ear, whispering that if I was a good boy there would be more than that available when the kids were asleep. She stepped back, winked at me, then raised her eyebrows with seductive invitation. A solicitation that I would accept with pleasure, or was that have pleasure in accepting.

Her invitation reminded me of a time before we had kids. I'd been out of town for close to a month. When I flew back she was at there to meet me, looking extraordinarily beautiful, all decked out in a long overcoat, high black boots, and stockings that climbed up under the overcoat. Her makeup just right, with brightly coloured glossy lipstick that looked extra sexy. I noticed guys getting off the plane wishing it was them she was meeting instead of me. As we hugged, she helped me slip my arm inside her coat. Boots and overcoat alright. That's all she had on. She often said she wished there had been a hidden camera on me that night, telling me that the look on my face had been beyond description. I remember thinking that if it was possible for one's jaw to dislocate and touch their chest like in a cartoon, mine probably would have done so. The ride home that night had been one of the most sensual of my life. I discovered that she was wearing something else, even if it was only a garter belt.

My R-rated memories were quickly shattered as I heard the kids screaming that my bag had arrived. Bag in hand, we headed to the car. On the way home, the girls brought me up to date on all their goings on, down to the last detail.

After supper, we carried on with the evening ritual of baths, teeth brushing and story time, ending another day like dads all over the world. Trish and I sat in the hot tub outside for close to an hour, finishing a bottle of wine as she told me about her last few days. I told her in great detail what we had accomplished. I failed to mention the idea that was forcing its way into my mind between every pause in conversation.

With the wine done, we left the hot tub, headed to bed, where she kept the promise she made to me at the airport, managing to snuff out any other thoughts.

CHAPTER 16

By Monday I was back in the groove, back on the road peddling my company's wares. Customers were aware of what I had just been through, and while working or talking to clients, my mind was constantly thinking of just how quickly life could be taken away. I had spoken to numerous customers about the accident, the strange turn of events at the hospital, about what my mom had said to my brother, even telling some about her seeing the man with the beard. Although in the company's eyes they were just customers, there were things many of my customers and I shared over the years, and many had become more like friends than clients by inviting me into their homes to meet their wives and kids.

The other item that kept bombarding my waking thoughts was the crazy plan that had begun to develop while I examined that key on the couch at my parents' house. I could never tell customers about the idea that was incubating up there. That crazy idea would be reserved for only four people.

I was scheduled for an early morning breakfast with a customer is Osoyoos on Wednesday, and would have to leave the house by 6:15. Being a news junkie usually had me watching the nightly news at 11:00, even when I had to be up early. Tuesday night was no exception and I stayed up to catch the headlines from Lloyd Robertson as Trish headed off to bed. I missed the lead story as I let the dog out to do his thing, gave him a Milk-Bone to chew, then put him in the garage for the night. I returned to the house in time to hear the teaser for the next segment about a shooting at an office in Florida.

After the commercial I watched the report about a situation in Tampa. The story was about a disgruntled employee who had been fired eight months earlier. He had returned to the office to visit former colleagues. He had appeared very calm, leaving the office after having coffee with them. The man had then returned at lunch time and proceeded into the cafeteria, bought a soft drink and calmly walked to where his old boss and supervisors were eating. Reaching into his suit jacket, he pulled out a pistol and opened fire as he screamed, "This is what you get for firing me."

His ex-boss as well as two of the supervisors died from their wounds, while two more were taken to the hospital with non-life threatening injuries. The gunman ran from the building and was later found dead in his car. Police reported that the gunman had shot himself. They found a notebook with a list of seven employees on his body. Three of the deceased were on his list, but the other four had not been in the cafeteria during the lunch period.

Then Lloyd carried on with the rest of the news. I really didn't even see it or hear it. I just sat in my chair thinking, unable to fathom anyone wasting their own life just to settle a grudge with their boss. Sure, there had been numerous cases, including one guy who was fired just before Christmas who showed up at the Christmas party and shot his boss, and of course, former postal employees were notorious for exacting murderous revenge, hence the term "going postal."

I finally turned off the tube and headed to bed. I would wake at 4:48 like every weekday, but checked to make sure the clock radio was set for 5:45, ensuring I would be ready to leave the house by 6:15.

I did wake at 4:48, then promptly fell back to sleep. Thinking my head had just settled back on the pillow, the clock radio woke me. I hit the off button, rolled out of bed and went through my morning ritual. I was ready to head out the door when the phone rang. It was just 6:08 according to the clock on the stove. I grabbed the phone quickly before it began its second ring.

"Hello," I whispered hoping I wouldn't wake the rest of the family, although the ringing had probably already done that.

"Hello, Chris?"

I recognized the voice as that of my regional manager from head office, Paul Calder.

"Paul? What the hell are you doing calling the house so early? You'll wake up the whole household."

"Sorry about that," he offered in a voice that did not sound all that sincere.

"You told me yesterday when we spoke that you were heading south today so I wanted to catch up with you before you left. I need to see you before you go."

"Well that will be a neat trick. I'm in Kelowna, you're in Vancouver."

"Actually, I'm in town right now. I got in on the last flight from Vancouver last night. I'm at the Capri Hotel. Can you stop by and see me? We have a bit of a problem."

"What's the problem?"

"I'll tell you about it when you get here."

"Alright, I'll give Wally a call, tell him I'll be late. Maybe I can buy him brunch. I'll give him a call on the way to meet you."

"Better tell him you have to postpone it to another day."

"What's going on?" I asked, but Paul had already hung up.

I didn't bother with my travel mug. I was sure I would get enough caffeine at breakfast with Calder. Something was definitely going on. That son of a bitch would never show up unannounced like this. There had been a lot of rumours floating around since the beginning of the year that the bottom line had not been that good.

Our branch has had good profits. I wondered if maybe head office wanted to find out why our bottom line was better than the others. "No, he wouldn't have come up here unannounced for that. He would've had us doing all kind of reports," I said aloud.

I went in, kissed the girls, and then popped into our room to give Trish a kiss.

"Who was on the phone?" she asked as I leaned over to kiss her.

"Calder."

"What did that sleaze ball want?"

"Never did like him, did you?"

"Nope," came her sleepy reply.

"Looks like my morning is off with Wally. I'll give you a call later, maybe we can get lunch if I can ditch Calder."

"Okay, give me a call."

I got in my car and headed off. As I drove I was thinking that the Peter principal was alive and well within our company. The new president thought the sun rose on Calder, and Calder's nose was so far up the boss's ass I wondered if he could even sleep at night. Yet when I talked to Calder's former customers after his promotion to Regional Manager, they all thought he was a bit of a jerk. Their opinion was that he was a legend in his own mind. I had watched him at head office on numerous occasions when I had been down there. I marvelled at the fact that he had never been charged with sexual harassment. His comments to various women and the way he demeaned them made him look like a total pig to me. Trish had seen him doing the same thing at numerous company functions.

I made it to the Capri Hotel just before seven, going to the coffee shop where we always met when we had visits from various managers from Vancouver. Calder was already sitting in a rear corner booth. I could tell from the empty creamers and sugar pouches that he had already finished numerous cups of coffee. The waitress was giving him yet another refill.

Calder stood and shook my hand, then got the waitress to pour me a coffee as I sat down. "Well this is certainly a surprise to see you here—you look like you slept in those clothes," I quipped as I took a mouthful of steaming coffee.

"Well, this has been one hell of a week and it's only Wednesday," he sighed.

He looked down at the table, then picked up his coffee cup with both hands. "I just want you to know that I'm only the messenger here. Everything that is happening here and at other locations today came right from the top." The coffee I had just swallowed went straight to my gut. I knew what was coming next. I closed my eyes and gritted my teeth. I was breathing hard through my nose. If that shit Calder had the balls to look at me he would have seen my nostrils flaring.

"So how much notice do I get?" I snapped.

Calder still didn't look up, reaching down to the seat of the booth. He brought up an envelope and handed it to me without saying a word. Snatching it out of his hand, I tore it open and quickly scanned the contents of the letter of termination, which was effective immediately. During our last regional sales meeting, my sixth sense had picked up vibes that people in my position within the organization could be part of a round of cuts to help stop the bleeding from the bottom line. Talking about it with Trish, she had assured me that I was getting all worked up over nothing. I should have trusted the intuition that had saved me from numerous car accidents in the past.

I decided that I wouldn't give the smug son of a bitch the satisfaction of seeing me lose it. I took another sip of my coffee, then took another look at the very formal letter from head office. It was not only formal, but very cold, in the way they used Mr. Porter throughout the letter.

One of my better customers had been correct. When our Mission Statement was produced, it had a bunch of airy, fairy paragraphs about how the company saw the employees and their families as their most valuable assets. I had proudly, if naively, showed him the statement. He just looked at me and asked. "So, what is the real mission statement?"

"Well its right there," I had said, pointing to how they valued our skills.

"Wrong," he responded.

I read another of the seven paragraphs of the statement.

"Wrong."

"Okay," I said. "Just what *is* our mission statement?"

"To make money. That's it."

As I finished reading the termination letter I realized he had been right. Nobody really gave a shit about the people, no matter what they said in a fancy proclamation. They probably spent a fortune on an expert to help them come up with all the drivel that the statement pronounced. I recalled that it took a weekend away with all the upper management to come up with the bullshit it spouted.

Bottom line. Money. My customer had been bang on.

I calmly placed the letter back in the envelope, put it on the table, staring at Calder across the table the entire time. "I need your phone!"

"What for?"

"I need to make a call, what else do you use one for?" I asked sarcastically. He handed over his brick-like portable phone, watching while I punched in the number for head office. It was still too early for most of the staff to be in, but I knew that our switchboard operator was always there early, along with the current CEO.

"Hi Ruth. Clinton Russel, please," there was no reason to be nasty with the receptionist at head office. She had nothing to do with this. Calder looked like he was ready to wrestle the phone away from me. I'm sure he thought I was going to lose it on the president of the company. I gave him a look that Lana would have been proud of. A look that said, "Go ahead and try it, you son of a bitch. I'll stuff this phone right down your throat and you'll have to use your belly button to dial the thing."

Russel picked up the phone. I calmly told him how much I had enjoyed working with such a great company, going on to say that I was sure that things would be great for each of us in the future. "My wife has always said there is a reason for everything," I said. "We don't always know what the reason is at the time, but down the road we will look back only to realize that this was a pivotal juncture in our lives."

My comments caught him off guard. He stammered and stuttered, as he told me that he was sure that things would work out for me. He also dropped a hint that maybe it was time to change industries. It had nothing to do with my future, but more that he hoped I wouldn't head directly to one of the competitors taking my customers with me. I got a chance to give him a gut shot and took it. I told him, "I appreciate the fact that this termination is taking place within weeks of my parents dying."

I finished off with a thinly veiled threat. "At least you didn't do it just before the Christmas party. I saw a story on the news last night about a situation like that—it was tragic."

He was laughing nervously as I hung up the phone without saying goodbye and handed the portable phone back to Calder. He took the phone with one hand, then held out the other and said, "I need your keys to the office and the company car."

"How the hell am I supposed to get home?"

"I'll call you a cab. You can put in for it on your final expense report," he stated with a malicious grin. I realized at this point that while he was indeed only the messenger boy, this prick was certainly enjoying being the one making the delivery.

"Don't do me any favours," I calmly stated as I got up from the table. "How many others?" I asked.

"How many others what?"

"How many other loyal employees got fucked today?"

The slime ball actually looked giddy as he replied with a grin, "Six."

I pulled the keys out of my pocket, removed my personal keys from the ring and dropped the rest in his glass of orange juice. "Oops, sorry about that."

Turning to leave, I saw him sticking his fingers into the juice to retrieve the keys. Fighting to keep my composure, I walked through the restaurant, stopping to say hello to people I recognized.

It's funny, I thought to myself. When some little thing goes wrong at home, like trying to hook up a hose on the dishwasher, no matter how small the problem I can totally lose it and become a complete asshole, to the point that no one wants to be in the same room as me. Now I receive the most devastating blow of my career, within weeks of losing my parents, and other than some pettiness with the keys and the phone call I just calmly took getting screwed. No screaming hissy fit, just wham, bam, thank-you ma'am, I'm outta here.

One of the things that the termination had given me was a full year's salary to be paid out like a regular paycheck. The letter had stated that if I found full employment before the year was out, I would be given half of the balance that was left. Guess I'll have to get a couple of part time jobs and let the bastards keep paying me for a year, I thought to myself.

As I continued out of the hotel I zoned out and wondered what song might be playing on my life's soundtrack right now. Maybe Springsteen's "My Home Town," the part where he sings about the boss telling the workers in a factory that all the jobs are done and that nobody would be coming back to work. "How am I going to explain this to Trish and the kids?" I wondered, then the understanding of Trish's words about everything happening for a reason hit me.

The vaults. The idea that had been baking in my mind suddenly changed to a destiny. I now knew that everything that had happened in the prior weeks had been predetermined as soon as the heart attack and accident had claimed my parents' lives. It was now a certainty that I was destined to rob the vaults. The icing on the cake would be if any of Calder or Russel's families had any prized possessions locked away in there. As I left the lobby of the hotel, I heard Trish calling. *What the hell is she doing here?* I wondered.

"Chris ... Chris? Aren't you supposed to heading down to Osoyoos to meet with Wally this morning?"

My eyes flew open like a broken roll-up blind in a cartoon, doing extra turns when it reaches the top. "What time is it anyway?" I asked as I rolled out of bed, stumbling to the bathroom to relieve myself.

"6:00 a. m. you're running late. You slept right through the alarm," I heard as I emptied my bladder.

I hung my head down. "Man, am I ever glad that was just a dream," I sighed aloud. I took a deep cleansing breath. "Now that's how I spell relief." I shaved quickly but decided to pass on the morning shower.

"You better not make a habit of sleeping in, or they're liable to fire you," Trish mumbled from under the covers. I gave her a quick kiss, then did the same with both girls and let the dog in to take my place in the nice warm bed. He should be able to get along without going outside till Trish got up. I don't know why I thought about it, but I realized that I hadn't let the dog out in my dream.

I'd never been so happy to see 6:25 in my entire life. What a nightmare. It seemed so real. Heading to the car, I swore I heard the house phone ringing as I got into the car. "No fucking way am I going back in to answer that! No bloody way!"

I started up the car and reversed out of the driveway. I didn't let the car slow down as I jammed the shifter into overdrive directly from reverse. The car lurched to a stop before instantly shooting forward. I jammed my foot on the accelerator, speeding off away from the house without so much as a glance back. I felt like a character in a disaster movie that keeps looking in the rear-view mirror only to see a tsunami or volcanic ash getting closer as he speeds away from impending doom. On the bright side, the leading man always manages to find a safe spot just in time.

I was no more than two minutes away from the house when my own oversized car phone started to chirp. "Shit! Shit! Shit! Shit!" I screamed as I slammed my hand against the steering wheel. I had screamed so hard and loud that my throat felt raw.

I grabbed the phone out of the harness and shouted, "Porter here!"

"Whoa. Did you get out of the wrong side of the bed or what?" said Trish. "You missed a call as you headed out the door," she continued. "I tried to catch you, but you took off out of the drive-way like a bat out of hell."

"Who was on the bloody phone so early? That peckerhead Calder?" I practically shouted.

"Don't shout at me just because you're having a crappy morning. For your information, it was Wally calling to tell you he wouldn't be able to make breakfast this morning. He fell down the stairs at home last night. He's home from the hospital with a broken leg, which is now in a cast, as well as a broken collar bone, so he can't even get around on crutches."

"Wow. Well that knocks the crap out of my day. I have another customer to see down there anyway, so I'll just keep on going. Maybe I'll get take-out for him for lunch instead of our breakfast. Either way, I'll call him when I get down there."

"Why the heck were you so pissed when you picked up the phone?"

"It's a long story. I'll tell you about it in the hot tub tonight over a bottle of wine. I was upset, but I'm fine now. Sorry for barking at you."

"Alright. Just drive safe. I know how you drive when you get in a mood like this."

"No problem. Thanks for letting me know. Love ya."

"Love you too. See you tonight."

I put the phone back into the cradle, relaxing for the first time since I had woken up. The rest of the day was just another day in the life of an account rep: calling on customers, answering questions, taking orders and solving problems. Nothing special, no drama. No different than a day experienced by millions of people in similar jobs around the world.

I did take lunch to Wally and Trish and I did get our alone time in the hot tub. I told her all about my nightmare of losing my job. The final comment she made as we headed into the house was, "You really do watch way too much TV. You need to stop watching the damn news."

"This was the second time I'd had that advice today. Another customer used the line, if you want to cut down on stress in your life, don't watch the news before you go to bed."

I thought this was starting to sound like good advice indeed.

CHAPTER 17

By the following Sunday, I felt everything was back to normal. Well, relatively normal. The nightmare I'd had on Wednesday still haunted me, making me realize that our hopes and aspirations were out of our hands. Ultimately, not much of the world's population was in control of their own destiny. The abstract notion of robbing the safe deposit vaults would be my conduit to take control of my own life once and for all.

Part of getting back to my normal routine was being on the golf course for our weekly game just as the sun came up. I began studying my friends in a manner I had never done before. I puzzled over how I could convince them to help me with the insane scheme I was devising. I wasn't sure where the other three would fit into my plan. I'm a salesman, not a psych major, but I still tried to analyze them as we golfed. What would they think when I told them what I had in mind?

Harry Bentley might buy in, I thought. Since he'd taken over running the Starlite Motor Inn, which his mom and dad had owned and operated for years, things hadn't been going well. It really was a second-rate establishment; a family motel with forty rooms on the outskirts of the city, far from the hub of the tourist district. He was lucky to fill the place at the height of a busy tourist season. The Starlite's saving grace was its proximity to the highway leading to the Big White ski area. This location provided more traffic during the winter season than he got during the summer.

Harry had entered adulthood with a bright future He married Pam, his high school sweetheart, in his third year of university when she had become pregnant. They had always planned on marriage, the pregnancy just pushed up the timetable.

Pam had lost the baby in the seventh month. And worse, she also lost the ability to ever bear children again. The loss of what would have been his son had been very hard on Harry, yet he still managed to finish at the top of his class. He had been recruited by a large aerospace company back east. Years of stress got to him, and he and Pam had moved back to Kelowna, where they had grown up. There were not many local high-tech jobs in those days, so he had ended up working as repairman in an electronics shop.

Eighteen months earlier, Harry's dad had passed away. He had made a promise to his dad similar to what Vic and I had promised our mom. Harry's promise had been to take over running the motel and not to put his mom in an old age home or care facility. He now struggled daily with that promise.

Harry used to have a lot of ambition—he proudly wore the coveted engineering ring on his right pinky finger, and had worked for great companies earning good money over the years. When his dad got sicker, he had been required to do more around the motel. If not for the promise he made to his dad, he would have sold it right after he'd passed. For years, he had helped his dad keep the place looking neat and clean, but now he tended to sit in the front office watching television, waiting for customers to come through the door.

Harry was just shy of forty years old. Born in Lancashire, England, he'd immigrated to Canada with his parents in the fifties. Harry had started going grey when he turned twenty-one and now also had full-blown male-pattern baldness. What was left of his hair was completely white. He had to wear a hat when we golfed or his head would turn the colour of a ripe tomato, and his pale skin never really seemed to tan. He was either very pale or a bright blotchy red anywhere that was exposed to the sun.

He wore long pants to hide the scrawny white legs that supported his slender, five-foot eleven frame. Considering how little exercise he got, I was always surprised by how he could keep so slim. He couldn't weigh more than one-hundred and sixty pounds I thought as I watched him take another swing. It would take a lot carbs and plenty of work in a gym to get him into shape.

Harry and Pam had attempted to adopt for years, but with each passing year the pool of young people willing to consider them as prospective parents dwindled because of their age and limited means. When they had taken over running the motel, Harry and Pam had sold their home and moved into the manager's suite, using the proceeds of the sale just to keep the motel afloat. There was no way Pam wanted to raise a child at the motel, and neither child services nor private adoption agencies would be thrilled at the idea of a child growing up there either. Harry had kept his promise to his dad to keep his mom out of a home—she now lived in one of the rooms on site, occasionally helping to check in customers to give Harry a bit of break.

Pam still had a job in a small accounting office, which helped to pay for groceries. On rare occasions, she would also help in the front on an evening shift. All customers ever saw was her bright, cheery attitude, never knowing she loathed being there. In private, she never let a chance go by to let Harry know how much she hated having anything to do with it.

The only time maintenance got done any longer was when a group of us got together for a work party to help him get things repaired and repainted or to tidy up the grounds.

Harry often told us that if he won the lottery, he might just disappear, go off the grid and start fresh somewhere else. My plan might be able to help him get that fresh start. I knew he still loved Pam and still wanted her to be part of his dreams.

What about Dan Kramer? I wondered as we continued our round. Dan had a job with a local chemical resin company. He'd worked there since graduating from university with a chemistry degree.

Dan loved gambling, and bought lottery or raffle tickets all the time. I pointed out to him more than once that if he spent less on the tickets, he might be able to afford some of the things he said he couldn't afford.

He was one of the smartest guys I knew. Over the years, he has designed processes that improved his company's profits considerably. All he got out of his ideas were small bonuses because his contract specified that any patents resulting from his research belonged to the company. He'd told us that he kept some of his ideas secret. His dream was to start a research and development company for the plastics industry. Financially, he was in no position to realize that fantasy.

One thing I'd learned about Dan years earlier was that it was best to stay on his good side. He tended to have a very quick temper. If you got on the wrong side of that, you would get a tongue lashing that could slash your feelings to ribbons.

The tallest of the four of us, his six-foot one frame was well toned from constant workouts at the gym. He never missed an opportunity to tell us that he fell into the ideal weight range for his body type at one-hundred-ninety pounds. He also had incredible endurance thanks to jogging rather than driving to work each day. These two things kept him in good physical shape. At thirty-five, he considered himself in his prime. I wouldn't have wanted to tangle with him physically—he would have put me on the ground faster than I would like to admit.

If we managed to do what I had in mind, Dan just might have the opportunity to strike out on his own. He had told his wife, Rita, that when they started having a family, he didn't want her working any longer. It had been a great idea in theory, but after having two kids, Rita still had to take on work through a temp agency. With some seed money, maybe Dan could kill two birds with one stone: open his own facility and let Rita be a stay at home mom.

Then there was Robert Michael Tarleton. Also just thirty-five, Bob was a GP and a partner in the prestigious Okanagan Valley Medical Clinic. It had its own x-ray clinic, optometrists, orthopedic doctors and their own independent pharmacy. Each of the various practitioners had a share in the three-story structure.

How would Bob be described in a missing person's report? He was five-foot ten, around one hundred and seventy-five pounds. His curly, jet black hair was cut short. By the end of a sunny Okanagan summer, his complexion darkened so much that new patients to the clinic might mistake him for someone from south of the equator. One of Bob's distinguishing features was a large, bushy moustache. One thing we all had in common was good looking moustaches.

Bob's first wife had divorced him four years earlier and it cost him a lot of money each month in both alimony and child support. His new wife, Gwen, worked at the clinic with him. They both seemed extremely happy, considering that they were together almost every hour of every day.

After the split with his first wife we had been a little leery of the new one, thinking we were turning our back on our friendship with Claudette. They say when a marriage breaks up, friends become community property and can be harder to divide up than family heirlooms. Trish had stayed friends with Claudette, but she now lived in Nelson with their two kids and as the time passed they had talked less and less.

Even though Bob was my doctor, it was still difficult for me to get in to see him when I had some sort of malady. There was no denying his passion. If he suspected there might be something hiding below the surface, he would not hesitate to order up a complete battery of tests. Bob had told us how frustrated he had become, watching too many young children and many of his patients in their prime die of cancer, or senseless accidents like my mom and dad.

Despite growing up going to church and serving as an altar boy when he was younger, he had lost his concept of God, considering himself a practising agnostic.

The four of us had occasionally been able to get away for some guys' weekends. We had done a rafting expedition down the Fraser Canyon, and some back-country skiing. Since Harry had taken control of the motel it had ended up being only three of us on these trips.

While Bob's compassion appeared endless, he had started to see through the phony crap of a lot of the people he dealt with, including prima donna surgeons and medical specialists. He was sick to death of the endless paperwork, the potential lawsuits and malpractice insurance. He said on more than one occasion he was ready to tell the whole lot of them to get stuffed. Since his divorce, he had cut back his work to four days a week.

One thing everyone loved about Bob was his quick wit and snappy comebacks. He was so fast with the witty retorts that he kept us in stiches. I usually thought of a great comeback hours later, and by then it had no meaning at all.

I thought that maybe, just maybe, he might not think my idea was totally crazy.

Who knows? I thought. Maybe they would all buy in. Each of them had a least one reason to give it a shot.

After the ninth hole, I talked them out of our usual snack with a promise I would buy them all a big breakfast after we finished the round.

CHAPTER 18

Twenty minutes after we finished our round, with each of us having made enough decent shots to not quit playing for good, we were sitting in a corner booth at the local IHOP restaurant. Since I had offered to pay, everyone had ordered the works. Omelettes, pancakes, bacon and eggs with toast and hash browns, with tall glasses of orange juice all around. The waitress had also left us with a large carafe of coffee.

"Why did you want to have breakfast here this morning?" asked Harry. "Something wrong with the club food?"

"No, it's just that what I want to talk to you about is confidential. This place is noisy enough that nobody can overhear us. The club has too many busybodies who might just want to stick their nose in at the wrong time."

"Ooh, sounds so clandestine," Dan commented.

"That's closer to the truth than you realize, as you'll understand when you hear what I have to tell you."

"So, what's on that conspiratorial mind of yours?" inquired Bob

"You might think that what I tell you over the next little bit is right off the wall, but I just want you to consider it. In my opinion, each of you has a reason to go along with the idea."

"The other thing is, that once I tell you what I have to say you can't—I mean absolutely cannot—tell another soul, especially the wives. I know we've shared lots of secrets over the years, but I assure you, never anything like this. If you don't think that you can give me your word about keeping it to yourselves, we can just have a quiet, friendly breakfast, then go about our days. If you do want to hear what I have to say, in the not too distant future, none of us will be just normal guys." As I finished my spiel, our breakfast arrived and I paused as the plates were put in front of us.

"What the hell are you going on about?" Dan asked, growing impatient. "You know that anything we have ever discussed in private has never gone beyond the four of us."

"Come on, admit it, Dan, I'm sure you've told Rita at least some things we've talked about over the years."

Dan looked guilty as he replied. "Well, maybe little things."

"What about you Harry, do you tell Pam things we discuss?"

"Hell no, we've hardly said two meaningful words to each other since we took over the motel. Hell, we don't even sleep in the same room any more. If I'm lucky, I might get a little hallway sex once in a while—when we pass each other in halls of the motel, she says 'Fuck you' and I reply with the same."

"Bob, do I have your solemn oath that you will treat what I am about tell you, as doctor patient confidentiality?"

"I solemnly swear," said Bob as he raised his hand as if to take an oath. "I promise that I shall not divulge anything about the conversation we are about to have to anyone. The Supreme Court will not be able to pry anything from my lips. Satisfied?" he asked with a grin.

"Firstly, you are all going to think I am certifiable. Secondly, when we're done you might want to have me committed. And thirdly, I just might need to hold you to that Supreme Court promise."

"Enough!" barked Harry in a hoarse whisper. "You've got our word. For Christ's sake, get on with it so I can finish my breakfast and get going."

"Sounds like a definite medical problem, Doctor Bob," laughed Dan. "Although, if you had seen him talking to his ball on the course today you might think he was more in need of an exorcism."

"Alright, I'll take you all at your words." As I was about to continue the waitress came to check on our progress, asking if the meals were okay. I picked up the empty carafe, telling her we could use a refill. She returned with another pot of coffee and more creamers, set them down, then was gone in a flash. "By the way, I'm buying breakfast, but you guys can look after the tip."

With their coffee cups refilled, I began to lay out the facts of the Vancouver Safety Deposit Vaults Company. How I had discovered the key for it, where it was. The five thousand safety deposit boxes it held, including what we had found in my folks' personal box, explaining that there was only one guard and occasionally two office people there on weekdays. "There wasn't a burglar, fire or smoke alarm system that I could see. I left out the part about Vic's suspicions about the vault being used for illicit purposes.

Although the restaurant was still crowded and noisy, I had kept my voice low, just slightly above a whisper. "Sounds like a good place for your parents to have kept all their stuff. If you need a place to invest some of your inheritance I know this little motel in need of a major makeover," suggested Harry.

"What do you want to do Chris, rob the place?" Dan blurted out.

I shot him a look. "Keep it down. That is precisely what I have in mind," I whispered.

Harry had just refilled his coffee. He had raised the cup to his lips, and as I finished my last statement, he sucked in a mouthful of steaming liquid, burning the roof of this mouth. The coffee he didn't spew out half way across the table scorched his throat all the way down to his esophagus. He was gasping, coughing and sputtering. An older man and woman at the table across from ours gave us a disgusted look. The waitress rushed over to make sure everything was alright. Bob instructed Harry to lift his arms up to help him catch his breath. Dan looked at the waitress and told her that I had just told an off-colour joke. "A *very* bad joke," he explained.

The table and plates were splattered with coffee and the front of Harry's white golf shirt was stained. His coughing and sputtering finally subsided as the waitress wiped up the table and removed our plates, which were mostly finished anyway. We all thanked her as she headed off.

"You guys are going to have to leave a bigger tip," I quipped.

"You're serious, aren't you?" Bob said.

"Sure. With the mess Harry made, she deserves a bigger tip," I replied.

"You know damn well that's not what I was talking about."

In a tone that my friends had grown to recognize as the one I used when I was serious about something, I simply stated: "One-hundred percent."

If someone had dropped an anvil on the table, not one of them would have heard it. They were all staring at me. I finally broke the silence with a whisper that oozed conspiracy: "Don't tell me you guys have never thought about something like this. Doing this just might let us fulfill some of the dreams we've always talked about. If you don't think that the basic idea has possibilities, no problem, we head home right now. The matter will never be discussed again. If you decide to consider it, then we'll get together at a more private location to discuss it further."

After an awkward silence as they each seemed to consider the idea, Bob finally spoke: "Chris, before any of us even thinks of going any further, are you sure you've really thought this through?"

"I have thought of nothing else. Today on the course, or while talking with customers over the last week, it is all I've been able to think about. Not to mention, it even popped right back into my head after some great welcome home sex."

"But look at who you're talking to. We know nothing about what would be needed to do something like this. As you've told us too many times to mention, we're just ordinary guys. They could make up nursery rhymes about us. The doctor, the salesman, the engineer and the hotelier. Not as catchy as *Tinker Tailor Soldier Spy*. I'm not ready to buy in. Part of me says you've got my interest, but another part tells me you are definitely sounding unstable."

"Thanks, Bob. Your confidence in my mental state truly underwhelms me."

"You're welcome. The floor is yours to continue."

I leaned in toward the centre of the table, once again lowering my voice, requiring the others to also lean in. "Thank you, Mr. Chairman. I have given this a lot of consideration. I think we can do it. People have been breaking into bank vaults for hundreds of years. Most of those that were caught were career criminals. Unless I am mistaken, that's not an issue here."

"Remember that guy who was caught embezzling here in a town years ago? His problem was that once he started, he had to keep going, each deal had to be bigger than the last so he could take the money from the last deal to cover the loans he took out when he started. They say that guy could sell you the shirt on your back and you'd be happy to pay for it." They all nodded as they recalled the guy who had become the talk of the town.

"This is different. This will be a one-night-only performance. You're probably wondering why I would spend so much time thinking about robbing this place." I told them about the nightmare in which I had lost my job and how it led to the conclusion that I wanted to be in control of my own destiny, not sitting around like some chump waiting to become a statistic. How I came to the realization that I didn't want to live the rest of my life waiting to end my days in self-imposed poverty trying to make sure I left something for my kids. "I want to enjoy life. Like we always say, 'To life. Our way.'"

"Just what is *our way?*" I asked. "If it means travelling, good wine and no financial worries, then I want that life," I said. "As I told you earlier, my parents have left us a decent legacy. I'm just not sure if that's enough. The bottom line is that I want more."

"What good will it do, when we go out in a little puff of smoke during our pit stop in the crematorium? We are a long time dead my friends, so why don't we take the opportunity to live life to the fullest while we're still here? We can all have a new beginning. It starts with what's in that big concrete and steel box in Vancouver. It's just sitting there waiting for us. It's loot for the taking! If my parents had this much stuff put away, can you imagine what might be in the boxes of people who had something to begin with?" I stopped talking and took a drink of my now cooled coffee.

I pointed at Harry, cutting him off before he began to talk: "Harry, you're a smart guy. You finished at the top of your class in electronics engineering. You can fix damn near anything ever built. Yet here you are in that miserable motel that you hate, doing a job you despise. Your wife isn't happy because you sold your house to make ends meet. You just finished telling us again that your love life is non-existent. Wouldn't a windfall change all that? Maybe you could hire people to fix up the place or to run it for you, or even sell the damned thing. You might be able to get your life back." Harry began to object to what I was saying, but I again cut him off with a wave of my hand. "I'm not making this shit up. Everything I've just said is based on things you have told us more than once."

"As for you Dan, my hot-tempered friend: you say your job is okay. Okay! Don't you want more than okay? When, not if, we pull this off, you could start your own place, like you've talked about doing for so long." Dan began to nod, then grinned as his own imagination started getting the better of him.

"And you, Herr Doctor," I continued, nodding at Bob. "You keep telling us that you're fed up with an underfunded system, surgical waiting times, bed closures, and sections of newly-built hospital wings sitting idle because there's no money to staff them. How many times have we sat at the nineteenth hole, listening as you told us how much you would like to pack it in? How you thought you might like to join Doctors Without Borders to practise medicine that would really make a difference? You don't want to sit in your office while I tell you that the growth on my foot must be cancer, only to tell me it's just a bunion, exactly like my wife told me in the first place."

"Your job has lost you one wife already, and you've only been practising ten years. How many will you go through in another thirty years? This could be a new start. Let the clinic run itself. Travel the world with Gwen, do medical work you truly have a passion for."

"That's it guys." I thought as I finished that if my life was a movie, the poor bastard playing me would sure as hell have a lot of lines to memorize. "I hope I've made compelling arguments for you each to at least consider the idea. As far as a 'let's get the dynamite and blow the sucker open' plan, I don't have that yet. Keep in mind our big advantages: A. None of us has a criminal record; B. We are unknown in Vancouver; and, C. I'm the only one without a university education. You might not agree with me at this stage, but we're all smart guys. And yes, I am including myself despite your misgivings."

"Oh, and lastly: deep down each of you just really wants to do this." None of them said a word.

"Harry. Book us a room at the far end of the motel for a week from Wednesday. I'll be there at 8:00 p.m. If you're there, you're in. If you're not, I'm okay with whatever you decide. Dan and I are going camping with the families for the long weekend, so neither of us will be golfing next Sunday. If your wives want to know what we are doing on the Wednesday night, tell them we're thinking of starting an investment club. Tell them I want to use my inheritance money as seed capital."

"Have a great week, and fun long weekend. Dan, I'll see you up at the lake."

I got out from the booth. "Don't forget a big tip," were the last words I spoke to them as I left, stopping at the cashier to pay the bill, knowing I would now just have to sweat it out for the next ten days. I hoped I would be able to keep my own big trap shut, especially after too much rum while camping with Dan and his clan.

CHAPTER 19

We didn't find out about the fire until we got back to town after lunch on the holiday Monday. Harry's Starlite Motel had been engulfed in fire on Saturday night. The fire department had managed to save the office area and the opposite end of the motel, but most of the motel had been consumed by the flames. The motel had been at seventy-five percent capacity, but everyone had escaped safely, including Harry's mom and Pam.

Fire Inspectors still hadn't come up with the exact cause by the time we saw Harry late Monday afternoon, but they were fairly sure that it had been started by a guest using a portable hot plate in their room. None of the rooms other than the manager's suite had a stove, so it appeared that the guest had brought his own.

Harry told us that his insurance broker had shown up Sunday morning to inspect the damage before he called the adjustors. It was while the broker was looking at the motel's file that he discovered a major problem. The last appraisal on the building had been done five years earlier, and Harry had not updated the value on the building since taking over. There was a line in the fine print stating that if the policy didn't cover at least 90% of the current replacement value, there would be a penalty in the event of a claim. Based on Harry's premiums, he would be lucky if the insurance covered half the loss, meaning he was going to have to come up with over two hundred thousand dollars to rebuild—money he didn't have.

Pam was livid. She hated the place, and if it had been insured properly, she would have been happy to see it burn to the ground, letting the insurance company pay for a place to stay while it was rebuilt. That was not to be. One of our friends from the golf course had a few houses he rented out. One of them was currently empty and he offered it to Harry and Pam for as long as they needed it. By supper time on Tuesday friends, relatives and people they had never met had arranged for furnishings, food and toiletries to be delivered to Harry and Pam's temporary accommodations. The show of compassion and assistance was overwhelming.

On Wednesday, Pam had headed out for the evening with co-workers from the accounting office. Harry's mom was staying with one of her brothers in Penticton, so he was going to be alone for the night. I called the other guys, telling then we needed go and keep Harry company, have a few beers and help to get his mind off his problems. My idea of getting together to discuss the heist had literally gone up in smoke.

The front door to his new residence was open a crack. I knocked, then stepped inside. Harry was sitting at the kitchen table, watching the second game of the Stanley cup finals between Philadelphia and the Edmonton Oilers on a portable television that was sitting on the kitchen counter. It had come from the manager's suite at the motel. The house that had been loaned to them was clean but well worn. The red and orange shag carpet was dated, as was black and white fleur-de-lis crushed velvet wall paper on the walls of the living room. The donated furniture that now decorated the room had a Mediterranean flair, dark wood with scrolls made of plastic adorned the end and coffee tables.

"Probably very stylish in the early or mid-seventies," I suggested to Harry. All I got from him was a grunt. The couch had wooden accents, and it might have also been covered with a crushed velvet material, but it was so worn that it was hard to be sure. "If all that material was red, you could add a red light on the porch, but that might make the neighbors a little nervous as to your intentions while living here." He continued to ignore my comments, watching the game as he sipped on a Coke.

"Who's winning?" I asked.

Flyers are up two to one.

"Out of nowhere, he piped up, "I'm in. Just tell me what you need me to do and I'll get it done. This might be my last shot, and if things don't get better soon I'm going to lose Pam as well.

"Whoa, slow down, buddy. You've just been through hell in the few last days. I wasn't even planning on talking about it tonight."

"You're convinced we can do it, aren't you?" he continued.

"I think we have as good a chance as anybody. Quite possibly better, if we make a good plan and stick to it. Who would come looking for four humdrum guys from Kelowna with no criminal records? If we play our cards right, they will be looking for professionals elsewhere," I said. "But let's just back off a bit. We don't need to get into it tonight. We just wanted to come over to be with you and watch the game, maybe share a beer."

"Will Bob and Dan be in?" he asked, then answered his own question. "Dan for sure, if only for the adrenaline rush. I think what you said about his own lab will be the deciding factor. I'm not so sure about Bob. He already seems to have it all."

"More or less, I suppose, but I think we all secretly want an opportunity to be a little larcenous, especially if we can do it without anyone getting hurt. And I really do think he's done with grumbling patients. He loves to golf, ski, and boat. Hell, he can probably do those things for the rest of his life with Gwen, without joining us, but with the extra loot, he could really do it in style and still make a meaningful medical contribution."

"I'm sure Gwen would love to be wined and dined around the world," added Harry.

We heard a car pull up and park in the driveway, and then a single car door opened and closed. Just before the knock came, I pulled the door open. Dan stood at the door wearing a cheap kid's disguise with big glasses, an oversize nose, bushy eye-brows and mustache. He was also wearing a tartan driving cap. "Excuse me, sir. Is this the new home of the Kelowna Investment Corporation?" he asked as he handed me a case of beer. "I hope this small token will help me gain entry to this prestigious gath-ering." Shaking my head, I let him into the room, then peeked outside to see if Bob was out there as well.

"Glad you decided to join us, Dan," I said, "and by the way I just told Harry that we weren't here to talk about any plan I had suggested earlier."

"I wasn't coming here tonight to discuss your plan. Just wanted to come over and spend time with you guys. But, if we were going to talk about it, would you be in, Harry?" asked Dan.

"Sure. My life is so close to being in the shitter, I think if we don't manage to pull it off then the next thing I'm going to hear is the sound of the toilet flushing anyway."

Dan nodded and turned to me: "Have you really considered all the consequences and ramifications for us all if things don't work out?"

"In a word, yes!" I replied. "I think that if anyone can do it, it's us. Have I thought about consequences? Yes. Have I thought of everything that we need to do? No. But that was my plan prior to the fire. Like you I told Harry that we were here for him tonight, not to come up with a hair-brained plan for a bloody robbery."

"Would everybody quit fucking well feeling sorry for good old Harry, I can take care of myself. If we did manage to rob the bloody place—and get away with it—a great deal of my problems would be solved."

"Okay, does this mean you guys want to try to come up with a real plan? We can't be part way into this only to have one of us getting cold feet," I said. I looked at my watch, and just like when you see a person yawn, others seem to follow suit, I saw the other two take a quick glance at their own watches. "Look, it's now 8:20. The last time I spoke to Bob, I was sure he was going to join us for a beer."

"Let's just say we do decide to try this idea of yours, Chris—do you think Bob will join us? And if he doesn't, do you think he would tell anyone?" asked Dan.

"I think we all know him well enough to know that what I said last week was just between us. But it's 8:25, so I guess we can count him out as a partner. Can it be done with just the three of us?" asked Dan.

"Well, let's put it this way: it sure beats me having to go out to find three guys I don't know. Running an ad in the classified section of the Vancouver Sun might have been tricky."

"I can see it now," laughed Dan. "Help Wanted: Three people for temporary, part-time position. On the job training provided. Must not be bondable, must have a criminal record. High earning potential. An opportunity for lifetime security. If job does not work out, we offer guaranteed accommodations complete with three meals a day." Harry and I laughed at Dan's imaginary advertisement.

"Keep in mind that the last part of that ad could be more of a chance than I think we have considered," Harry added soberly.

"No! No more negative talk. Harry's fire is going to be the last negative thing to happen to any us from here on in. To paraphrase Donald Sutherland in *Kelly's Hero's*, 'Enough with the negative waves.' We can't afford negative attitudes. The next little while must be filled with positive attitudes. If we don't stay positive, then it will all go to shit and we will be the ones getting those three square meals a day. I don't know about you guys, but my arse is nice and tight right now, and I intend to keep it that way." They both signalled their agreement with two thumbs up.

"Let's get to it then. I'll give you a quick recap. From there, we can divvy up everything we will need to do before D-Day. We'll split up the tasks so that we don't bring too much attention to ourselves for any single action." Before I could go on with the details, a loud pounding on the door stopped me cold. I hadn't heard any cars come into the driveway, like I had when Dan had arrived.

"Sorry I'm late, but I had a delivery at the hospital," said Bob as he burst into the room. I was on my way home to get supper before coming here when I got a call from the delivery room saying that one of my very pregnant patients had arrived there with no time to spare. They weren't kidding. I managed to get there just in time to catch the little bugger as he slid out the chute."

"Congratulations Doctor Kildare. I've just finished telling these guys that we weren't here to discuss our conversation on Sunday, but they want to talk about it. What about you, Doc? You here to comfort Harry or plan a heist?" I asked.

"Well, first and foremost, I think we all need a beer—doctor's orders," he said, so I passed around four of the cold Kokanees Dan had brought with him, as he continued to talk. "I figured you guys just might buy into Chris's crazy ass idea, especially considering what's just happened to Harry."

"Chris, you told us how most of your waking hours have been consumed by the thought of robbing the vaults. I'd be lying if I told you that I haven't been doing a lot of thinking about it as well. It will not only take money to get Harry's motel running again, but it's also going to take time. I can help with some money to get Harry and Pam back on their feet, but with the insurance shortfall, it's going to take a lot more than that to rebuild the motel. I don't remember you having a rich uncle anywhere, do you have any other options?"

"The only thing I have left is the raw land where that pile of charred wood sits. I'm sure I could get something for it, but it wouldn't even cover what's left on the mortgage," said Harry.

"How much of a shortfall are we talking about, Harry?" asked Dan

"Early estimates are now over three-hundred grand, and that's why I already told Chris that I'm in. It could be my only shot. I don't expect you guys to risk everything to help me out just because I screwed up on the insurance," Harry explained.

"I thought it might be something like that, and the more I kept thinking about it the more I realized that Chris was right. I do want to do more with my life than hear about colds, indigestion, and sore backs. There are people in the world dying from very treatable diseases but not a lot is being done about it. I can make a difference," said Bob. "Besides, if you guys go ahead without me, you'll be so busy I won't have anyone to golf with, and if they do catch us upstanding citizens, we might get put into one of those nice country club prisons, like the one outside of Victoria. I've heard they have their own theatre group."

We had just been holding our beers until Bob finished talking. We popped the tops at the same time then lifted our cans in our salute. "To life. Our way," we chanted.

"I would much rather be doing this with a snifter of Grand Marnier," whined Dan.

CHAPTER 20

"Okay, now that were all in, let's get back to where we were before Doc arrived," I suggested. I began explaining how important it was that we keep to our regular schedules and routines, including our weekend golf games. We could golf and talk over plans at the same time. "It is critical that we carry on like normal, both before and after the heist."

I gave a brief description of the layout, and told them how the main hallway and vault door could easily be seen by anyone coming down the stairway or elevator. Even though the place was closed on weekends, there could still be people coming into the lobby on the way to any of the offices on the upper floors. Another concern was that there would be no way to prevent any noise from radiating throughout the building. It would also be impossible to get any equipment to the doors without being noticed. It wasn't like we could just carry everything down Pender Street and traipse into the building. It didn't take long for them all to agree that we had to go through the steel and concrete wall.

I described my investigation of the rear of the building, telling them about my conversation with Jakub and how he'd explained that the vault was on the other side of the boiler room.

Harry would be in charge of making sure we had a good exit plan in case we had to bug out early and leave everything behind. He was also tasked with finding a way to get the loot safely out of town. His other responsibility would be to come up with plausible alibis for while we were out of town.

We talked about using one of our annual guys' weekends as the best cover to get away without anyone being the wiser. Even though we had given up curling for various reasons, including the demand for family time, the four of us still tried to get in a weekend getaway once a year. Harry, who had missed several recent getaways, said that he would have to make it sound like an economy excursion because Pam kept track of everything he spent, and now there would be even less.

"No problem, Harry. I'm sure you'll come up with a way," Dan assured him.

Bob offered to take care of financing the operation. We had no idea of how much we would require, but Bob told us of a secret account with a decent slush fund he had set up prior to his divorce. He assured us that he could not only help out Harry over the next while, but likely also cover most of our costs.

I would do more reconnaissance on the building and neighborhood and find out what was in the surrounding buildings. Once we had a list of required supplies, we would buy them at different places around the interior. My travels took me from Cache Creek to Castlegar, and from Osoyoos to Blue River. I figured we could get anything we needed in that geographic area. By purchasing things in a variety of locations, it would be more difficult to trace any items back to us should things go wrong.

Though I had insisted that no notes were to be taken, I drew them a diagram of the building, showing Pender Street, and the back alley, including the position of the fire escape and door to the boiler room. I then drew a plan of the lobby, illustrating where the elevators were as well as the stairway down to the vault area. I would come up with more detailed plans for the building and surrounding areas when I took my next trip to the coast.

We had been at Harry's for over two hours, going over general ideas. Everyone had come up with good questions, which I either had answers for or spelled out how I would find answers for those I didn't. "You don't need to have all the answers, you just need to know where to find them," I said.

We discussed the fact that it was Bob who would be funding our endeavour and he had the most to lose financially. I said that I would arrange to reimburse him with a part of my inheritance money if things didn't work out. When we did finish the job, he would get his costs returned to him off the top before we split the rest.

"Let's call it a night. We have enough to think about for now, and I'm sure you'll wake up in the middle of the night thinking of other things. As I told you before, I have not had many waking hours without thinking about it one way or the other. If you come up with any ideas or questions, save them for Sunday. Remember, just don't write anything down."

"One last question. Just when did you plan on this taking place?" asked Dan

"That will depend on how long it will take us to take care of all the logistics. Let's see if we can figure that out in the next two weeks. Once we have that, Harry can work out the time frame for our trip."

Harry tore up the papers I had drawn on and flushed them down the toilet. As the three of us filed out of the house, we met Pam arriving home from her dinner out. We knew the fire had made things worse between her and Harry, but as always, she had a big smile on her face and gave each of us a big hug, thanking us for helping them out in the tough times they were facing. We all assured her we were there for them both, said our goodnights and headed home, praying that things would turn out okay for all of us.

CHAPTER 21

As we walked the course and stood on the tee boxes and greens during our second game of golf since our meeting at Harry's, we discussed the ideas we'd all been coming up with. The prior week, our first decision had been that since Bob would be financing us he should get a look at the spot our adventure would begin. We decided that the two of us would drive down to Vancouver together and I would attempt to get him inside.

Bob had his staff reschedule his appointments to arrange a Tuesday off. It wasn't unusual for him to take a one day trip to Vancouver. Gwen had a lot of work to catch up on, so fortunately she didn't suggest that she should head down with him. I let Trish think I was heading off on my regular route when I left the house early on the Tuesday morning. I would be back in Kamloops that evening, staying at my usual hotel in case she tried to get in touch with me. I advised my branch manager that I would be in the Merritt area for most of the day and that I would be calling him on Wednesday.

Bob drove to Merritt, leaving his car across the street from Aspen Planers, one of four lumber mills in town. As soon as Bob's car was parked, we headed down the Coquihalla to the coast, arriving at 402 West Pender in Vancouver without incident just after noon. We had decided that when we did our survey we would get a video of the area, and if possible the vault itself. The video would let Dan and Harry see the location almost first hand.

On the Saturday after our first meeting at the motel, Bob had headed up the valley to a Vernon camera shop where he purchased a Sony Handycam and the accessories we needed: extra tapes, a recharger for the cigarette lighter and three extra batteries which should each last for about an hour. The sales clerk had headed home that day with a decent commission and Bob's investment in our project was already over eighteen hundred bucks.

Harry had given Bob the requirements for a good video recorder. The make and model would be up to Bob at the time of purchase, but it had to be able to fit into a briefcase, have a full automatic mode and a ten-power zoom lens. The sales guy had told him this unit would be good in low light environments, and with the lens on wide angle it would give a high-quality picture in tight indoor locations.

Harry had purchased an old hard-sided briefcase at a second-hand store. It was the perfect size to fit the recorder. He modified the case by attaching Velcro straps inside to hold the recorder in place, and cut a hole on the end of the case big enough to ensure that the lens would fit flush with the outside. When Harry showed us his modifications, I had to look hard at the leading edge of the case to notice the lens. We agreed that Q from the James Bond films would have approved.

We practised carrying the case and taking pictures, trying to find out how much movement it could take and still get clear video without a lot of ghosting. We determined the key was to make sure he didn't swing the case as he walked and held the case steady as he took slow turns. I also practised walking with the briefcase in case I had to take over.

When we arrived on Pender Street, Bob began taking footage of the buildings around the vault building, continuing to record as we turned the corner on Richards Street, as well as down the back alley of the four hundred block of Pender. Bob commented on just how clean the back alley was. I told him that I had thought the same thing the first time I saw it. It was not strewn with garbage like so many alleys and the dumpsters were pushed up neatly against the building. It could have passed for the main drag of many major cities.

The power poles looked to be thirty to forty feet high, rising to the third story of the buildings on either side of the laneway, spanning the alley like goal posts. The cross members supported three transformers large enough to power the entire block. He panned the camera up the back of the building, getting good footage of the fire escape.

Feeling that we had enough exterior footage, we parked the car. Bob placed the camera in the briefcase, fastening it into position with the Velcro. We headed down to Pender, entering the lobby through the main entrance. Bob noted that my description of both the front of the building and the lobby had been very accurate. I steered Bob over to the stairs that led to the upper floors, located to the rear of the elevator shafts. We wanted to check out the businesses on each floor to determine if any of the people that worked in the building would have reason to be there on weekends.

We stopped on the second floor to take a close look at the fire escape window and its locking mechanism. While we were looking at the fire escape, I discovered another set of stairs that led to the main floor. While Bob took the video of the alley, I ran down the stairs, which ended at a door. Thinking it must lead to a part of the lobby I hadn't seen earlier, I received a pleasant surprise when I pulled the door open. It wasn't the lobby, but rather a direct entrance to the boiler room. From where I stood, I could see the door that I knew led to the back lane only feet away. I also noticed a deadbolt that I hadn't observed when the door to the alley was open that first morning.

This was not going to be a problem because I had already come up with a plan to gain access to the boiler room. I ran back up to join Bob and got him to concentrate the camera on the locking mechanism of the window that led to the fire escape. We then headed further up the stairs, walking each of the hallways of the eight-story building, taking note of the names that were stencilled on the frosted glass panels of the doors.

The marble and mahogany features that had been prevalent in the basement area continued throughout the building. The hallways were brightly lit and the floors were all clean and shiny. Jakub certainly maintained a nice, clean building.

The style of the stencilling made me wonder if we might come across a door marked with a name like Philip Marlow - Private Detective. There was a collection agency on the fourth floor, and the third floor was home to the BC Writers Association office. Overall, we didn't see anything that caused us concern. Before we checked out the tenants on the eighth floor, we peered out the window that overlooked Pender Street, giving us a great view of the Woodward's Department Store with its iconic W mounted high on the tower atop the building. We could also see the mountains of the North Shore as well as the huge gantry cranes and containers at Centennial Pier.

We checked out the rest of the tenants on the eighth floor, and as we neared the end of the hallway we noticed that the window at the end leading to the fire escape was wide open. From that window, we had an unobstructed view of Holy Rosary Cathedral with its French Gothic architecture and asymmetric bell towers. Beyond that was the Scotia Bank building, with the top of the BC Tel building in the background. Looking off to the right we caught a glimpse of the green copper roof of the stately Hotel Vancouver.

While we stood admiring the view, Bob decided to do a quick change of the tape and battery. Standing at the open window of the fire escape, Bob set the case on the sill, and then removed the camera. Having practised this quick change umpteen times on our trip to Vancouver, he had the time required down to thirty seconds or less. He had finished strapping it back into place and was ready to close the lid when a voice behind us startled him so much he came close to knocking the briefcase and its contents right onto the landing of the fire escape.

"You boys planning on using the fire escape? I didn't hear the alarm?" asked a female voice. I spun around and found myself staring at a remarkably attractive woman wearing an extremely tight, very short dress that hugged her curves nicely, accentuating a pair of very shapely legs. She must have come out of one of the offices when she saw the two of us standing at the window.

I tried not to stare. "Oh, no. No, I was just showing my buddy the view from up here. My dad used to have an office in the building back in the sixties. I used to come down here with him all the time. I'd sit at this window for hours on a Saturday and watch the city grow while he was working."

"I love to sit right there on my coffee breaks," she replied. "Lots of fresh air, and in the summer there's always a nice cool breeze. It's not like we have central air or anything. These offices can get real stuffy."

"I remember," I replied.

Bob managed to close the briefcase and tapped me on the shoulder. "Come on, there are other places you promised to show me," he said, breaking the spell that this beauty seemed to have cast on me.

"Well, I have to fill the coffee pot. Have to get the water from the restrooms at the end of the hall. No office plumbing in this old building," she explained, holding up the empty pot as she turned and headed down the hallway. "Enjoy the rest of your tour," she called over her shoulder.

We waited before proceeding down the hallway behind her. Bob glanced over at me and whispered, "Very nice, Very short, but very nice."

I looked up at the woman we were following down the hall. Bob was right, she wasn't very tall at all; maybe five-foot one. It definitely wasn't the first thing I had noticed.

We didn't speak again until we were closed inside the elevator. "You never told me your dad actually worked in this building."

"He didn't. It was the first thing that came to mind as I was looking at her."

"Not bad, quick thinking. She scared the crap out of me when she spoke, I almost dropped the damn case out the window."

"I know. You should have seen the look on your face when you turned around."

"My face? Your eyes were popping out of your head, Christopher," laughed Bob.

"Never mind. She was a knockout, wasn't she?"

Before the doors opened on the bottom floor, Bob looked up, then crossed himself and muttered the beginning of a Hail Mary.

"I thought you were a devout agnostic."

"Even those as committed to being a non-believer as I am pray when the pilot tells us to assume the crash position," he laughed. "I'm just praying we all don't end up crashing and burning."

"Well, now is a great time to find religion again. Remember the fifth commandment. Thou shall not steal," I said

"Actually, that's the eighth. I could always try going to confession afterwards, but that probably wouldn't fit with my being agnostic," commented Bob as the doors opened and we stepped out onto the floor that held the vault.

"Well," I whispered to Bob, "it's show time. *All that Jazz*, 1979." I flung out my arms and turned my palms to the air.

"What?"

"Never mind, just a little quote from an old movie. My brother hates it when I do it."

Bob just shook his head and gave me a strange look. I don't know why, but I get that head shake from a lot of people when I do my movie or music quotes. I thought they were usually appropriate for the occasion, and as far as I was concerned, they were usually funny.

Mr. Unger was on duty again. He gave me a look of recognition. "Mr. Potter, isn't it."

"Close, it's Porter," I corrected him. I then introduced him to Bob.

To ensure anonymity, we had looked in the phone books, each of us coming up with a list of names from different places around the interior that we would use in a situation where we might require a name and address. Bob and I had practised reciting our aliases to each other during the drive to the coast.

We had thought about using Bob's alias, but decided that it would be best to just use his own name. I was about to explain our cover story to Unger when Bob cut in: "I just came along to spend some time with Chris. I can wait here while he does his thing, if it's okay."

In the weeks since I had returned to Kelowna, Vic had managed to get box 383 transferred to our names and arranged for a second key to be waiting for me the next time I came into town. He had no idea that it would be this soon.

"I probably need to see Mrs. Hayward to get my new key. My brother Vic has it all arranged."

Unger escorted me to the office, introducing me to the vault's secretary. After filling out a small card, I was given the key to our box. Bob was waiting patiently in the hallway when we returned. "I'll need my briefcase," I told him.

Glad that I had practised with the video recorder, I took the briefcase from Bob, continuing the surveillance. Once I was signed in, Unger went through the ritual of taking me inside. This time, giving me a walking tour that would have made him a worthy guide in any historic building. I lagged behind as Unger recited facts and figures of the vault Vic and I had not heard when we were here the first time. I couldn't exactly bring out a tape measure to get any measurements of the size of the room, but the floor was covered in the same one foot square floor tiles as the hallways, so I angled the briefcase down as I walked, in hopes we'd be able to count the how many tiles there were in each direction, giving us a rough calculation of where the centre of the room was. This would help determine where we had to drill through the wall from the boiler room.

Unger explained that the safety boxes were made by Gross and Fieble of Hillsboro, Ohio, and that the framework was built from three-sixteenth-inch steel plate. The vault itself was built right into the foundation of the building during construction.

Right in the middle of the floor was a steamer trunk that I hadn't noticed the first time we were here. "Sorry, Mr. Unger, what's with the steamer trunk? I don't recall it being there when I was here with my brother."

"Oh, it was there all right. Been sitting right there since before I started. Never have seen the owners. According to Mrs. Hayward, the storage fee is paid up right till the early nineties. I've always wanted to take a peek inside just to quell my curiosity, though I never have."

Unger showed me a glass panel built into the back of the vault door. It housed the time lock mechanisms, one of which was a backup. His history lesson continued as he explained that the time lock was first introduced in the late 1870s to make sure that if bank personnel were kidnapped and tortured for the combination, thieves wouldn't be able to enter until the time set on the clocks.

The guard used his key to open his lock and I tried my new one, which worked the first time. I removed my box and headed to the cubicles. I was in and out of the cubicle in a jiffy, then slowly walked back to replace the drawer. I panned slowly around the room one last time as I left. While doing so, I saw a large tag taped on the wall. Upon closer inspection, I discovered it was a log for when the time lock had been serviced. The first date entered was April 18, 1913.

It wasn't like we would be going through the front door, but I still found this information fascinating. Bob was waiting in the hallway where I had left him, and was talking to Unger at his station. Unger released me from behind the bars, and I prayed that none of us would be on the inside, looking out of a barred room in the future.

"You know, in seventy-plus years, no one has ever lost anything from here," he said proudly. "In the early years, there was a night shift, but that was discontinued in the sixties. Unger went on to say, "It would probably be easier to break out of a maximum-security prison than to break into this steel and concrete bunker." We both agreed, said our goodbyes and headed on our way.

Back in the car, Bob replayed the tape as we drove, complimenting me on keeping the case steady while taking turns slowly. I had managed to capture a full three-hundred-and-sixty-degree video of the deposit box room, and although I had been in there twice now, it still sent shivers up my spine thinking about what we might find in those five thousand boxes. "The room is a lot smaller than I'd expected from your description. Based on the video and the tiles on the floor, I figure it's only forty feet long by twelve feet wide not including the deposit boxes," said Bob.

When we got back to Merritt, Bob got back in his own car and headed back to Kelowna. It would end up being a very long fifteen-hour day for Bob by the time he got home after nine. I continued on to Kamloops to make my sales calls the next day.

CHAPTER 22

Over the summer months, we continued to gather the equipment and supplies we would require. Using the name of Cam Cunningham, I rented a garage in Kamloops where we could store everything. Mrs. Trimble, a widow who no longer owned a car, had advertised the space in the local paper and it proved ideal for our purposes.

Giving her a six month advance on the rent, I told her that my friends and I would be using the space to fix up an old vehicle for a friend that was starting a new business. I went on to tell her that I was only in town every other week, and most of my work would take place on evenings when I was in town.

I often didn't leave the garage until after one or two in the morning, heading back to my hotel for a few short hours of sleep before making my sales calls the next day. The flames at both ends of the candle were getting dangerously close to each other, and I had to make sure that sales didn't falter. If that happened, that peckerhead Calder might want to make a sales trip with me.

Harry managed to find a Grumman cube van for sale in Armstrong. When we had watched the video together it had been Harry who pointed out a Vancouver Public Works vehicle in the alley behind the four hundred block Pender that neither Bob nor I had even noticed when we scouted the location. The idea was to get a similar vehicle and replicate the look with decals and striping so that it wouldn't appear out of place if it was parked behind the building for a period of time.

The one Harry found cost Bob another fifteen hundred cash. The van was okay, considering it was a 1979 model with 225,000 miles on it. It had a five-speed manual transmission, and the tires were in decent enough condition to get it to Kamloops. There was very little rust on any of the exterior of the cab. As a bonus, like a lot of step-in vans, the box itself was white painted aluminum. The van's interior was twelve feet long behind the driver's seat, and had a partition behind the seats to protect the driver and passenger from flying objects.

Harry found a copy of an outdated transfer permit used to transfer unregistered vehicles from one location to another, as BC only used paper temporary permits. Harry produced a good-looking fake, which would serve our purposes to get the Grumman to Kamloops. The van hadn't been registered with the motor vehicle office for years. Despite being in relatively good running order, we told the seller it would be used for parts. The current owner had not bothered to transfer the vehicle into his name after he bought it for another company to use as a second delivery truck when that company's business had faltered and the customer had never taken delivery of it. He wasn't concerned with transfer papers. It was a perfect scenario because it eliminated another paper trail. Harry had used one of his aliases while buying the truck. Little did he know it, but Mr. Andrew Hurtle was now the proud owner of an unregistered 1979 Grumman Cube van.

Fortunately, the city of Vancouver had stopped painting their trucks a pumpkin colour. They were now all a basic white with an orange stripe and city logo on the side doors and rear box. I would arrange to get a better picture of the decal so that Harry could make up magnetic signs for us. Because the aluminum body would not attract a magnet, we might have to rivet sheet metal on the sides of the box where the decals would be placed.

One of the requirements was that it would fit into the garage in Kamloops. By chance the one I rented didn't have a roll up door. Instead, two swinging doors made from two-by-four framing with sheets of plywood overtop kept the elements out of the garage. Instead of golf one Sunday, Harry and Bob drove to Armstrong to pick up the van before meeting me in Kamloops. We managed to get the van into the garage with only inches to spare. It was a tight squeeze, but once inside we still had three feet on each side to walk around. On an earlier trip, I had changed the locks on the garage and covered the windows with plywood, explaining to the Mrs. Trimble that I didn't want to break any of the windows while I was working.

I spent an entire evening cleaning all the surfaces, paying special attention to any area that either Bob or Harry might have touched on the drive to the garage. I had purchased boxes of disposable medical gloves that would now be worn any time any of us even thought of touching the van, or anything that we would put either on or in it.

Harry arranged with a friend to use a photography room at the local high school. He bought a roll of magnetic vinyl in Kelowna. We would blow up the photograph of the public works logo and then glue it to the magnetic material as soon as I got a good picture.

At one of the earlier meetings, we had asked Harry to find a way for us all to communicate. It was also up to him to design an early warning system that could be placed at the rear door of the boiler room. Our plan called for at least one of us to be near the van at all times, but if for any reason we all needed to be downstairs at the same time, we would be able to put the deadbolt in place. These were all just precautions, but as the Boy Scout motto said, "Be prepared."

Despite his motel lying in ruins, Harry headed to Penticton on the premise of attending an Independent Motel Owners meeting in Penticton, telling Pam he would also visit his mom while he was there. Harry went there expecting to find most of what we needed at the local Radio Shack, but they really didn't have anything but basic two-way radios and baby monitors. He did manage to get an intrusion alarm in the form of a small optical warning buzzer that stores used to alert staff when a customer entered the store. The other item he found there was a decent police scanner. Because it was a retail store, he paid cash for these items, eliminating any reason to provide identification. Bob was now out another hundred and fifty bucks. He continued his search for the communicators. When we had decided that we needed these, Harry had said, "Sounds like something from of Star Trek. While I'm at it, why don't I try and find us a transporter? That way we won't even need the van or any of the other stuff," he had mumbled.

With two of his three purchases made, Harry thought he had finally found a place that could fill our communication needs. He told the clerk that he needed a way to communicate with his staff at the back of a large warehouse. The clerk explained that the ones he had were also very much like kids' walkie-talkies or baby monitors. All the units he carried were on the same basic frequency, and they were also subject to a lot of static when under fluorescent lighting ballasts. "One of the big grocery stores tried them, but ended up bringing them back because of the interference. They had to get them specially made. I think they went with Motorola. They might be your best bet for what you want, but be prepared to pay a lot more than what these ones go for," he told Harry.

Harry phoned the local Motorola dealer and spoke to one of the technicians. Harry is a smart guy, especially with electronics, but his mind was drowning in facts before the call was done. The bottom line was that there were no private frequencies available in Canada. Anything he did get would still be on a common frequency. If we wanted transmissions that were scrambled, we would be looking at twelve hundred dollars apiece. The Motorola sales guy said that if we went with low power units, people would have to be right outside a building to allow the radio waves to be picked up.

Armed with this wealth of facts, figures, signal strengths and costs, he explained it all to us between the seventh and eighth holes the next time we golfed. The consensus was to purchase a product on the lower end of the price spectrum. We shouldn't really need them a lot, but we all agreed that we needed radios.

Harry managed to make another trip to Penticton, telling Pam that he was getting assistance from another motel owner, who was negotiating with a large motel chain to take over the property. She was thrilled at the prospect of getting out completely, so she told him he should head down there. In the end, he bought four Maxon 49sx, single-channel, three-frequency communicators that seemed good enough for our purposes. The units were voice activated so we would not need to press a button every time we spoke, had thumb wheel frequency controls, and came complete with batteries, belt clips and adjustable headsets.

Again, Harry paid for them with Bob's money, telling the clerk that his kids and their friends loved Star Wars and wanted to look like Han and Luke. "All I wanted when I was a kid were a pair of pearl-handled cap guns," he joked as he handed the clerk the two hundred and sixty bucks. As he was leaving the clerk handed him extra sets of batteries for each of the units.

"I think those kids are going to go through those things pretty quick"

CHAPTER 23

It was Dan's job was to find a way to get through the concrete wall. With his background in chemistry, he knew there were no combination of chemicals that could eat through that much concrete in a reasonable time. Muriatic acid was fine for cleaning cement but not for penetration. He worked on a couple of formulas, including $H2SO4$, commonly known as sulphuric acid, but heavily concentrated concoctions would still take too long to work through that much concrete. The fumes would be caustic, and could cause severe, painful chemical burns if spilled.

Based on the location downtown—and having no idea how to use them—explosives were out of the question. He figured a mistake using any explosive might end up a giving a funeral home a windfall of clients.

Dan's next avenue of attack was to find a mechanical way to cut through the wall, quickly realizing that no matter what they chose, it was going to be expensive. He hoped that Bob's resources would be able to handle whatever he came up with. Dan considered concrete coring equipment and diamond saws. The problem with drilling would be the size of equipment required, and just how long they would take. The depth of the required cut was another problem, depending on just where the armour plating was in relation to the thickness. Small diamond coring bits would require too many cuts to make a hole large enough to crawl through.

Dan was the tallest and broadest of the four of us. He needed to figure out what size of a hole they required to be able to crawl though. In his garage one evening he used a jigsaw to cut an eighteen-inch diameter circle in an old piece of plywood, then tried to slip it over his shoulders and hips. It did slip all the way to the floor, but it was tight. He repeated the process with a twenty-inch hole, which slipped easily over his head and hips, but he still wasn't sure everyone could easily fit through a deeper channel of that diameter. While using the jigsaw, he wished they could cut out the wall as easily as the plywood.

He finally settled for a hole twenty-four inches in diameter, which would be plenty large enough for any of them as well as any equipment they might require inside. He then confirmed how difficult coring might be, concluding they would have to drill at least twenty, three-inch diameter holes through the thirty-four inches, with a possibility of a lot of rebar in the concrete as well as the armour plating. "Cross that one off the list," he commented to the empty garage.

Then he had an aha moment, remembering conversations at work with co-workers who had taken up diving as a hobby. These guys had helped in salvage work years prior. Many days during lunch they would talk about how they had assisted in the recovery of artifacts from a ship that had sunk in Barkley Sound off Vancouver Island. They had not been qualified to do the work but had acted as dive buddies to an archeological crew that was working on the recovery of pieces from the *Tuscan Prince*, a freighter that had gone down in 1925. The crew they assisted had cut the name plate off a boiler. The dive crew had used an underwater cutting system that would cut just about anything.

Instead of taking a coffee break the next day, Dan used his time to check with the local welding supply outfits about what kind of systems might be available. The first was a small operation and didn't have a clue what he was talking about. The next place he called was a little better, knowing what Dan was inquiring about but didn't really know a lot about them. "The guy you want to speak to is Brian over at Industrial Welding Products," he was told. Dan got the contact information and gave Brian a call, explaining that he was going to be helping friends dismantle parts of an old train engine so that it could be put back together at a heritage site.

Brian told him about a model that would probably fill his needs: "Thermal lances can burn at temperatures up to ten thousand degrees. They'll burn through cast iron, stainless steel as well as concrete."

The last statement made Dan sit up and take notice. Brian continued to tell Dan more about the unit, including the requirement of an oxygen source and regulator. Many units had twelve-volt ignition systems, which could be attached to batteries. Brian explained it was better to use an oxyacetylene torch to ignite the rods.

"How much money are we talking about?"

"Around a grand for the basic system. Two hundred bucks for a twenty-five pack of half-inch diameter, 36-inch long quick-connect magnesium burning rods. They're a little pricier, but will go through anything like shit through a goose."

"I don't know just how big the pieces we will be cutting might be, but I know there will be some hard to get at areas. What if I needed to reach in a little further than the three-foot bars?" he asked.

"We can get longer bars, but they don't cut as fast as the magnesium, with the quick connect bars you shouldn't need anything longer. Will you have oxygen tanks available? "

"Yeah, we've got some basic equipment. How much oxygen do you think I need?"

"You can cut through around thirty-four linear feet of one-inch steel plate with each large cylinder of oxygen." Brian talked about ensuring everyone was safe while cutting, and how long the cutting might take. Dan thanked him for his patience and help, saying he would check with the project guys and get back to him.

At home that night, Dan started calculating how long it might take to do the cutting. He had just finished figuring out a time frame when another thought occurred to him. "Once we get the piece cut, how the hell are we going to pull the plug out of the hole?" He did more calculations for a twenty-four-inch-diameter, thirty-inch-thick piece of concrete plus a four-inch piece of steel and realized they would have to remove a donut hole from the rest of the wall that weighed over 1700 pounds. He pondered that problem for a while before settling on a plan, then worked out what other items they might need in the in the boiler room, as well as in the vault itself.

During Sunday's golf game, we spent a lot more time talking than golfing. We had taken the tee box well before any other golfers were in the parking lot. The first hole was played to keep up appearances, then the four of us just walked and talked until we came to the ninth hole and played our way onto the green. There were a lot of people now out on the course, waving and saying good morning to us, so we just put our heads down and played the back nine.

On the front nine, Dan told us about his findings, including why he had ruled out a concrete coring machine. He reluctantly told Bob how much more his investment would be. "The biggest problem we're going to have is that this process is going to create a lot of smoke," said Dan. "I'm not sure how we can get around that. I think I noticed a manhole on the video of the back alley. We might be able to exhaust the smoke into it."

In principle, we all agreed with the plan that Dan had laid out. Bob would take care of getting the cash needed and Dan would arrange to pick up the thermal lance and rods. I also thought I might have a way to arrange for the oxygen. We would all try to find the rest of the supplies that Dan had listed.

We finished our golf day and headed off to start the week with very specific goals and targets to be reached before we got together next Sunday. If problems cropped up during the week we would arrange an investment club meeting somewhere.

CHAPTER 24

Dan made more phone calls, tracking down another dealer for the thermal lance that Brian from Industrial had told him about. Interior Welding Supply in Castlegar had the exact same model. Dan concocted a story for Rita, telling her that their friend Bill from university was working at the pulp mill in Castlegar and had called to see if he was interested in coming over to give him a hand. Bill had his own lab in Calgary, and his services always seem to be in demand. He told Rita that this would be a great chance to pick Bill's brain to see if maybe he could finally strike out on his own. Knowing that opening his own lab had been Dan's dream for years, she said she would support him no matter what he wanted to do, and that yes, he should take this opportunity to meet with Bill.

Dan arranged for time off work, and headed to Castlegar. His old roommate had indeed called, but not because he needed help. It was because he was out of town and hated being alone for a long time and wanted company. They would meet at the Sandman Hotel to catch up, and Dan would certainly get as much information on starting his own lab as he could.

Originally, he thought he would have to rent a vehicle to head to the welding supply place. Discovering prior to leaving that Bill owned a pickup, Dan was sure he could swap vehicles with him for the day so that he could use it to pick up the lance. It wasn't that the unit was big—he just didn't want to pick it up in a vehicle he could be identified with. Using a rental would require him to use his own identification and there would definitely be a paper trail.

Dan had made the call to the lance dealer, arranging to have one there for pickup later in the week, as well as three cases of the thirty-six-inch magnesium rods that Brian suggested would be best for the job. This was one more box than what Brian had suggested, but it wasn't like we could run down to the 7-Eleven at two in the morning to get extras if we ran out.

On the drive over, Dan had thought about their university days, when he and Bill had roomed together. They'd been really close, but their girlfriends had never really gotten along. Finally, after two years, Dan had moved out to live with Rita. Things between him and Bill had never really been the same. Dan and Rita were still married, but Bill had divorced within two years. Dan and Bill had not kept in touch a lot, except for sporadic visits when Bill stopped in Kelowna on his way to the coast.

Dan and Bill met for dinner and talked about old times. The evening ended up just like the old days, in a bar drinking way too much. Dan had to stop himself numerous times from telling Bill all about what he and the others had planned. Bill was a big, heavy-set guy and had always been able to drink a lot more than Dan. Before he was totally wasted, Dan had arranged to swap vehicles with Bill the next day. He told Bill he wanted to head out on the local logging roads while Bill was working. They finished off with the same night cap that they had both enjoyed in their younger days: a double shot of Southern Comfort.

Dan woke to a pounding in his head and a banging on the door. Through half-closed eyes, Dan saw that it was still early and that Bill was probably heading off to the mill. He answered the door in a haze and they swapped keys. Dan got a ribbing about not being able to hold his liquor any better than when they used to shut down the Student Union Building at university. Dan was leaning on the doorway while talking to Bill, who looked bright-eyed and bushy-tailed. Perhaps the doorway was holding him up. He asked Bill. "Did I say anything offensive to anyone last night?"

"No, nothing stupid. As usual you ended up asking or telling me the same thing at least three times. You really do tend to kill more brain cells than the standard person when you drink."

"I think Rita would agree with you. She never lets me forget it after I get tanked. Thanks for the use of the truck today. I'll meet you back here tonight, dinner will be on me and I'll head home tomorrow morning."

When Bill left, Dan headed back to bed. If he was pulled over it wouldn't be because he had a hangover—he would still blow over the legal limit. He struggled to get the alarm set to wake him at 11:00, then promptly fell back asleep.

He was still a bit groggy when he woke, but headed off in search of the welding supply store anyway. Before finding it, Dan needed a gas station with a washroom that would not require him to go inside. He drove past three stations before finding an old Shell station that fit his needs. He lucked out when he discovered that although you normally had to go inside to get a key for the restroom, the door he tried had not been closed properly, saving him from having to ask for the key, which was probably attached to a horseshoe to make sure you didn't walk away with it in your pocket.

He had packed old coveralls, work boots and other props for a basic disguise in a separate gym bag. He got changed in the relatively clean bathroom and checked himself in the cracked mirror that hung on the wall. The coveralls had seen better days and were at least a size too big even for him. He had a set of old horn-rimmed safety glasses he had found at work and finished off his working man look with a Band-Aid on his forehead and a ratty old Caterpillar ball cap. Rita might not recognize him if she drove past on the street, he thought as he looked at his reflection in the mirror.

After finding the location of the store, Dan headed off to find the dirt roads. Bill's truck was just too clean. Fortunately, it was registered in Alberta and they only used rear license plates in that province. He finally came across an active logging road and headed down it in search of mud. Logging roads are usually well maintained, but you could always find a spot in the shadows of the trees where the road never seemed to dry up. It took him close to half an hour to find the perfect dip in the road where a diverted culvert sent a small stream of water constantly traversing the road. Dan ran the truck back and forth through the mud, creating an oozing muck with a consistency thicker than chocolate pudding and twice as sticky.

By the time he was done, there was mud everywhere, including some that had been flung onto the windshield, which the wipers spread into a hazy film. Pulling off to the side of the road, he grabbed a big glob of the oozing muck and threw it against the rear licence plate, attempting to obscure it. Satisfied that it looked as though he had partaken in a mud bog race, he headed back to the welding store.

When he had got out of the truck to dirty up the plate, he made sure that his boots were covered in mud and had wiped his dirty hands on the sleeve of the coveralls. Rehearsing the name he would be using and his storyline while he drove back, Dan was sure he could be convincing in any manner of conversation.

There were only two guys behind the counter at the small welding shop. "Can we help you?" they both asked at the same time.

"I'm looking for Roger," Dan answered. "He was going to put a thermal lance and rods aside for me."

One of the guys came out from behind a desk and came to the counter. "You must be Mr. Engle," said Roger as he stuck out his hand.

"That's me, Gerome Engle," replied Dan, shaking hands with Roger.

"Got your stuff all put together out back. You want to put all this stuff on a credit card?"

"Any discounts for cash? We've been getting a lot donations for our project."

"Afraid not. Have to cover the overhead whether it's cash or credit card," Roger looked at the bill. "The total with taxes in going to be $1982."

Dan pulled a fistful of bills out of his pocket and peeled off twenty one-hundred-dollar bills. Roger gave Dan back a five, a ten and three of the new one dollar coins everyone was calling "loonies." Roger then stamped the two-part invoice as paid and gave the bottom part of the form to Dan.

"What exactly is your project?" asked Roger

"I thought I told you on the phone."

"Nope."

Dan had read up on old trains and rail lines as part of his back story, and proceeded to give Roger the spiel he had memorized just in case anyone started to make inquiries related to the purchase of the thermal lance equipment.

"I'm helping with a reclamation project, trying to get an old locomotive out of the bush off an abandoned rail line between here and Cranbrook. It was built by the Canadian Locomotive Company way back in 1914. Damn thing weighs over three hundred thousand pounds. It used to run on the old Cranbrook and Nelson Railway. Derailed back in the forties and been sitting in the woods ever since. Our project is to take it apart and then put it back together in Nelson."

"That sounds really cool," commented Roger. "Come on through the back and we'll get you loaded up."

Dan followed behind, leaving little clumps of mud all the way from the front counter to the loading dock. "Sorry about all the mud. Got stuck this morning around Ymir."

Roger gave a run through on the operation of the unit and how to hook up the oxygen, and what pressure to set the gauge at. "The ignition switches are okay, but you probably already know that you get the rods started a lot quicker with an oxy-acetylene torch."

As they loaded the boxes inside the back of the truck that was covered with a matching fibreglass canopy, Roger pointed to the Band-Aid. "What did you hit your head on?"

"Smoked it on a branch when I got out of the truck when I got stuck this morning. Bled like a son of a bitch for a bit."

Roger pointed at the back of the truck, "Better get that mud off your plate. Cops don't have a lot to do around here, other than busting hidden grow ops or giving out speeding tickets. You'll get a ticket for sure with a plate all covered like that."

"Thanks for the warning, I'll head right over to a car wash and get that looked after. I guess the whole thing could use a bit of a cleaning. Think I saw a wash bay over by the Shell station."

Dan thanked Roger again for all his assistance, got into his truck, about to head off when he saw Roger run up to the side of the truck and bang on the window. *What the hell does he want now?* Dan wondered as he rolled down the window.

"Forgot to give you all the warranty papers. It's got a lifetime warranty. This envelope has everything in it. If you need any more rods, let us know. I might be able to bring them up to you. I'd love to see that old locomotive."

"Sounds great," Dan said, now wondering if he'd opened a can of worms. "I'll let you know if we need anything else." Dan put the truck in gear and headed directly over to the wash bays. He cleaned the truck up completely, including the floor mats, then he changed out of his disguise and was back at the hotel having a drink in the lounge well before Bill returned.

Before returning the truck's keys to Bill, Dan said, "I need to get some stuff out of the back of the truck and into my car." With the transfer complete, he treated Bill to a great dinner at Michael's restaurant, a place that Chris had recommended. It was a terrific meal and the veal was just as good as Chris had promised. Dan and Bill spent the rest of the evening discussing the pros and cons of running your own lab, as well as tipping back more drinks. Dan left with a much better understanding of the sacrifices and hard work it would require in the years to come.

They made it an early night and Dan returned to Kelowna invigorated by the thought of having his own lab in the near future.

CHAPTER 25

We continued to refine our strategy during our Sunday golf games. We still didn't know when we would have all the equipment. I was getting concerned with how long it was taking. In movies or on any television show I've ever seen, it never seemed to take much more than a scene or two to come up with everything that's needed to rob a bank or an armoured car. The time we had invested already would have filled a mini-series. As the summer waned, we came to the realization that we wouldn't be having a weekend getaway this fall.

After Dan had acquired the thermal lance, our next step was to make sure we had the oxygen to run it. During sales calls throughout the interior, I had seen many oxygen cylinders over the years. The complication was that you had to rent the bottles from the welding gas company. Each cylinder has a lot of labels, including the serial number, date of the last hydrostatic test on the bottle, as well as other identifiers. These numbers could identify the last location of the cylinder, and that could be a problem. When we pulled off the heist, we would not be able to return any bottles we rented. Leaving rented bottles behind would become evidence that could be traced back us.

Taking the thermal lance away with us would be easy enough, as the pieces were small enough to cart away and dispose of when we left. Based on what Brian told Dan, we would need at least six, three-hundred-cubic-foot cylinders, each weighing close to two-hundred pounds when filled and measuring over five feet long. There was another tank that might do the job. It was just over four feet long and weighed only ninety pounds, but only held one hundred and fifty-four cubic feet of gas. We would need to steal at least thirteen of these smaller bottles.

I wondered how the hell we were going to get that many bottles. I thought about my trips around the interior, knowing there were small welding shops that kept extra bottles around, acting as rental depots for the companies that supplied the cylinders. A lot of welding shops used small exterior areas closed off with chain link fencing; however, there were shops where the enclosures weren't consistently under lock and key. It seemed that some of the machine shop operators storing these bottles didn't consider theft an issue. As I went about my sales route, I noted the places I might be able to get the bottles. I wouldn't be able to take them all from any one shop. A bad operator might not pay a lot of attention to their inventory, but I was sure they would notice if there were thirteen bottles missing.

Ideally, I would get them from smaller towns around Kamloops, making it easy to take them directly to the garage. I found likely sites in Ashcroft, Barriere, Clearwater and Vavenby, but it would require more than one overnight trip to get all the ones we needed.

The idea of stealing the oxygen bottles was causing me more anxiety than the idea of robbing the vaults. Taking them was not going to be just a one-time occurrence, and each time I stole a cylinder I ran the risk of being caught. Before we committed to stealing them, I had to be sure there was no other way to get our hands on them.

While I was at a job site in Kamloops, I happened across one of the ideas Dan had earlier eliminated. While on a sales call, I noticed a building being erected on an adjoining lot. I was watching the progress on the site, and then I saw a coring machine being used. I always had a hard hat with me, so I put it on and went to check out what they were working on. A crew of men were operating the core drill, putting a hole right through the concrete. I asked if the job super was around and the drilling crew informed me he was currently off site. I struck up a conversation with them, asking them about the big holes they were drilling.

They explained that the cribbing crew had made a mistake in positioning the hole for sewer lines, water services, gas lines and electrical conduits that would be going into the building. The crew from a specialty coring company was drilling a sixteen-inch diameter hole right through the foundation wall. I stood spellbound as they worked, asking them to explain exactly what they were doing. They made the process seem easy. The drill was mounted to a stand, in turn the stand was mounted to the wall. The concrete was green, enabling them to drill through the eight inches of concrete and rebar in no time.

As the diamond bit was working its way through the wall, I found out that these guys had experience in cutting exhaust vents in various older buildings, including banks. They had drilled holes with bits three feet in diameter, and had drilled others up to six feet in diameter by drilling a series of smaller three inch holes, overlapping each hole as they made their way around the circumference. The deepest hole this crew had drilled to date was four feet.

I pointed to the rig that was set up on the wall, "That equipment must cost a pretty penny." I said.

"Well what we have sitting here right now would probably run you fifteen grand," said the guy who seemed to be in charge.

"That include the big bits?"

"No, those will run two to six grand each, depending on the size, but they'll drill a lot of holes if you go slow enough and use enough water to keep them from overheating.

I kept asking questions, trying to soak up all the information I was getting from them, with the hope that it would assist us with getting the right equipment if we decided to go that route.

"That looks like quite the power cord you're running." I said, pointing to a heavy-duty electrical line.

"Yeah, this hydraulic unit is a twenty-horsepower rig that needs 230 volts. We have another unit that requires a 575-volt power supply."

Thanking them for the demo, I asked them for a business card. "My customers include mines and sawmills throughout the interior. If I ever come across clients needing your services, I'd be happy to tell them to call you."

I would get together with Dan when I got back and tell him this might be a better alternative than having to steal all those cylinders. We'd still need oxygen bottles, but certainly not thirteen of the smaller ones. This process would also eliminate a great deal of the smoke generated by the thermal lances. The other bonus was that the whole thing could be stripped down to individual components and carted away. We would still need the lance to cut through the armour plate, but if what we had been told was correct, we would only be cutting through a total of four inches of steel.

I had no idea where we could get our hands on a coring drill, but thought Dan would probably be able to track down a supplier somewhere. It sounded like the coring equipment and bits weren't going to be cheap. I spent the rest of the day hoping that Bob's funding was as solid as he claimed.

A bit of luck came our way late in the summer. My head office needed personnel from the branch offices to help with new product promotions. I volunteered and ended up spending an entire week in Vancouver. During the week, guys from the head office staff had invited us out of towners out for dinner or drinks. I used the excuse that I needed to use my time to continue to go through Mom and Dad's things. I was even happier about being there when I realized that Calder was on vacation.

One evening, I headed out to play photographer. I got good pictures of the public work vehicles used in Vancouver, using two rolls of film to get three good shots of one of the trucks. I also took pictures showing a variety of dumpsters and their locations around the city, interspersed with a variety of pictures of flowers and statues.

London Drugs was one of the best places for one-hour development of pictures in the city. The shots were perfect for Harry to make our magnetic signs and also showed us how to do the stripes on the van. The colour of the shots was good enough that we could locate spray paints that were close to city colours. When we finished with the decals and paints, I was convinced that if parked beside another city unit, our replica would pass a cursory inspection.

When Dan had calculated the weight of our concrete-and-steel core at over 1750 pounds, he realized that we would need a five-ton lever-action hoist to pull it out from the wall. I managed to find one of these in a surplus store in Vancouver.

After the first large items had been bought, Bob gave each of us a thousand dollars in cash, which allowed us to buy the things we needed without having to go to him each time. We assured him on more than one occasion that he could take what was owed to him off the top of anything we managed to steal.

During the lunch hour on one of my days in Vancouver, I went to one of the local welding supply stores and purchased leather welder's aprons, chaps, and spats to cover our boots. I also got four sets of expensive welder's gloves. There were going to be a lot of sparks and slag coming off the steel and concrete when the cutting started. We didn't need anyone getting burned. Dan's research on the thermal lance indicated the noise of the oxygen charging through the lance could be deafening, so I also purchased some top-end ear protectors.

CHAPTER 26

It took us until mid-November to finally get all the equipment transferred to the garage in Kamloops. Prior to that time, I had taken extra out of town trips, giving me more time to work on the truck and get the oxygen cylinders.

My conscience was bothering me, making it difficult to steal the cylinders of oxygen outright. When I did permanently borrow them, I left $200 cash in an envelope with a photocopy from a newspaper that simply read "TANKS" for each of the cylinders I had taken. I wondered if the proprietors would get my attempt at humour. I hadn't asked anyone what the cost of an empty cylinder would be, but thought the money might help them offset the loss.

It had been easier to get the tanks than I'd figured. I started with four tanks, which would be at least one more than needed to cut through the four inches of plating. If we had no luck with a coring machine, we might need as many as seven bottles. Dan had recalculated the cutting rates for the oxygen, then rechecked his calculations, making sure we would have a surplus. The bottles had been awkward to handle, but were easier to get into the back seat of the car than I expected, and I would worry about the extra three if we needed them.

To this point, we had managed to make all our purchases with cash. I had found coveralls the same colour as those used by the works crews for the city of Vancouver. Heavy work boots came from a surplus store in Kamloops.

When I first told Bob the cost of the drill rig, he balked a little, even though he had told us on numerous occasions not to worry about the funding. At this point we could have walked away from the entire plan, but he would have been out close to ten grand from his slush fund. If we could find a core drill, his output was going to nearly double on a single purchase.

Dan located a company where we could buy the drill and bits in Savona, a thirty-mile drive west of Kamloops. I didn't go to the same extent as Dan when he picked up the thermal lance, but I did do a bit of disguising. I put a small pebble in my shoe and the pain induced a fake limp. It was just before Halloween, so I had gone to a variety store that carried costumes and bought a high-quality long, stringy wig. I completed the look with a pair of reading glasses, a ball cap and old leather coat. If it had been sunny out I would have used sunglasses, which would have given me a Kim Mitchell appearance if I do say so myself.

They had taken a used electric hydraulic power unit weighing over five hundred and fifty pounds on trade. The drill they had was a heavy-duty unit, able to handle up to twenty-four inch bits. It weighed in at fifty-seven pounds, complete with a water connection to help keep the bits cool. They had two of the twenty-four-inch diameter bits that could drill up to two feet deep. I told them I would take both. I knew we only needed one of the bits, but we couldn't take a chance of having one crap out on us without a spare. I hoped two-foot-deep bits would be long enough to reach the steel plate embedded in the concrete. The used unit also came with an anchor rig that would mount to the wall and support the drill while it did its job. We also needed a hand-held hammer drill to mount the anchor rig to the wall, along with anchor sleeves and bolts.

I used the same basic story that I had given Mrs. Trimble, explaining to the owner of the equipment store how a friend of mine on Vancouver Island was just getting set up in the business. My friend had been the one who had called about the unit earlier—he was thrilled to have found one. I explained that I didn't know much about the process. I was just there to pick up the equipment for him.

While talking to the owner, he told me that most of the turn of the century buildings didn't have a lot of rebar in them and that concrete back then used a larger stone aggregate than was used today, making concrete from that period easier to drill than modern hardened concrete.

The owner said, "Your friend should be able to drill as much as thirty to forty linear feet of holes in reinforced concrete with a single bit."

I explained that my buddy said he wanted to make sure he had at least two of the twenty-four-inch bits to start with just the same. His first contract was with the Department of National Defence at the naval base in Esquimalt. He didn't want to be partway through and run into a problem by only having the single bit. He would start adding other size bits as he required them for new jobs.

The owner was sure a second bit wouldn't be required, but agreed it would be good insurance in case the concrete on the base had been mixed to a higher standard than similar buildings of the same vintage. He offered to take one of the bits in trade if it didn't end up being required

The hydraulic unit was on a cart with wheels, measuring forty-nine by twenty-six by forty inches high. I wanted to ensure the whole unit would fit through the back door of the boiler room. A plus was that this was a 230-volt model. I knew from my conversations with the crew in Kamloops that there were other models that would require much higher voltage. I wasn't sure what our power supply would be like, but Harry had been confident he could work it out.

In the end, I managed to get the entire package we needed from the shop in Savona. We dickered on the price a little. Since he hadn't entered the used unit into his inventory yet, he was more than happy to do a cash deal. "Harder for the tax man to keep track of. This will help pay for my next vacation." The only paperwork he gave me were the operating manuals. I was also relieved that I wouldn't need to steal any more oxygen bottles.

I had handed him an even eight grand. I had used the thirty-five-minute trip out to Savona as a test drive for the Grumman. Over the past months, we had found a pair of old licence plates and Harry had produced counterfeit license plate decals. These decals would not stand up to a close inspection if we were ever pulled over, but if we obeyed the rules of the road and avoided accidents, there was nothing to worry about. Without the logos, the painted stripes on the box shouldn't draw any unwanted attention, after all, I often saw old ambulances that had been converted to a variety of purposes.

The ride back to Kamloops was uneventful and the truck ran as well as I could expect for its vintage and the miles it had on it. With the addition of the coring equipment, the van was getting full. We had the oxygen tanks, boxes holding an assortment of other tools that might be required, and four sets of barriers we would use while the van was parked in the back alley. One evening while I was in Kamloops, I painted the barriers in the colour scheme of the blockades I had taken pictures of while I was in Vancouver.

Another night was spent taking serial number tags off every piece of equipment. I dismantled the compressor cart and reassembled it using wing nuts, allowing us to rapidly break down the unit when we were finished with it. I usually hated wearing any type of gloves, but I was diligent while working on all the equipment, and wiped down everything as it was stored to ensure I left no prints on any parts.

I don't know where I heard it or who said it, but I couldn't help but agree that the trivial things are the most important, and tried to remember that in each step of the process. If we took care of all the little things, then the big things we were doing would be a lot easier. I had gathered up all the serial number plates, discarding them at an array of locations along my Kamloops to Kelowna route.

Getting the Grumman from Kamloops to Vancouver could be prove to be a challenge. We had tentatively set a date early in the new year pull the heist. We knew that the new Coquihalla highway could be hazardous in winter. It had only been open since May of the previous year and the accumulated snow its first winter had been over four feet. The summit of the highway at the Coquihalla Pass rises to almost 4100 feet, with instances of snowfalls during last winter of ten to twelve inches in a twenty-four-hour period. Those sudden snow storms had brought the entire highway to a standstill. The slick conditions caused tractor trailer accidents as well as sending buses off the side of the road. Though the trip would take close to two hours longer, we determined our best route was going to be the less-travelled Fraser Canyon highway. This route did not get nearly as much snow, nor did it have the same physical challenges as the Coquihalla, making it easier on our older Grumman.

To be on the safe side, we changed the tires to good winter treads. All we needed in this whole endeavour was to end up in a ditch if we did encounter a winter storm. Bob would drive us all to Kamloops, then Dan and I would transfer to the Grumman, with Bob and Harry following us in Bob's Suburban. Under normal driving conditions, it would take five or six hours, but we factored eight hours to make the trip.

CHAPTER 27

While I was in Kelowna plotting a crime, Vic was in Vancouver trying to solve one. He was attempting to find out who had killed three men on the Vancouver waterfront several months earlier. Police had determined that the victims had arrived on the container vessel *Neptune Pearl* after they'd been taken on board as deckhands in Buenaventura, Colombia.

Containers from the ship had been traced to locations around the site. With help from the port authorities, they had discovered a container that had been opened. Sniffer dogs had been brought in, and even though the drugs were no longer in the container, the specially-trained canines confirmed that there had been drugs in there at some point. The dogs also discovered a point on the causeway where investigators felt confident the drugs had been opened, probably for testing.

The forensics team had found shell casings from a variety of different weapons and empty clips from a Scorpion machine pistol. The Luger and Uzi were also taken into evidence, noting that neither weapon had been fired. When the mangled body of Emilio had been recovered, they found the H&K he had been carrying, confirming that it had been fired. All the clues pointed to confirming their initial assessment that the carnage was a result of a drug deal gone very badly.

The major crimes task force was certain that Chang was at the top of the triad chain for the west coast. If drugs were arriving in the area, he would be one of the major players that could have brokered the deal. If they could prove his involvement in the shootings—before, during or after the fact—they might have a chance of putting a dent in his empire.

The information Vic had reported about seeing Chang at the vault had rekindled the interest of the task force in the possibility that this place was being used by criminals. They requested to have Vic temporarily assigned to the task force. He was now involved in the surveillance of Chang and his entourage. Watching him was for the most part extremely boring. As he had explained to Chris back in May, this guy looked like a model citizen, and a gut feeling that Chang might be involved in criminal activity including drugs and murder had not been enough to convince a judge to authorize any form of electronic surveillance. Failing to get approval for wiretaps, the task force had been required to observe, wait and report.

Chang lived in a penthouse suite that took up the entire top floor of a high-rise condo on Beach Avenue, less than three miles to the heart of Chinatown, and Vancouver's Chinatown started just over four blocks from the vault.

Chang had been born as Da Chang to wealthy parents in Hong Kong in 1935 and was educated in private British schools before being sent to Canada in 1946. With his colonial schooling, he spoke flawless, barely-accented English, so he integrated easily into his new schools and it didn't take him long to adopt his new country.

By sixteen he had become interested in many of the traditions of his homeland. It wasn't long before he was noticed by prominent members of the Vancouver triad community. By twenty, he became an initiated member, referred to as a 49 or soldier in the numerology-based rank system of the triads.

It was soon after his initiation to the triad that Chang began to discover the changes in the pigment of his skin. The taunts, jeers and name calling he had subsequently received forced him to become a hardened street fighter and by twenty-five, everyone knew to steer clear of him. Early on, many Chinese people referred to him as Nanzi Buding, which translated to Man with Patches. Those that had dared to call him that in those days were left with scars on their faces that made his patches of vitiligo look mild in comparison. It was now well over thirty years since anyone had dared say it to his face.

At the University of British Columbia, he became an accountant while continuing his rise through the triad's ranks as an administrator. By the time he was forty, he had become one of the youngest Deputy Mountain Masters with a numeric code of 438 and was being groomed as the successor to Ki Yee, the Mountain Master of the Vancouver Triad. At age fifty, shortly after Yee died in a suspicious boating accident, Chang ascended to numeric code 489, the top position of Mountain Master, or Dragon Head. On the streets of Chinatown, it was understood that he was the leader of his triad, which controlled drug and human trafficking, prostitution, money laundering, smuggling and counterfeiting of everything from music and video tapes to watches and clothes along the west coast all the way to northern California.

On the surface, Vancouver's Chinatown is a place that is appealing to visitors from around the world. A place where they could experience delicacies and culture that had been part of Vancouver's heritage since the 1890s when thousands of Chinese workers were hired to build the Canadian Pacific Railway. Behind the scenes, a lot of people would compare it to their impressions of the mob in Chicago or New York, the Cosa Nostra in Italy or the Japanese Yakuza.

Chang kept an unobtrusive office on the second floor of a modest looking building in the one hundred block of East Hastings. This office allowed him to carry out his supposedly legitimate business and philanthropic activities, as well as overseeing all operations of his triad.

With such a large Chinese population, many of whom were now second or third generation Canadians of Chinese descent, there was a large contingent serving in the police service. Although, there were also rumors that Chang had informants within the police department, often making it difficult to get officers involved on clandestine operations looking into the organized crime of the triad. The department did have many trusted officers that assisted in keeping track of Chang's activities in the Chinatown area easier. Asian officers took turns watching his offices on Pender Street.

They also set up surveillance on the second floor of the Montgomery Apartment Hotel, directly across from the vault building. The two-man detail only needed to stake out this location during the operating hours of nine to five on weekdays. Vic and two other officers were relegated to watching Chang's condo building, taking turns watching the parking garage at the corner of Harwood and Bidwell.

When Chang and his men left his condo, most often they headed down Beach to Burrard Street, then straight to Pender before heading east to his offices in Chinatown. Surveillance crews were surprised that they seldom changed routes to be unpredictable. This displayed extreme confidence, considering how ruthless members of other up and coming gangs were becoming, it surprised those on Chang's surveillance that he wasn't more cautious.

In the weeks that they had been conducting surveillance, there hadn't been a hint of illegal activity. Vic's confirmation of Chang using the safety deposit vaults had renewed the task force's interest in him, but things were going nowhere fast. There were hundreds of precious man hours of surveillance taking place with very little to show for it.

CHAPTER 28

Vic spent a lot of evenings on the rooftop keeping an eye on Chang's penthouse. Other than not being chewed to pieces by bugs or having to watch out for poisonous snakes while lying in a muddy rice paddy, the watchful isolation reminded him of his days on recon with the Rangers in Vietnam. Sitting alone on the roof, he realized he was a like his dad in many respects. He didn't talk of his time in Vietnam any more than his dad had ever spoken about his time during the Second World War.

Vic wondered if his dad had relived memories of the terrible times when he was alone like he did. Alone time was always the toughest, remembering things that no one should ever have to remember. Like thirty-thousand other Canadians, Vic had gone south and enlisted in the US military during the Vietnam War at the same time as twenty to thirty thousand young men left the US and moved to Canada to avoid the draft.

Vic's physical fitness and high IQ had qualified him to join the elite US Army Rangers, where he was selected for their Long Range Recon Patrols, or LRRPs, pronounced "lurp" in army lingo. The lurps went out in small patrols of four to six men and could be in the jungle behind enemy lines for weeks at a time, silently observing enemy activity without engaging or being spotted themselves. The intelligence work of the LRRPs saved countless lives during the war.

Whenever possible they would attempt to capture enemy combatants, as a live prisoner could tell the interrogation officers a lot more than a dead one. Capturing the enemy was one thing. Getting him back to a base was an entirely different matter and he had lost many friends while waiting for an evac-chopper to get them all out of the extraction zone.

Silent hours spent in the jungle had helped Vic develop the patience needed for the long-term stakeouts on which he had spent so many a lonely evening since joining the police force. As he sat on the rooftop of the building that overlooked Chang's, his mind returned to the scariest night of his life. Ironically, Vic had been on leave in the supposed safety of Saigon rather than in the jungles behind enemy lines when he received his only injury of the war. At three o'clock in the morning on January 31, 1968, under the ruse of the Tet holiday ceasefire, North Vietnam had thrown everything they had at the south.

Waking from a dead sleep to the sound of gun and mortar fire, Vic had raced from his hotel room. Far from his own unit, he'd automatically rushed toward the closest sounds of battle, which turned out to be the grounds of the American embassy. Two blocks from his hotel, he'd been passed by a jeep filled with American military police racing to the embassy. As he chased the vehicle on foot, he saw a figure step from an alley directly in front of the jeep and raise a weapon to his shoulder. The soldier fired at the jeep just as the passengers had opened up with their sidearms in his direction. The RPG screamed passed the jeep as the VC soldier fell, missing its target by yards and slamming into the building across the street from Vic. The specialist in silent, invisible jungle warfare was felled by a piece of shrapnel in the middle of a road under the glow of a neon bar sign.

Sitting on the roof in Vancouver, Vic closed his eyes and massaged the piece of steel hanging on a chain around his neck that the surgeon had given him for luck the following morning. "Don't know if it has ever brought me luck, but I've never been shot again," he said to himself. After being wounded he was awarded the Purple Heart. Like his dad's Second World War medals, it's tucked away in a dresser drawer and he has never brought it out.

After returning from Vietnam, Vic had taken a law enforcement program at the new Langara College and then joined the VPD in 1970. He had now been on the job for seventeen years and had spent many long nights on surveillance, often wondering if he had really made a difference. There were still guys like Chang, and the Hell's Angels were now fully entrenched in the lower mainland. Anytime the police managed to make headway on one gang, another was ready to take over their territory.

The majority of homicides he had investigated while on the force were connected to gang activity. Not often did they have a homicide that was committed by Colonel Mustard in the Study with a Candlestick.

"Christ, now I'm starting to think of things in reference to trivia just like Chris," he whispered to himself as he shook his head in disgust.

As dawn broke, Vic used his spotter scope as he had done throughout the night, watching Chang's condo, from the time the lights went on right up until Chang's assistants arrived to escort him for another day doing whatever it was they did.

The mobile unit had checked in just after seven. Vic turned the day's surveillance over to them. He was stiff and sore, the area around his old shrapnel wound ached as it often did when he was cold and tired. With his shift finished he headed home to get a bit of much needed sleep.

After six weeks, the Staff Sergeant in charge of the operation called everyone into the office. With hundreds of man hours of surveillance, hours of boring video and close to five hundred still photographs, they were no further ahead. The budget for this operation had run out and all the members on this detail would be reassigned back to their regular areas of operation.

Vic was disappointed, but he recognized the futility of carrying on with the surveillance. The three homicides from the terminal building were still unsolved, so he would rejoin the homicide team, putting his efforts toward that case, which had turned very cold. The Vancouver homicide squad was a quiet organization compared to most major American cities, but there were still a few other open cases that they had been pursuing since the dockyard murders. Vic was assured that if anything came up on Chang and his triad that he would be kept in the loop.

CHAPTER 29

When the golf season ended, we returned to curling for the first time in five years. Joining an evening men's league gave us an opportunity to get together at least one night a week to finalize the details of our planned escapade. Pam had made it known to Harry that she wasn't happy with the fact that Harry was spending their limited cash on curling, but as always, she had given in since he was going to do it anyway. Things were proceeding slowly with the insurance company. If not for the goodwill of their friends, they might be living in a homeless shelter.

The curling league also gave us an excuse for an early-January getaway. Using the premise of a bonspiel on the coast, we set D-Day for the weekend of the seventh of January. Dan and I booked extra days off work for both the Friday and Monday and Bob made sure he had no appointments for either day. We added the Monday just in case weather or other events beyond our control made it tough to get back in time.

Harry had produced an excellent set of decals for the side of the truck at the high school photo shop. They were glued and laminated to the magnetic sheeting, ready to be attached to the metal panels that were now riveted to the van. All our equipment was secured in the cargo area and all mechanical checks had been completed as though we were parents sending our daughters away on their first long-distance car trip.

I paid Mrs. Trimble an additional two month's rent, telling her I would be taking the van to my friend in early January, but that it would be early February before the garage was cleaned up enough for her to rent it again.

December is always a hectic time of year for all parents. Between Christmas concerts, music and dance recitals, this year was no exception, but we all got through our busy holiday schedules. Bob had tried to get his kids to spend the holiday season with him, but his ex-wife had wanted no part of it, so he and Gwen headed off skiing for the Christmas break. Dan's festivities were hectic like ours, but he had a lot of family in town, making things even more stressful. Harry and Pam spent time in Penticton with his mom.

Then it was over, the weeks of hectic schedules, and months of searching for just the right presents, like the year every little kid had to have a cabbage patch kid, or the year I stopped at every department store in the interior looking for a Princes of Power Castle. This year it had been Care Bears. Then in a flash it was all over and done in just over twelve hours. Trish and I ended our Christmas Day with a glass of wine in the hot tub, turning our attention to the year ahead.

One of the hardest parts of the entire plan was not letting little details slip out. I couldn't imagine what unfaithful spouses did while they were having trysts outside of their marriages. A poorly-chosen phrase or weak excuse or uttering the wrong name at a totally inappropriate time could ruin years or decades of trust in the blink of an eye. I had been keeping a fairly normal schedule and wasn't having an affair, but I felt guilty just the same.

There were times when my mind would wander and I'd be staring blankly ahead, thinking of what the four of us would be attempting. Trish always noticed when I got that blank look and asked what I was thinking. I'd managed to come up with reasonable explanations so far, with replies that varied from "Just thinking about how much soggy dog crap I'll have to pick up after the snow's all gone," to one that worked well lately: "Just thinking about the time Dad helped me build the deck."

One of my recent go-to excuses that always seemed to work was, "Just thinking about how short life really is. How it can be snuffed out in a heartbeat." During my melancholy moods, I told her how I would prefer to go out like Dad did. Better that than to linger on like numerous friends and family members who had suffered from various hideous forms of cancer.

One of my best friends once told me that if he found out he was suffering from a terminal disease, he was going to have a big party. He had a shop full of tools, and he wanted to be the one to give away his possessions. At his pre-funeral party he would give out gifts to all his friends. He would be there to say goodbye on his terms. After that party, he would arrange for a permanent sleeping pill, then relax on his deck as the sun was setting, with a good glass of scotch and his loving wife beside him and fade to black like the sunset.

"Enough of these morbid thoughts, after all it's Christmas," said Trish.

I sang a little of Burl Ives' "Holly Jolly Christmas," about what the best part of the year was, and as usual I was slightly off key. Then we finished our wine and headed off to bed, exhausted from another full Christmas Day.

D-Day was approaching quickly and getting to sleep was proving difficult. Each night as I closed my eyes, my mind raced with various scenarios, both good and bad. I had been seeing the clock radio alarm flip to three in the morning on too many occasions as the date drew nearer.

"What the hell have we got ourselves into?" I asked myself over and over. I was sure the plan was foolproof. We could pull it off, but self-doubt kept creeping in, causing me nights of fitful sleep. I wondered what was going through the minds of my partners in crime.

We had one more get together on Tuesday after curling.

"This is it guys," I told them. "Any second thoughts? Everyone still in? I have to admit, I'm scared shitless. As you might be able to tell by the sacks under my eyes, I have not slept a lot in the last while. I'm sure we can do this, but it's not too late to call it off. It might take a while to pay you back, Bob, but if anyone wants out, now is the last chance. Otherwise, we leave on Friday morning."

I looked at the other three who seemed just as nervous as I was feeling. They all took turns talking, each of us listening intently to their various apprehensions. Waiting for them to finish with their concerns, I thought of a movie I had watched late one night called *Houston, We've Got a Problem*. It was a 1974 movie with Robert Culp about the near disaster of Apollo 13. Tonight, I was playing Gene Kranz, mission control director.

"Okay guys, you have all had your say, last chance for a go/no-go."

"Bob? Go/no-go?"

Bob looked at the three of us and raised his thumb. "Go."

"Harry?"

Harry started nodding affirmatively and raised his thumb up. "Go."

"What about you Dan?"

"Ah hell, we only live once, right?" he stated then put out his fist with a thumb in the air. "Go."

"Well?" they all piped up in unison.

"Let's make it unanimous," I said as I clenched my hand with my thumb up, thrusting my arm in the air. "Let's Go."

Bob got up from our table, went to the bar and bought four snifters of Grand Marnier, handing one to each of us. The price of those four snifters wasn't much to Bob, but would have blown my weekly allowance. A week from now, we all hoped to no longer have to deny ourselves treats like this ever again.

We all lifted our glasses and proudly chanted, "To life. Our way."

CHAPTER 30

D-Day had arrived. Bob was our chauffeur. I was the last to be picked up. We left my place just after six in the morning and headed to Kamloops to get the Grumman. As we drove, I pointed out the spot where I had pulled off my imaginary armoured car robbery, telling them how we could have pulled that heist, including the part where Bob would have been driving the Kenworth and Dan was driving the bus.

"What about me?" asked Harry?

"Didn't need you on that one, pal. But it was your wife who helped with stopping the traffic. By the way she looks great in shoulder-length red hair."

We arrived at the garage shortly after eight. Dan and I would drive the van. We eased it out of the garage, locked up, and set course for the coast with Bob and Harry following close behind in case we encountered mechanical problems along the way.

The weather gods were on our side, giving us clear skies all the way to Vancouver. We'd agreed to stop in Boston Bar to give the Grumman a rest, then stop again at Hope for lunch. After leaving Boston Bar, we would be passing through the seven tunnels that were blasted through the rock of the canyon during the fifties and sixties. As we approached the first, called China Bar tunnel, we saw the concrete sign embedded into the rock that told us the tunnel had been built in 1961. "I remember trying to hold my breath all the way through the tunnel when I was a kid," I told Dan.

"Not sure which one it was, but I heard a story about a tragic accident in one of these tunnels. Apparently, kids out for a joy ride tried to pass another car while they were in the middle of the tunnel and ended up slamming head-on into an oncoming semi-truck. By the time the trucker came to a stop, the car had been reduced to half its size. All four kids were pronounced dead at the scene. The story I heard is that the trucker got out of his truck that day and never drove again."

"Well, you better keep your eyes open and stay on our side of the road," suggested Dan.

It was after one thirty by the time we stopped for lunch in Hope. The drive had gone very well. Our Grumman had performed better than expected. Knowing that over the coming days our meal times could be sporadic, we all enjoyed a nice greasy trucker's platter at one of the many roadside restaurants that dot the landscape around Hope.

Leaving Hope just after two thirty would put us in downtown Vancouver around five thirty or six. With the sun setting just after four thirty, the back alley should be dark enough for the first phase of the operation. It would work out perfectly for the closing time of the vaults as well.

Before leaving Hope, we picked up sandwiches from the local Subway. These places had sprung up everywhere recently. Hope is the perfect place to stop for a rest, or to fill up the car or belly before tackling the highways that lead in or out of the interior. Close to nine thousand vehicles a day passing through town kept all the fast food franchise's hopping.

We felt that heading all the way in on the Trans-Canada highway, keeping a steady speed of sixty miles per hour with fewer places to easily pull to the side of the road might be a little much for our 1975 Grumman. Opting instead for Highway 7, travel distance would be the same, but it would add at least half an hour to our trip, due to the varying speeds of the two-lane highway. On the plus side was the proximity to small towns where it would be easier to conduct roadside maintenance if required. The extra time would get us to Pender Street closer to six o'clock. With the route settled, we again headed off. Our Grumman made the trip with no difficulties, but we arrived at Broadway and Boundary right in the middle of rush hour.

Prior to leaving Hope, the hand-held radios were handed out. Arriving in Vancouver, our vehicles were stopped beside each other at a traffic light. Opening the window, I held up the radio to show Harry that we should turn them on. We had previously agreed that Harry would start monitoring the police band radio at the city limits to get a feel for the way calls were being dispatched.

Bob knew where he was going, so he set off ahead of us. On scene, he and Harry would drive by the building, circle the block once or twice to establish the rear alley was clear of any vehicles, then park at the end of the block and do a full walk around the block. Dan and I detoured to an industrial area just off Terminal to change into our coveralls, boots and vests. We had been wearing utility gloves since we got into the truck in Kamloops. We then attached the magnetic signs to the sides of the van.

We headed north on Main after leaving Terminal. Although there was no reason to be concerned, I was happy that we would be turning west on Pender a block and a half before passing the Vancouver Police headquarters.

The range on our two-way radios was not that great, so we didn't hear from Harry until we passed Cambie Street. We had worked on various code words to use on the radios when we communicated, using the fake names we had generated months earlier. Our codes would not cover all contingencies, but they should cover the basics.

"Gerome, this is Duane. Do you copy?"

Dan replied, "Loud and clear."

"Looks like it will be a good night on the water."

I showed Dan three fingers and he relayed our ETA to Harry. We also toured past the front of the building, turning up Richards street and into the alley. With the all clear, it was our job to stop behind the vault building to set up the barriers. Once they were erected, we would back up to the fire escape, and I would climb the ladder on the back of the van, and then from its roof to the second-floor platform of the fire escape, where I would open the window lock.

From the video of the window lock leading to the fire escape, Harry had found a similar lock and fitted it to a mock-up of the window. I had practised often enough that I was sure I could get it open in thirty seconds or less.

I was glad the owners of the building had never upgraded to modern windows. The concern I had was whether years of painting the window frame would make raising the window too hard. I couldn't chance breaking the window in case an office worker came in to catch up on paperwork over the weekend and noticed a draft coming from a broken window.

Opening the catch on the window had gone smoothly. Yet again, my mind briefly went off on a tangent, thinking if this had been a movie, now is when I would discover that they had just changed windows or put in an alarm system. Thank goodness it wasn't a movie and the window slid open with little resistance. I climbed inside, heading immediately downstairs. Approaching the boiler room door, I spotted a problem I hadn't noticed the first time I went down these steps: this door had a lock. It had been open the first time, but it made sense that Jakub would keep it locked on weekends.

Even though our radios could be voice activated, eliminating the need to key the microphone, we had decided to use the push button when communicating, otherwise every time we spoke we might end up transmitting. "Everyone stand by." I walked down the last steps, put my hand on the handle and twisted. "Shit, it is locked. God damn it." I looked at the door, encouraged by the fact that it wasn't a steel door embedded into a metal frame. I pounded on the door, discovering it was a solid-core heavy wooden door in a wood frame.

I activated the mic, "I'll be right out" I said as I ran back up the steps and climbed onto the fire escape. I pantomimed using a pry bar and Dan hopped into the van, reappearing a few seconds later with one of the big pry bars. He swung onto the van's ladder and clambered to the roof.

"What's the problem?" he asked as I emerged

"Fucking door to the boiler room is locked. I should be able to force it open, unless you know how to pick a door lock?"

"As a matter of fact, I do. But you're holding my lock pick," he said as he passed me the tool. "Great minds think alike, I said, "I should be out in a minute."

I returned to the boiler room door. There was no deadbolt, only a locked door handle. Jamming it between the door and frame right in front of the handle, the pry bar easily squeezed into place. On the third pull the frame split as the handle latch forced the striker plate to give way. Kicking the door caused the leading edge of the frame to break off completely. Reaching inside, I unlocked the handle then pulled the door closed again, checking to see how obvious the damage was. I was pleased when saw there was only a slight compression of both the door and frame. I verified there were no bits of wood sitting on the floor outside of the door.

There was a hook and eye on the inside of the wooden door, after setting it, I ran up the steel staircase to the rear door. While I had been getting the interior door open, Bob had taken his Suburban away, leaving it at a self-park lot a block away. We would swap parking areas at times over the weekend to make sure it didn't get hauled away because a well-meaning parking lot attendant thought it had been abandoned.

When Bob returned, he and Harry climbed into the back of the van to get suited up in their city works disguises. While I had been prying open the door, Dan had pulled the truck tight to the rear door. He was ready to start unloading equipment as soon as I opened it. Once he was changed, Bob would act as a flag man, ensuring no other vehicles attempted to come down our section of the alley past the barriers—there were always some people who thought barriers were for everyone but them.

There was just enough room between the rear door and the sidewalk to park the van. In front of the door in the centre of the alley was the manhole we would use to complete our charade. The rear of the van was parked just ahead of it.

Using the chain pulley system and slings that Harry had purchased for each of our major components, all our gear was lowered to the floor of the boiler room. Using the manual chain hoist wasn't fast, but it was easier than carrying the heavy items down a circular stair case without being able to see where you were stepping. Harry went to the bottom of the staircase to operate the hoist while Dan and I unloaded the van and set up the slings. Bob was doing his job as flagman.

We had the van unloaded in forty minutes. Harry turned it around so the rear bumper stopped just ahead of the grate that was embedded in the asphalt. Bob then used a pry bar to remove the grate, set cones around the uncovered hole, then placed a ladder down the shaft, giving the appearance there was a worker below.

Considering it was January, it wasn't an especially cold night and all of us were all glad we weren't doing this in the heat of the summer. Between the physical exertion, adrenaline rush and a deep-down fear, we were all hot and sweaty.

With everything done for phase one, we gathered at the back of the van. "Next time we do this let's make sure we spend a little time in the gym first. Golf in the summer and curling once a week didn't prepare me for this much exercise," said Harry.

"Not going to be a next time. Right?" said Bob.

"Well at least we have a doc on staff in case one of us has a heart attack like the guy in *Ocean's Eleven* with Sinatra, Sammy Davis and the rest of the Rat Pack," I said, using yet another movie reference.

I checked the time. Since arriving in the alley at 6:15, a little over and hour and a quarter had passed, figuring we'd lost ten minutes to the locked basement door.

Harry set up the buzzer system on the door leading to second floor, just in case Jakub decided to stop in over the weekend for any reason, and confirmed that the door looked normal from the outside. While unloading the equipment, we had debated the merits of whether to leave the hook and eye on the basement door and decided to use both.

CHAPTER 31

The next few hours flew by. Our first job was to get everything arranged in way that would make our task more efficient. We started with an inspection of our entire work area, finding the electrical panel and a hose bib, allowing us to run a hose to the drill that would keep the bit cool. There was a floor drain to carry away the three and a half gallons of water that would be streaming onto the floor every minute.

Harry and Bob had gloved up as they donned their disguises. "Leave no prints," had become our constant mantra. Because of the issue with the door, we knew that our radios were working well. We checked with Bob once more to ensure that we had good reception from the floor of the boiler room. The number of transmissions would be kept to a minimum, and those would be very short to reduce the chance of anyone picking up any suspicious communications.

"George, this is Cam. What's the weather like?"

"Hey Cam, it's a clear night," came the reply.

Our police scanner had been set up in the back of the van. If our outside workman heard anything on the scanner relating to our area of the city, he would advise us by radio. The outside man would then try to monitor any further movements of units in the area. If there was any danger of the police getting closer, whoever was outside would make sure the door was locked and closed tight, then pack up the truck and be ready with our prepared cover story. The interior crew would put the deadbolt in place and pray. That was all well and good if a warning came over the scanner. It wouldn't help at all if a patrol car just happened to take a drive down the back alley unannounced.

Based on the rough measurements I had taken from inside the vault, we located the spot on the boiler room wall where we would drill our entry hole. My best guess was that it would come out two feet right of centre of the inside wall. When I had been inside on the two previous times I noted that one of the tiers of boxes didn't extend the entire width of the back wall. It was offset from the centre, leaving a three-foot gap where another tier might have been located at one time between it and the stack of drawers on the other wall. Marking the spot on the boiler room wall with a big X, Dan and I set up the wall mount while Harry opened the electrical panel. He hotwired a plug directly to two breakers, giving us the 230-volt power the drill would require.

Harry hooked a garden hose to the source and was ready to attach it directly to the drill when we were ready. We geared up with the goggles, ear protection, and dust masks. Dan was gung ho, wanting to be the one to drill the first hole.

The hammer drill bit used for our first pilot hole penetrated the old concrete better than expected. When he bought the hammer drill, Harry had purchased several of the longest bits available. Dan started with an eighteen-inch long, three-quarter-inch diameter carbide tip bit capable of cutting through any rebar it might encounter.

As the hammer action of the bit contacted the concrete we could hear a muffled chattering noise right through our ear protection. The initial contact sent small bits of concrete out from the wall, but Dan kept steady pressure on the bit. Harry and I watched as the bit penetrated the wall deeper and deeper. There was a steady flow of powdery concrete dust emerging from the wall as the flukes of the bit carried it out of the hole. The inward progress of the bit halted and Dan reversed the direction of the drill until the bit came clear of the hole. He stopped the drill and removed his ear protection.

"I think I hit the steel plate already, I don't want to ruin the bit on the first hole."

"Try the next hole", Harry suggested. Dan did as he was told and when the bit reached the same depth as the first hole he stopped again and reversed it out of the hole.

"I'm definitely hitting a substance more solid than the concrete. It must be the steel plate. If it was rebar this bit would have chewed right through it."

We checked the depth he had drilled. It was right around twelve inches. Dan then drilled the three other holes we required. We inserted sleeves into all five holes. The first two would allow us to attach the drill stand horizontally. The others would be fitted with rings, then attached to the chain hoist to pull out the core. We drilled the same size hole on the opposite wall, inserting a sleeve and ring into it as well. These rings would give us a straight horizontal pull of the slab. With the stand mounted on the wall, we got the drill attached, then connected the hose. After two hours, we felt we were ready to start drilling the twenty-four-inch hole.

One of the other pieces of equipment we had picked up over the last while was a used Shop-Vac. Harry had been holding the hose below the holes Dan had been drilling. It was collecting all the fine powder as it emerged from the three-quarter-inch diameter hole, preventing the particles from floating around the room, as well as keeping that same dust off the bottom of our boots so we wouldn't be tracking it outside and leaving a path that might look suspicious if anyone was trying to figure out what a city crew was doing in the alley late in the evening.

It was time to give Bob a break. Dan took the next shift outside. I wanted to make sure Harry was in the boiler room when we began drilling the larger hole in case we had any electrical issues.

When Bob arrived, we made sure we were all in our safety gear, then gave Harry a thumbs-up. Harry had read through the drill's instructional manuals and even though he was the smallest of us, he felt comfortable about operating it. We couldn't see the huge smile on his face because of the dust mask, but I was positive I detected a twinkle in his eyes through his goggles as he fired up the drill. We had drawn a big black line eleven inches from the bit's teeth as a depth guide. He wanted to slow the drill from that point to the spot where we figured steel plate started to ensure we didn't destroy the teeth.

We signalled Dan with the two-way radio to advise him that we were ready to start the drill. This was his cue to start up the small gas powered compressor in the back of the van, a purchase that had set Bob back another grand. There were extension cords plugged in and fed down the manhole, giving even more of an appearance to having workers below. Our hope was that it would also mask any noise created by the drilling in the boiler room. Once we had the all-clear from him, Harry flipped the switch and I started the flow of cooling water. As the water hit the drill bit, the first revolutions created a pinwheel effect on the dull grey concrete wall. The drill itself wasn't very loud, but the instant the teeth of the bit engaged with the concrete, the noise increased tenfold.

Once again, as the bit started penetrating the wall, it sent pieces of concrete flying through the air. The colour of the wall turned a light grey at two feet around the bit, turning to a full dark grey circle as the water soaked deeper into the pores of the concrete. Silty water now streamed down the wall, running in rivulets toward the drain in the floor. The unit we had purchased didn't come with an auto feed, so Harry slowly turned the spoked arm, forcing the drill to bite deeper into the wall. I grabbed another of our smaller purchases: a long-handled squeegee allowed me to guide the extra slurry into the floor drain.

The drill was amazing, reaching our first guide mark in just seventeen minutes. Harry reversed the drill and removed it from the hole. When the drill was shut down there was a weird silence that was still there when we removed the ear protection. Bob ran up the stairs, checking with Dan to see if things were still quiet outside. He reported that one car had tried to come down the lane but he had managed to get the driver go around our position without incident.

"Did you hear any noise from the drill?"

"It wasn't that loud out here. A very astute passerby would have to really be listening to know where it was coming from. It sounded more like it was coming from a long way off."

Bob came back down, relaying his conversation with Dan, while I continued to use the squeegee to push more slurry toward the drain. "I'm going to fire this puppy back up and see if I can reach the steel plate," said Harry.

Dan was advised that we were starting again. Bob got the flow of water started, Harry fired up the drill, inserting the bit back into the existing cut. When the bit started to dig in, Harry reduced the pressure on the feed arm, advancing the bit more slowly. Minutes later, we heard a distinctly different sound coming from the cutter head. Not quite as bad as nails on a chalkboard, more like an engine grinding as it ran out of oil. The high-pitched squeal sent shivers down my spine and up the back of my neck.

Harry again reversed the bit and pulled it out of the hole. "Okay, we have to get the rig off the wall then see if we can pull this slug out of the wall," he said.

It took us ten minutes to dismantle the drill from its stand and unbolt the stand from the wall. Harry and Bob set up the chain hoist to pull on the slab by attaching a chain to the three outer rings and then hooking it to the hoist. This configuration would help us to pull the slug evenly. My concern was whether there would be any rebar attached to the plate that might prevent a clean pull.

Dan had calculated how much the concrete was going to weigh, so we knew that each cubic foot was one hundred and fifty pounds. Bob used the felt marker we had made our depth mark on the bit and did a little quick math on the boiler room wall. "Probably at least four hundred seventy pounds, maybe five hundred pounds if it has a bunch of thick rebar."

Harry ratcheted the slack out of the chain, slowing down as the chain grew taut. The ratchet made a rhythmic ticking noise as its lever moved back and forth. At first there didn't appear to be any change in the resistance on the chain. Then the slug appeared to start moving. Bob was looking intently at the concrete slug. "I just saw movement. Keep going, Harry," he giddily announced. Harry and I both got big grins on our faces. My fear of the concrete slug being attached to the steel plate proved unfounded.

"Want me to take a turn?" I asked.

"I got this," he told me.

Harry kept the rhythmic push-pull on the handle of the hoist. Bob and I were now watching with rapt attention as the slug eased further and further out of the wall. We grabbed two forty-eight-inch pinch-point pry bars, jammed them into the void between the slug and the wall, and tried to force the slug out further to assist Harry. I looked at Bob as Harry continued ratcheting the hoist, "Did you give him something to increase his strength, Doc? I don't think Dan could have kept going this long."

Our assistance seemed to be helping. The slug was coming out of the wall easier with each stroke of the lever. It seemed like a slow process, but within minutes, we had over six inches of the slug protruding from the wall.

"Hold on Harry, let me get the cradle," I said.

Harry paused as I pulled out another piece of equipment that Dan had rigged up. Using a two-and-a-half-ton rolling floor jack, he had built a wooden half-moon cradle with a steel collar inserted into the bottom of the wood to hold it in place on the jack's saddle. We hoped this rig would support the slug as we pulled it out of the hole. Dan was concerned that when the heavy slug passed the half way point, it could tip, causing the upper edge at the back of the slug to bind with the sides or top of the hole.

Once the jack and cradle were in place, with the wheels of the jack aligned with the direction of the chain, we raised the jack so that it lifted the leading edge of the slug ever so slightly. With the jack in place, Harry again began to work the lever on the hoist. The addition of the jack cradle helped ease the slug from its hole. The slug continued out the rest of the way with ease.

We stopped and checked the depth of the protruding slug. "Eleven inches," announced Bob. "One or two more reps on the chain and it should pop right out. Everyone keep clear of this sucker, if this thing lands on your foot, I might have to amputate."

As predicted, with two more strokes of the hoist lever the slug did indeed pop out of the hole. The floor jack had moved forward with the slug as it had emerged. The four hundred seventy-pound circle of concrete edged past the wall. We should have made the cradle higher on the sides, because as the slug came completely free, it rolled to the side off the cradle then hit the floor with a thud. The bottom of the hole was just eighteen inches off the ground but the impact of the slug still left a four-inch-long, half inch-deep gouge in the floor.

"You're right, Bob. If that had hit my foot it would have ruined my pedicure," I laughed.

Harry removed the hoist hooks from the slug, then put the rig against the back wall while Bob and I pushed the jack and cradle off to the side. We grabbed the pry bars and rolled the slug well out of the way.

The three of us gathered around the gaping hole in the wall. The outside edge of the concrete looked almost polished. There was no indication that any rebar had been used in the construction of the vault. The steel plate at the end of the hole showed no rust, as though it had been put in place the day before.

It was now 11:30, over an hour and a half had passed since we had started drilling. We were now into the fifth hour on site. So far so good.

"Good job guys, if your information about the depth of this wall is correct, Chris, there should only be about another twenty-two inches to go. At this rate, we should be inside early in the morning. Right now, though it's time for a bit of break and to get ourselves fed," said Bob. Harry agreed, and then using our pre-arranged signal for anytime we would emerge from the building, Harry gave the mic on his radio two quick and two long clicks, then waited for the all clear which was four quick clicks. When we got outside we decided to sit in the back of the van while we ate and rested.

"After the break, I'll give the lance a go. By the time we're ready to start cutting it'll be after midnight. That sucker is really noisy, I hope that the compressor can mask the sound from it as well. Either way, we might want two guys outside while we do it. We'll also get the exhaust fan set up to extract the smoke."

"I hope it doesn't make so much smoke that a looky-loo going by thinks the whole building is on fire," said Harry.

"Me too," I said as I held up crossed fingers.

CHAPTER 32

We sat in the back of the van, sharing the sub sandwiches we had bought in Hope. We told Dan how pleased we were with how the first phase had gone. Although the water on the drill had kept most of the dust down, the only parts of our faces that were clean were where our protective gear had covered the skin. None of us had worn a hat, so our hair was covered in fine dust. This layer of fine powder gave us the appearance of instant aging. In my case, it also made my fine hair feel a lot thicker than it ever had been. The perspiration had left long dirty streaks across any skin that had been exposed to the dust.

The alley running behind the 400 block of West Pender was quiet as a graveyard. The building next door was only half as deep as the one housing the vault. At the end far of the alley was a ramshackle block building with metal siding on the upper half. It was the only other structure in the alley that extended all the way from the frontage of the buildings on Pender to the back alley. One of the things that surprised me most about that structure was the lack of graffiti. After we finished getting through the wall we would park our Grumman in one of the empty lots further along the alley. For the time being, we needed it right outside the boiler room until all our drilling and cutting was complete.

Each time we headed out from downstairs we made sure we had our city worker disguises including our hard hats. The building directly across from the one we were working in was undergoing major renovations and was currently gutted and empty. Another thing in our favour was that other than the big unlit three-foot-high letters on the upper floors of the building, there was nothing else to indicate that the building contained a privately-run vault. I doubted people other than those renting a box even new of its existence.

"What do you think the process will be when they find the place has been emptied out?" asked Dan.

"That's a damned good question. You know, in any of the discussions we've had since we first decided to go on this adventure, I don't think we've ever talked about that. My answer is that I don't have a clue," I said.

We finished up our sandwiches and put the wrappers in a garbage bag. Our break had taken twenty minutes. It was getting close to midnight, and it was time to get back at it.

"Okay," I said, "as I said before our break, I've studied up on the thermal lance, so I'll give it a go first. Harry, I want you down there with me to light up the rods with the torch. I'm not sure how long this part will take, but it might be a while depending on how thick the plating is. Unger told me it was four inches. If that's the case, it could take three or four hours. Bob, you and Dan set up the fan. Be ready to vent into the drain. I hope that will help dissipate most of the smoke. Keep an eye on the other manholes out on Homer and up the lane. We don't want to have a bunch of smoke coming out of those."

"Also, after we start, take a walk down the side of the building to check out the noise level." Harry and I headed down the stairs to the boiler room while Bob and Dan took care of getting the fan and exhaust tube set up. It took us half an hour to set up the oxygen cylinders with their hoses and valves. We geared up in the welder's outfits and Harry sprayed down the floor with water, hoping it would keep sparks or slag from starting any secondary fires, although there really wasn't anything in the boiler room to catch fire.

The operational instructions for the lance had confirmed that using a torch to ignite the lances would be better than the twelve-volt system. With the lance inserted into the handle, I gave Harry the thumbs-up. He got a good flame going on the acetylene torch and set the flame to the end of the burning bar.

It took less than a minute for the bar to ignite. The sparks flew off the tip like a volcanic Halloween cone. He backed away as I stepped forward to attack the steel plate. Going to the oxygen cylinder, he increased the pressure to one-hundred pounds per square inch, which the instructions said should be optimal for the job.

The loud hissing grew exponentially as the oxygen flow increased. During his research on the bar Dan was surprised that the sound produced by the lance could hit 125 decibels. That's more than the 110 dB his power saw produced or the 115 dB from a loud rock concert, but less than the 140 dB given off by a jet engine at one hundred feet. His research suggested that even short brief exposure to a hundred and forty decibels could cause permanent hearing loss.

When I heard the noise through the ear protection, I was glad that we had splurged on the best available. I put the tip of the bar right against the centre of plate. Once contact was made with the steel, the smoke started to get thicker by the second. I hoped the exhaust fan was doing its job. Despite the welding helmet shielding my eyes, the intense brightness made me squint.

Immediately upon putting the lance against the plate, I felt a change in the blow back coming from the tip. It seemed I had already penetrated through the plate, so I made a five-inch circle in in a matter of seconds, then pulled the lance back, motioning for Harry to shut it down.

I lifted the helmet to inspect the cut I had made. The five-inch disc fell out and I was now looking at molten concrete behind where the steel had been. Using the welder's gloves, Harry picked up the steel disc and showed it to me. He motioned to the ear protection and we both removed them.

"Damn, that's only around half an inch thick," he said.

"That's got to mean there's another chunk of plate further in. I wonder just how far in it might be?" I asked him.

"No idea. Let's get this piece out, then we can use the hammer drill to see if we can find the next piece of plate like we did with the first holes."

Harry signaled with the two-way radio, then went up and told Dan and Bob what we'd discovered. They told him the noise hadn't really been that noticeable and the smoke coming out seemed minimal. "It was a really small piece, so when we get going on the next piece, keep a close watch and let us know if it gets worse," suggested Harry.

Harry came back downstairs and we started up the lance again. I started cutting at the top of the plate, slicing a line right down the centre, then I began on the circumference of the plate. I was flabbergasted at just how quickly the rod was eating through the plate. The rod was getting short, compounded by the fact that the tip was starting a foot from the edge of the wall, making it harder to reach the plate, and the further I reached in, the more that the molten metal was shooting directly back at me.

We stopped, inserted a new rod and I finished cutting the rest of the circle. The two halves dropped away from the concrete. Harry took hold of each piece, setting them beside our twenty-four-inch slug of concrete. With the lance burning again I reached into the hole, holding it on an angle to clean away any slag or rough edges of the steel that might hinder us putting the drill bit back into place.

We were ready to start drilling again just after 1:00 in the morning.

I got out of the welding clothing. It was my turn for a shift outside as the other three looked after the next phase. The weather was cooperating and there was no sign of rain. January could be a miserable month, usually recording the fourth highest rainfall each year, often getting between four and six inches of rain. The temperature was also decent, as January could often get down to almost zero on the Celsius scale, but the day had been close to eight degrees and the cloud cover had kept a thermal layer over the city, so the temperature had only dropped down to six degrees.

The fact that it wasn't raining might work against us, I thought. If it was pelting down, foot traffic would be less, cars driving past the alley with windshield wipers flapping and foggy side windows would be unlikely to notice a works vehicle sitting in the back alley At least there was good breeze swirling in the alley which helped to dissipate the smoke that the extraction fan didn't take away. It wasn't the kind of gale that blew in the valleys of the high-rise buildings at Georgia and Granville but it was doing the job.

I spent my time outside pacing back and forth between our barriers. Each time I got back to our end of the alley at Homer Street, I glanced both ways. Downtown Vancouver traffic on a Friday night could be quite heavy in certain parts, but this area wasn't exactly tourist central. I tried to stay focused on the task at hand and not let my imagination get the better of me. Each time I felt my mind start to drift, I pictured the inside of the vault, thinking of the treasure that might be there waiting for us.

CHAPTER 33

I heard our signal that one of them was on their way out. I checked both ends of the alley once more, taking a peek along Homer. Looking at my watch, I couldn't believe it was three-thirty in the morning and that two and half hours had passed since I took over the outside watch. Bob met me at the doorway and we changed places. He didn't say a word, but when I saw the huge grin on his face, I knew that things must have gone well. He silently stepped into the alley in his workman's duds.

From the top of the spiral stairway, the first thing I noticed was the sludge that had flowed over the floor. It looked like an aerial view of a river delta. Then I spotted a new slug of concrete protruding at least a foot out from the wall. "Wow, great job, guys," I said. "Any problem drilling past the first steel plate?"

"It went really well, seemed to get hung up a bit when we first started, but after that, smooth boring, same as the first hole," pronounced Harry. "We all took turns on the drill. Thought we could use your help to pull it out the rest of the way."

"How much further to get it out completely?"

Dan said, "We used the long bits to see if we would hit another section of steel plate. We hit it around sixteen inches in. Then we replicated what you and Harry did with the first slug."

"Bob figures this piece is just over 625 pounds," said Harry.

The rolling jack and cradle were in place. "Let's do it. Then we can cut the rest of the plate out. That first slug was twelve inches plus the half inch piece of steel. Now another sixteen inches means we'll only have around six to go."

Harry took his position on the chain hoist, while Dan and I used the pry bars to help move the slug out further. We had pulled it out at least another inch or two so I measured depth. "One inch to go. Dan keep your toes out of the way. Let Harry do the rest of the pull."

Harry activated the lever again. For a guy I had thought could use time in the gym and protein shakes to bulk him up, I was amazed at his stamina. We watched as each pull brought the slug another quarter inch out. "Okay, Harry. One, maybe two more pulls," Dan announced.

It ended up being only one more, then the slug tipped out of the leading edge. It fell off the cradle, taking another chunk out of the floor.

"Alright," shouted Harry.

We used the pry bars to roll the slug off to the side while Harry bundled up the hoist. Then he began hosing away the silt, using the squeegee to send it down the floor drain while Dan and I got the thermal lance ready to go again.

"Time for another break," said Harry when he had finished cleaning up the silt.

It was now close to four in the morning. I agreed to a short break. "I want to make sure we're through to the inside of the vault with all the cutting finished before sunrise. In fact, I want to be finished at least an hour before that. Sunrise might not be till ten after eight, but we'll start getting glimpses of light by around seven, maybe a bit later in these urban canyons and depending on how overcast it is. We could see traffic start to pick round then, but with it being a Saturday, we probably have more time than on a weekday. If the next cut with the lance causes a lot of smoke, I don't want to take the chance of a passerby noticing it."

We wetted our whistles with drinks of the pop and water we had in the back of the van, then Harry and I headed back down to start cutting. We knew we hadn't used much of the oxygen to cut out the first half inch of plate, but still switched tanks regardless. This would give us an idea of how we were making out with our consumption rate. If we ran low we could always put the first tank back on.

Using the quick couplers to create a longer lance, we were now working with a seventy-two-inch section. The more Dan and I had studied and investigated the science of thermal cutting, the more confident I had become, and with the practise of cutting the first piece of steel, I was sure that I could get this cut done well ahead of my self-imposed deadline.

The research had suggested that a suit much better than the welder's outfit I was again wearing should be worn by the operator. We didn't have one of those, so I just hoped what I was wearing would hold up and keep me from getting burned to a crisp by any molten metal being kicked back.

Harry lit the rod. We followed the same routine I had used on the half inch plate. I felt like Luke Skywalker using a light saber as the lance penetrated right through the centre of the steel plate. "The Force is with me," I mumbled from under the helmet. With the shrieking of the lance, I was sure that Harry never heard me. The resistance on the lance disappeared and I realized I must have blown right through the concrete. Pulling back on the lance, I again cut a five-inch hole in the centre of the steel plate, impressed at how fast I accomplished it. The second of the coupled lances still had close to twenty-four inches on it.

When I removed the stub of the lance, Harry shut down the oxygen, and then grabbed one of the pry bars, pushing on the small slug in the centre of the circle I had just burned out,. He pushed the bar harder, finally shoving the five-inch diameter plug hard enough that we heard it clunk onto the floor. If it hadn't been for the noise of the slug hitting the floor, we really wouldn't have known it was through.

We had burned our way into a black hole. There wasn't a hint of light coming from inside. There was probably more ambient light in space than there was coming out of the vault.

With the new lances ready, we again struck a flame to the rod. As I had done on the earlier piece, I gouged a line right down the centre of the plate and concrete. It took me just under ten minutes to burn down the centre of the plate, including the time to change to a second set of bars halfway through. We changed oxygen bottles for the final cuts. The exhaust fan was doing its job, and there here was only a slight haze hovering in the boiler room. A lot of the smoke was probably being trapped inside. "I sure hope the vault is air tight," I said to Harry. "I think most of the smoke is staying right inside."

"Should we get one of the guys to go around and check around the side by the stairway to the upper floors?"

"Good idea."

"Give me a minute." Then giving the exit signal, Harry trotted up the stairway. He stuck his head out, telling Bob and Dan to check the side of the building, where there was another stairway to the basement. They checked it out, giving Harry a thumbs-up signal as they came back around the corner.

We proceeded with the final cuts, taking over forty-five minutes to cut the entire twenty-four-inch diameter piece, using eight sets of double lances and two bottles of oxygen, leaving us with what was left in our first bottle, and one full extra bottle. Money well spent, or stolen, surely beating the alternative of running out.

Each half of the circle I had cut probably weighed three hundred pounds. Harry grabbed one of the pry bars, inserted the curved end of it through the hole in the middle and hooked the end on one side of the circle.

He tried to pull it out, but the thickness of the plate and concrete wouldn't allow the piece to come out as easily as the first half-inch barrier that had fallen right off. After struggling with it for ten minutes, all we'd ended up doing was jamming the edges so that it wouldn't budge. Lighting up the lance yet again, I spent the next ten minutes slicing both pieces horizontally.

Harry reached in with the pry bar, managing to pull out the top quarter piece. It tipped over and with the bar hooked on the back side, Harry managed to drag it out far enough to allow us each to grab a side and lift it out of the hole. The pie shaped piece was still hot, but our welding gloves allowed us to take hold of it and we set it off to the side with the other slugs. Fifteen minutes later, the other three pieces were out and we were both sweating profusely.

The haze in the boiler room had cleared substantially. It was now just after 6:15 in the morning. After relaying our signal, we changed from the welder's outfits, putting on our vests and hardhats, then climbed the stairs, stepping out into the cool, fresh morning air. I knew I had been sweating, but didn't realize how drenched my coveralls were until I got right out in the alley. The cool morning air gave me an instant chill. "Damn, it's bloody cold out here," said Harry.

Bob and Dan joined us as we exited the boiler room. "Well?" asked Bob.

"We're ready to go in," said Harry

"What's it look like?" asked Dan

"Haven't looked yet. Thought you two might like to have the first peek," I said, "You two go down, grab the big flashlight and check it out. We'll keep watch out here for a bit." They didn't have to be told twice. Both their faces lit up like kids hoping to see Santa at Christmas.

"Now that we're through the wall and it's getting light, we need to move the van. I think it would have been more conspicuous just having two guys standing around the alley all night without their work truck. Can't let it sit here all day though. We'll move it down the alley to that parking area next to that decrepit looking building"

"No problem. What about the signage, might look a little funny having a city truck parked in there all day."

"We'll just take the signs off for now. I'm glad we made them with the magnetic sheets," I said.

Before we had a chance to move the van, there was another signal that someone was coming out. The back door to the boiler room opened and Bob stepped out, "We have a problem guys."

"What is it?" Harry asked.

"Come see," was his only response. "You want to go, while I keep watch?" I asked Harry.

"Alright. Bob you stay with Chris, he wants to move the van," said Harry as he disappeared through the door.

We stood in silence in the alley and I could feel my blood pressure rising and knew my pulse rate had climbed. What the hell had happened? Various scenarios about what they had encountered ran through my mind at the speed of sound. Was there another wall between the boiler and the vault? Just before I started to hyperventilate, I asked Bob what the problem was.

He could see I was almost in panic mode. "Calm down, it's nothing that can't be solved."

"What the hell's the matter then?"

"Our entry hole is a half covered by one of the banks of deposit boxes."

"Shit. I was sure I had accounted for that before we started. Can we squeeze past?"

"They're working on that now. Why don't you go down and see for yourself? I'll keep an eye on things out here."

I took a deep breath to calm myself down then headed back to the boiler room. Dan and Harry were standing in front of the hole. I took the flashlight from them, shining it into the hole. Sure enough, the centre of our hole was directly in line with a tower of boxes on the inside of the vault. The hole was a little left of where I had planned to penetrate. If it had been any further left, the first small plug Harry had pushed through never would have fallen to the floor.

"Fuck! I was sure I had gone far enough to the right," I said

"Doesn't matter how it happened, the question is how to get by it," answered Dan.

Harry hadn't said a word. I looked over at him. He was looking around with an expression I recognized as his thinking mode.

"Okay here's my thoughts," said Harry. He took two minutes to explain the plan to us. Both Dan and I agreed it was our best option, so we got right to work. Dan, and I headed to the van to retrieve an industrial strength cargo bar from the back of the truck that we had used on the trip to the coast to help hold the oxygen bottles in place. With the bar in hand, Dan headed back inside and I briefed Bob.

It was now getting close to 7:00. We were all tired, but knew we had to keep pushing ourselves. We could take a rest when we finally had a clean entryway inside. Bob and I got busy taking the barriers apart and loaded them into the van, then we covered the manhole and put the cones away as well. I hung the exhaust hose over the handrail of the stairwell in the boiler room and left the fan on the stairs in case it was needed again to extract smoke from inside the vault.

I removed the City of Vancouver magnetic signs, then moved the van down the laneway, retrieved the other barrier and then finally parked in the small lot I had pointed out earlier. I grabbed the scanner and locked all the doors before heading back to the boiler room.

It was now just after 7:00. Sunrise wouldn't be for at least an hour, but morning twilight was starting to filter into the alley. I couldn't hear any traffic sounds, but that would certainly start to change within the next hour.

In the boiler room, Harry, Dan and Bob had made progress on Harry's plan. Before I joined them all downstairs, I made sure the deadbolt on the back door was set, then plugged the scanner into a wall outlet.

"I think we're ready to give this a go," said Harry.

He had fastened a piece of four-by-four dunnage that had been found in the corner of the boiler room to the floor. After drilling holes through it with the hammer drill directly into the concrete floor of the boiler room, he had then fastened it using anchor sleeves and the rings we had used to pull out the concrete slugs.

With the cargo bar in its retracted position he had placed one end inside the thirty-six-inch tunnel resting it against the tower of deposit boxes, and the other end was angled down and wedged up to the four-by-four that had been bolted to the floor.

Dan was kneeling beside the cargo bar ready to start working the ratchet. "Okay Dan give it a go," said Harry. "Just pray that those suckers aren't bolted to the wall or all this will be for nothing," said Bob.

"Thought you were agnostic, Bob," Dan said sarcastically.

We held our collective breaths as the bar slowly inched forward. "How big a space do we need?" I asked.

"When I was working that out months ago I figured we could probably get through a hole no smaller than eighteen inches. That means we will have to push this sucker ahead by at least six inches," said Dan.

"That shouldn't be a problem, this bar has at least twenty inches of travel," said Harry.

I found myself biting down on my lips, again holding my breath. I watched as the bar slowly inched forward with each stroke that Dan made with the handle. Dan kept up a slow steady pace as he pumped the handle. When the cargo bar had extended out at least ten inches he said, "Let's see if that tower has moved ahead enough to squeeze in, I don't want to put any more stress on this bar than we need to."

"Where's the flashlight?" I asked.

"Right here," said Dan as he tossed it to me.

Reaching into the hole, I shined the light inside. It looked like Harry's plan had worked. I wiggled my way into the cavity. The bank of boxes had moved ahead a full eight inches. Enough that I would be able to squeeze in.

I shimmied my way back out, giving them the good news. Everyone took a turn to see our accomplishment.

"Once we're inside, we should be able to use the pry bars to move it further," commented Harry after he'd extricated himself.

"Let's get that done, then stop for a rest before we start tackling the boxes. Doctor's orders," said Bob.

"You got us in there Harry, so you go first," said Dan.

We all agreed, then Harry crawled into the vault. It turned out to be an awkward process, made more difficult by the fact that the last six inches of the hole was a jagged cut from the lance, compared to the first twenty-eight inches that were smoothly drilled.

Harry had to crawl with his arms straight ahead. Even so, there was just enough room for him to squeeze through. When he got to the end of the hole he stretched his arms toward the floor, pushed on the side of the hole with his feet and walked himself forward on his hands until he could drop his feet to the floor. Standing up, he shone the flashlight around the room. There was still smoke hanging in a cloud near the ceiling, but the flashlight penetrated the haze and he let out a shrill whistle when he got his first look at all the boxes arranged around the wall.

"This is amazing guys," he shouted back to us. "Dan, you come next. Bring the pry bars, and while you're at it, see if you can protect that jagged edge of the hole where we cut it with the lance. It's really sharp—don't need anyone bleeding all over the place."

I handed the welder's jacket to Dan. "Put this down," I said.

Dan then made his way into the hole carrying the pry bars, his feet disappearing as he made his way in to join Harry. All we heard from inside was a hollow sounding, "Holy shit."

In the boiler room, Bob and I stood and waited, unable to see what was going on as we peered inside. We heard the pry bars clunking and scraping on the bottom of the bank of boxes. As we watched, the light coming from inside slowly widened, like the moon rising over the horizon.

The light slowly became more fully circular as Dan and Harry pried the bank of boxes completely out of the way. Harry's faced appeared in the middle of the hole, reminding me of Jack Nicholson in *The Shining*. Although his expression was a little wild, it wasn't manic like Nicholson's. "Come on guys."

Less than a minute later, all four of us were standing in the middle of the vault, gawking at all the dazzling deposit box doors. "I had my doubts," said Bob, "but we did it. Now let's take that rest I talked about and then get started."

We clambered our way out before collapsing against the walls of the boiler room. I checked the time. It was now seven thirty; we had been at it for over twelve hours since arriving, and we'd all been awake for over twenty-four hours since leaving Kelowna.

Rest was exactly what we needed.

CHAPTER 34

I startled myself awake, quickly looked around, only to discover the other guys had fallen asleep sitting up just like me. *This is nuts, what a bunch of amateurs,* I thought. Like a bunch of old men falling asleep after a big turkey dinner. When we had emerged from the vault, we'd each found a dry place to sit and slump against the walls. It was only supposed to be for a few minutes.

Still groggy, I looked at my watch with heavily blinking eyes and was shocked to see that it was already after 10:15. While I sat there, I heard a variety of conversations taking place on the police scanner. There had been chatter going on most of the night, but we hadn't heard any locations relayed to patrol cars to give us any concern.

"Hey, guys. Time to wake up." The other three slowly came back out of their naps. "It's after ten. We should get ourselves into gear."

"Wow, guess we all zonked out, eh?" said Harry as he slowly rose, stretching out the kinks.

Within minutes, we were all up, yawning and stretching. "Who wants to head down to the restaurant for coffees?" I asked.

Bob and Harry volunteered. Before heading up the stairs to the door they got out of their coveralls, then used the hose to wash the grime off their arms and faces. Harry had found a roll of paper towels in the boiler room and they used numerous sheets to dry off. At the top of the stairs, they cautiously opened the door, surveying the alley before heading off. Suggesting they head down the alley to ensure the van was still sitting where we left it, I locked and bolted the door behind them. Upon return, they would make sure they were alone in the alley then give a rapid three rap signal on the door for us to let them back in.

While they were gone, Dan and I snapped up the equipment needed inside. Dan made his way inside and I passed the equipment down the tunnel. Finding a light switch inside had eliminated the need for a flashlight.

When I climbed inside, Dan pointed to the spot where the lance had burned through. There were blackened scorch marks fanning out in a circle and ricocheting off the back of the deposit boxes that had been against the concrete. We checked the back of the bank of boxes that had been pried away from the wall and found that it also had scorch marks on it. "Almost burned right through that as well," said Dan.

"Damn near, by the looks of it," I replied.

With all the equipment now inside, we climbed back out to wait for Harry and Bob. It was thirty minutes before we heard the rap on the door. Not only had they brought back coffee, they also had bacon, eggs and toast keeping warm in foam takeout containers. We all turned these ingredients into sandwiches and scarfed them down with gusto.

We had known each other long enough to know how each of us liked our coffee. Dan never drank the stuff, mine was mixed with both cream and sugar, and when Harry did drink coffee, his was always plain black. Bob had even brought back a can of Coke for Dan. With our sandwiches done, I raised my coffee cup in the air and we toasted in our traditional fashion: "To life. Our way."

Making sure all the garbage was in the bag, we were ready to go. Once again, I checked the alley for people or traffic before I bolted the door, turned around and gave the three below an enthusiastic thumbs-up. It was time to see the fruits of our labour. We crawled through to the vault, eager to see how rich we might become.

Dan had laid out an array of our tools in the centre of the floor. We had electric drills, grinders, cold chisels, and varied sizes of sledge hammers.

While I had been in Vancouver for the week working on the new marketing plan, Vic decided it would be best if we emptied out our parents' box and divide the contents between us because there had been surveillance taking place on Chang. He wanted to make sure there was no hint of conflict should they ever arrest Chang. "I think you're stretching that a little bit, but I can take this stuff back to Kelowna," I told him. On my own safety deposit box at the Credit Union in Kelowna, the key slots seemed to be made of brass. The thousands before us all had silver-coloured key slots, but the external hinges were all made of brass.

"I think we'll start right here," said Harry, pointing to a box at shoulder height. "Anything higher is going to be harder to work on. I'll start with trying to drill out he locks. Dan why don't you take one of the grinders to the opposite side and give those hinges a go?"

The heavy-duty drill had a three-eighths high-speed bit in the chuck, so Harry began to drill while Dan began on the opposite side with the grinder. I clutched one of the three-pound sledges to pound on a door near where we had made our entrance hole.

The discordant sounds were like a very bad set of musicians trying to tune their instruments. The screeching from the drill bit was the worst, my pounding on the doors not quite as bad, but listening to that all day would certainly give us all a head-ache. The grinder, though sending up showers of sparks, was the quietest of all.

It took Harry over five minutes to drill out the two locks. Dan had cut off the exposed side of the brass hinge in seconds. My pounding on the doors really didn't have a lot of effect. Drilling out the lock hadn't released the internal latch, so I pounded the door Harry had worked on without it opening. I did the same thing on the unit that Dan had used the grinder on, and after only two hard whacks the door bounced and the latch popped out of position, allowing the door to fall to the floor with a clang.

"Well I'll be damned, I think we've got it," I shouted, "Bob you do the honours. Get that drawer out here." Reaching up, he grasped the collapsible wire handle, pulling the box out of its compartment and laying it on the steamer trunk we had all seen in the video. We gathered around to see if all this work had been worth it, or whether we'd be a bunch of chumps who now owed Bob a ton of money to replenish his slush fund.

Bob flipped up the lid. We stared at the contents. The first thing we noticed was a stack of foreign currency. Bob reached down, grabbed the pile of bills from the drawer, examining them closely. "Danish krone," he announced as he flipped through the stack. "Don't have a clue what the exchange rate would be but there are there must be close to ten thousand kroner. Unless anyone's planning a trip to Copenhagen, I'd say these are worthless to us. Let's see what else we have."

The rest of the box wasn't any more exciting. There were sets of Olympic coins, a will, deed for a house, an old cameo pendant on a thin gold necklace and a small bag of Danish coins. We all felt quite disappointed.

"Come on guys, cheer up," I said. "It's just like hitting your tee shot into the water. The second shot's always better. It'll only get better from here." I said.

"Yeah," said Dan, "time for a hole in one."

We all agreed as Bob put the contents back in the box, then shoved it right back where it had come from. Dan got the grinder going, starting on one side and working his way across the entire row, then back in the opposite direction. I followed behind with the sledge, pounding on each of the doors he had cut the hinges from. Getting into a rhythm, the doors were falling off at my feet, while Harry and Bob started pulling out box after box.

When they started, they were slowly opening each of the boxes to check the contents. The first few weren't much more exciting than the initial one we opened, until Harry opened one that made him shout to the rest of us.

"Hey guys. Look at this"

We gathered around the box lying on the trunk. He had already pulled out thousands of dollars of Canadian currency, along with savings bonds and a bag of old coins. None of us were coin collectors so we had no idea what they might be worth. The savings bonds carried high interest rates, but they would be hard to cash in because most would be registered with the government. Harry took the cash and placed it in one of the suitcases.

"What are we going to do with all these boxes after we open them?" asked Bob. "It'll take too long to stuff them all back into the slots."

We looked around the room. "Why don't we open a bunch of boxes in the corner over there," said Dan. "We open them in that area, then start piling the empty ones over there."

"Sounds like a plan, Dan," said Harry.

"Paul Simon. 'Fifty Ways to Leave Your Lover,' 1975."

Harry shook his head in disgust. "Not again."

In typical Canadian fashion, I replied "Sorry about that, couldn't help myself."

"Yeah right," mumbled Harry.

"Anybody getting hungry?" asked Bob. "It's already one-thirty." I should move the Suburban to another lot, then I'll get us lunch while I'm out. Who wants to join me?" I was ready for a break outside. It would give me a chance to move the van if required. While Bob moved the Suburban, I would see if there was another place to get sandwiches.

While we were gone, Dan kept busy grinding off hinges, then pounding the doors off almost two hundred boxes, pulling them out and stacking them in the middle of the floor. Harry stayed in the boiler room waiting for us to return. Not wanting to sit idle, he began to dismantle the drill unit, which had been made easier and took less time than it would have if I hadn't taken it apart and reassembled it using the wing nuts.

Bob and I got to the back door at the same time. I had found a small deli on Richards Street that made home-style sandwiches, returning with a variety for each of us, as well as more cans of pop. The other thing we each found were clean washrooms and had taken care of business. During the night, we each had slipped out into the laneway to relieve ourselves, but hadn't wanted to just squat in the alley. After lunch, Harry and Dan also went out in search of the restrooms we had found.

By the time we were ready to start again, it was four o'clock. We began by emptying the drawers Dan had stacked in the middle of the room. We became more efficient, but a lot messier. Each of us would grab a drawer, empty its contents onto the trunk, then pick through the pile, grabbing any Canadian or US cash and any bearer bonds we found and putting all the loot into one of the bags. The first suitcase was almost full of cash by the time we finished the stack of drawers.

It was becoming repetitious, but there was the excitement of opening each box, a lot of which held great treasures. We began finding a quantity of loose diamonds, as well as numerous Troy-ounce wafers of gold. One of the drawers had at least half a dozen small ingots with the engraving "Five Tola" on the face. We would later discover these bars were from India, equal to just under two Troy ounces. We unveiled quantities of silver ingots, and one of the drawers contained a six-ounce bar of gold with Chinese characters engraved on it.

The floor was littered with the contents that we had no inter-est in. Rings of assorted styles, a lot of watches that definitely weren't made by Rolex, a variety of stock certificates and a lot of Last Will and Testaments, deeds to properties, and a surprising amount of baby and adult teeth. There were also bearer bonds from a variety of companies and governments, most of which we also put in the bags and suitcases.

With the last of the original set of boxes now emptied, Dan and Harry got two grinders going on the hinges, while Bob and I followed behind, pounding on the doors with the sledge hammers. Our efficiency improved and by the time we stopped for another break, we had opened and emptied another three hundred boxes. The loot would be put in a total of ten bags and suitcases ranging from medium-sized sports bags to hard-sided suitcases. With the first of the suitcases full, we were now filling the sports bags.

During the planning stages, Dan had suggested we bring along elastic bands. We wouldn't be counting the cash or separating it between Canadian and US currency. The bands would just make it easier to put stacks of cash into the suitcases in piles, rather than a bunch of loose bills, which would take up a lot more room. We grabbed handfuls of bills, then wrapped elastics around them before sticking them into a bag or suitcase.

If our large suitcases had been filled with new hundred dollar bills they could hold upwards of seven million bucks apiece. Our stacks contained every denomination from Canadian ones and twos, through to a handful of one thousand dollars bills. Except for the two and thousand dollar bills, which were uniquely Canadian denominations, we had the same variety of American currency. I figured there was getting close to a million in cash in the one suitcase alone.

Canadian thousand dollar bills were rare. Years earlier, my in-laws arranged to give one of them to both Trish and her sister for Christmas. It had taken my mother-in-law weeks to get her hands on them after specially requesting them from the bank.

We were getting quite a haul of gold, silver and loose diamonds as well. We had discussed the possibility of diamonds when we talked about the loot we might find, but had never arrived at a concrete plan for what to do with them. Harry was friends with a jeweler from the curling club but it wasn't easy to just come out and ask about the value per carat of loose diamonds. At the time, we agreed we would have lots of time to figure out those details in the future.

As we gathered more of the diamonds, we all agreed that they sure looked great—all bright and shiny—however, even in the poor light we could tell that some of them were not as nice as the others.

Bob looked at his watch. "Holy shit. Call the cops I think we've just been robbed of a few hours. It's already nine o'clock." We were all shocked at how quickly the time had flown by. We decided that after we got dinner, each of us would take turns trying to get a little sleep. Two of us would work on opening as many of the boxes as possible while two of us slept, then the other two would take care of emptying them out after we traded off.

It was Dan's turn to head out and find us some grub and Bob decided to move the Suburban again. I decided that while we took turns in the vault, one of us could start bringing up the equipment we no longer needed, so I fetched the van. While waiting for the other two to return, Harry and I set up the barriers again, once more removing the grate from the manhole, and setting the stage as though people were working below.

Bob and Dan returned with a bucket of chicken. We took a break, wolfing down the greasy fare in the back of the van. Between bites, I started bringing out the smaller equipment and putting it back in the van.

"Just stop and rest for a minute," said Bob.

"I'm afraid if I stop for too long, I might not be able to get moving again," I said.

As it turned out, nobody wanted to stop for long and we were soon back at work. Dan and Harry went back inside to open boxes. Bob and I got the slings in place then used the hoist to raise the equipment to the top of the stairs. By the time we had finished loading up most of the gear including the oxygen cylinders, it was close to midnight. We checked on Dan and Bob's progress. They had the doors removed from close to another three hundred boxes.

We were all getting a little punch drunk from lack of sleep. Bob decided that he and Dan would take a break. I would empty the drawers, and Harry would load up the van, and move it back to the parking spot, and then join me in the vault. We would shift the Grumman to the back door one more time when we were ready to load up the loot and make our getaway.

Doctor Bob suggested we limit our naps to ninety minutes. "If we go longer than that, it might do us more harm than good," he suggested. "The ninety minutes will give us a complete sleep cycle, allowing us to wake without that confused, sleepy feeling."

Taking the doc's advice, I said "I'll wake you both in an hour and a half."

Inside, I got busy emptying more drawers. The cash and empty drawers kept piling up. The entire corner where we had started to pile them looked like the jumbled pile of discarded boxes after opening presents on Christmas morning.

While working on my own, I made an incredible but frightening discovery when I opened four large boxes. The first one had nothing but papers. Up to this point we hadn't bothered to look at most of the papers we came across, but this was filled to the top with nothing but official looking papers. There were dozens of copies of deeds to properties. The properties all seemed to be owned by different corporations or companies, practically all of them had one thing in common: the principal signature on the bottom of the papers belonged to David Chang.

I gasped when I opened the second box, finding it full of tight plastic bags of what looked like icing sugar. "I might be an ordinary guy, but my momma never raised no dummy," I said to myself. It didn't take me long to figure out that it was unlikely anyone was paying to store icing sugar in a deposit box. "Heroine? Coke?" I asked myself out loud. The box beside it was full of even more bags of powder. Each of the previous boxes was hard to extract because of the weight inside.

It was when I opened the fourth large box that I discovered the mother lode. It had also been hard to extract from its slot due to its weight. I set it down on the floor and opened it up for a look see. I was stunned by what I saw. The entire box was filled with cash. Being so close to the one that had belonged to Chang, and given that Vic had told me that the cops thought Chang was up to his ears in illegal enterprises, I was pretty sure the two boxes of icing sugar and the one stuffed with cash also belonged to him.

I needed time to think about just what might happen if we took all of this guy's cash. It was one thing to be hunted by the cops, but if we took David Chang's stash—an amount that was probably in the millions based on the stacks of one-hundred dollars bills I saw—that was quite another. I'd seen enough movies and read enough novels to know that if we ripped this guy off, we would be asking for more trouble. I was sure we would never close our eyes at night without the fear of waking up like a character from Coppola's *Godfather* movies. We might not be safe anywhere.

Thankfully Harry did not return from parking the van until I had the drawer full of cash back into place for the time being. He had ended up waking Dan when he returned from parking the van but he now joined me we carried on pillaging the rest of the batch that had their doors removed. There wasn't a square inch of the floor that wasn't covered with rejected loot. Bigger gold and silver bars that would be useless to us, thousands and thousands of BRIC shares like Mom and Dad had in their deposit box. More sets of Olympic coins than I cared to count, stacks of personal papers with no value to anyone other than the families, we also came across a stack of very racy Polaroid pictures. Thousands, if not millions, in foreign currency now littered the floor. There were pesos from six or seven countries: francs from Algeria, France and Switzerland, rubles, and dollars from numerous countries besides the US and Canada. During the planning stages we had debated keeping the British pounds and Australian dollars, but in the end had opted to keep only Canadian and US cash.

One of the large boxes had a cardboard box inside. I opened the box and wondered why anyone would waste their money storing a boxful of cassette tapes. Leaving the tapes in the box, my mind drifted as usual, and I wondered aloud with Harry, asking him if he thought the tapes contained recordings which might be embarrassing to public figures or officials. Perhaps the missing Nixon White House tapes, or a confession containing the names of the assassins who had been on the grassy knoll when Kennedy has been shot. "Probably not in a box of tapes in Vancouver," he said.

Realizing we hadn't opened the steamer trunk where we had been sorting all the loot, I grabbed a bar, pried open the hasps, then lifted the lid. I couldn't believe it. The damn thing was full of old clothes. We pulled out the items, which included an old Canadian ensign flag, uniforms from various branches of the military from World War Two, several real-looking fur coats that might have been mink or chinchilla. We just put everything back in the trunk and closed it back up.

The amount of Canadian and US currency and bonds had continued to grow. We now had our original suitcase filled as well as four of the larger sports bags. Each one also contained enough gold pieces to make them overweight on the luggage scales at an airport.

It was just before 2:00 a.m., time to change the guard, and there were another two hundred boxes piled up in the coroner. We crawled back to the boiler room and woke the guys, telling them about the old steamer trunk.

Over the next six hours we kept trading off in shifts, managing to get a little sleep as our loot continued to pile up. Our ETA to leave with everything cleaned up and loaded was to be no later than four o'clock Sunday afternoon, allowing us to leave the area as the sun was setting. Progress had slowed down by breakfast time on Sunday morning, but when we stood back and did a quick calculation, we figured we had opened close to a thousand boxes.

None of the others paid attention to the drawers which I had persuaded myself belonged to Chang.

At eight on Sunday morning Bob left to get us breakfast. It was close to an hour till he came back, each of us wondering what was taking so long, but it had given us each an opportunity to find washrooms to use. Bob had ended up over on Main Street, at a McDonalds not far from the geodesic dome that had been built for the 86 Expo. He came back bearing coffee, juice, hash browns, and breakfast sandwiches.

We were all running on fumes, in a condition of both mental and physical exhaustion. And we still had at least sixteen hours to go before we were home safe and sound.

After breakfast, we took turns at one more nap. At 12:15 we were all back inside, grinding hinges, pounding off the doors, sifting through the loot and stuffing our remaining bags. One of the other drawers was so heavy I almost dropped it on the floor. When it was opened, we removed a huge silver ingot. "This sucker must weigh twenty pounds," said Dan as he hauled it out of the box. "Too heavy to do anything with. Let's just leave it," he said as he slid it off to the side.

I offered my thoughts "It's not really worth all that much. One of the guys at my warehouse has been buying silver since the early eighties. He said the most he ever paid was around twenty-four bucks an ounce around the middle of the 1980s. Last time I asked him about his investment, he told me he could now buy it for seven or eight bucks an ounce." I did a little calculating in my head then said, "If that sucker is twenty pounds, it's still only worth around twenty-five hundred bucks."

By the time we had planned to stop, all the bags and suitcases were full and heavy. One of the other items we had found in the last hours was a bracelet. We had found other ones previously but this one was different because there was a matching necklace. The matching set looked like the kind of bling a movie starlet might wear to the Oscars.

Bob said, "We'll have to draw straws as to whose wife gets these I guess."

"Better let you take it, Bob," said Harry, "You're the only one of us that has a salary big enough to justify a purchase like that. I'm sure Gwen will love them."

"Yeah, Bob, why don't you just count on those being yours and we'll call it square for fronting all the cash to this point." Dan said.

"I could live with that. Subject to appraisal of course," he laughed.

"Deal," said Dan.

I suggested that something that unique would probably be very traceable and asked, "Do you guys think it's all that smart to take something as identifiable as those, and then let Gwen wear it to the golf club's next gala?"

We spent the next ten minutes discussing the pros and cons of taking the jewels. In the end, they finally concurred with my reasoning, agreeing to just leave beautiful trinkets where we found them.

We had finished grinding off the hinges, and pounded the doors off as many units as we could. The last of the drawers had been removed. The very last drawer we opened contained a set of intricately painted lead soldiers. Taking a closer look, we realized the figures were pieces to a chess set. Leaving the pieces where they were, we set it beside another box we had set aside earlier.

The one we'd set aside earlier was one of the larger twelve-inch-square boxes, and had been full of old gold coins. "My doubloons" I screeched. Then I told them about the treasure we had found as kids. We knew we couldn't take these, as they would certainly draw a lot of attention if we ever tried to take them to an antique or coin and stamp shop.

"That's it guys," said Dan. "I think we need to call it quits, clean up and get the hell out of Dodge."

We looked at the mess on the floor and the stuffed sports bags, which were overflowing with cash and bearer bonds, taking in the ravaged rows of empty sockets where the drawers had been, now seeing a pile of empty drawers in the corners, stacked all the way to the ceiling.

"How many did we get?" asked Harry.

I figure the last batch we did at around five hundred giving us a total of fifteen hundred give or take a hundred," I replied.

Not a bad weekend's work," said Dan

"Time to get back to reality, boys," said Bob, then finished with one of the backwards sayings he often used: "Let's get this go on the show, and we'll be off like a turd of hertles," We all had a good laugh, gathered up the remaining tools, grabbed the bags and suitcases and then crawled through the tunnel back to the boiler room.

I stayed back, telling the others I wanted to make sure we hadn't forgotten anything. I made my decision about the boxes that probably belonged to Chang. I thought of spreading the contents, including the coke or heroine, on the floor, but if I did that, I might as well just take the cash.

I figured that one check of the log book would confirm that these boxes were his. Rules of evidence might make it difficult to charge him with anything. I was sure a good lawyer could argue that these items had been planted to frame his client. But they might help the cops to get more evidence on him, leading to an arrest in the future, so I left the four drawers right where I had found them.

Turning off the lights in the vault, I waded through the loot that reached to the top of my boots, toward the tunnel of light, hoping I wouldn't see the light of a spiritual tunnel any time soon, and then crawled back to the boiler room and unhooked the latch on the door leading to the second floor.

Bob and I headed off to get the vehicles. While we were doing that, Harry and Dan carried the remaining gear and cases to the top of the stairs. Dan needed to use two hands, taking the stairs one at a time with the bags because of the weight. "We should use the pulley," said Harry

"I got these," grunted Dan.

The barriers were set up again and the van was backed up to the door. Bob arrived, backing the Suburban into place so that it was also right outside the door. The other two were waiting with the last of the gear, including the scanner and door buzzer. The bags and suitcases full of loot were also waiting for transfer to the Suburban. We loaded the luggage into the back of the Suburban along with the grinders and sledge hammers, we then transferred the smaller items from the back of the van into the Suburban.

Before leaving Kelowna, Dan had mixed up twenty-litre pails of caustic chemicals. We had wiped down the tools and equipment as they were removed from the boiler room. Dan put on heavy-duty, chemical resistant gloves, immersing our clothing into the compound, then transferred the clothes into another pail full of water to rinse them off, finally tossing everything into the garbage bags. He used the same process on all the masks, ear protection, goggles and safety glasses. We double bagged everything and placed them in the back of the Suburban.

If the boiler room had still had an operational boiler we probably would have burned them all.

CHAPTER 35

Dan was in the back of the van as Harry pulled it away from the boiler room door and backed down to the corner. Bob and I made sure that the boiler room door was tightly closed and locked. I thought of locking the boiler room door with the deadbolt then going out the same way I had entered on Friday night, but decided that the basic door lock would do.

We walked to the corner, dismantled the barrier for the last time and tossed the pieces into the rear. Bob and I sat on the floor with the doors open and Dan pounded on the side wall of the van, signalling Harry to head to the other end of the alley to get the barrier there. When we were done, Dan got into the Suburban with Bob and I got in the front of the van, and just like that we were on our way from the scene of the crime.

Harry and Bob had each memorized the circuitous routes we would take to get out of the area. Even though we knew the routes, each vehicle still had a map inside in case we needed an alternate route. Alternate routes had also been predetermined and marked on the maps.

Harry had the scanner up front with him, and we all still had our two-way radios. The distance between the different routes we would be using would make contact challenging, if not impossible. The lights from the scanner were tracking back and forth. Occasionally, the lights would stop and Harry would hear communication between various units and the dispatch office. It was just after the Christmas season, and the last thing we needed was to come across a Counter Attack roadblock that might still be stopping vehicles to check for drunk drivers, a program that had begun in 1977 and was responsible for getting thousands of drunk drivers off the road.

We had plenty of time to accomplish the rest of our tasks before we left town. Our main priority was to get rid of our fake city works vehicle. We felt that the fake logo and stripes would withstand any elementary inspection. We knew we couldn't get right into the city yard, but close by would be the second-best thing, and there was an employee parking lot outside the gates of the Manitoba Street works yard. Parked in their lot, it might not draw attention for days. We only needed one night. The real license plates we had on the van should help. There wouldn't be any reason for anyone to run the plate until they discovered it wasn't a city vehicle.

Harry and I headed off in the direction of the south side of Vancouver where the city yards were located, following the main route we had chosen to get there. Bob and Dan were taking their own roundabout way and would meet us there.

The route to the works yard was definitely not the shortest distance between two points. During my time in Vancouver I had driven around, finding large dumpsters at various points around town. We didn't want to use any garbage containers in the downtown core, just in case a homeless person dumpster diving inadvertently found our bags of clothes.

The dumpsters I had chosen were from a variety of waste management companies. One was an old-style, City of Vancouver bright orange dumpster. All the garbage from the greater Vancouver area went to the same disposal site, but the bags would arrive at different times because the dumpsters were picked up on different days of the week. Bob and Harry each had notations on the maps where the dumpsters were located. One of us would jump out, put the bag in the dumpster, jump back in and we'd drive to the next. We had come up with alternate sites in case we arrived at one and found anyone in the chosen dump area or discovered that the one we planned on using was over flowing. The other thing I had made sure of was that none of these containers had locks or chains placed on them by the tenants of the commercial sites where they were located.

Harry and I had a lot of to get rid of and we made a detour to Mitchell Island. It was the ideal place to get rid of the equipment. On the island, Mitchell Road had several auto wrecking yards, as well as places that had direct access to the Fraser River. Once on the island, Harry proceeded down the unlighted road. When he arrived at one of the wrecking yards, he pulled over and I jumped in the back then pushed an oxygen cylinder out. All remaining oxygen from the cylinders had been purged to make them lighter, but it still took a great deal of effort to gather the one-hundred-pound cylinder in my arms like a Scotsman might hold a wooden caber and toss it over the fence. It might be years before anyone noticed it lying against the fence line.

We did the same thing with various parts of the drilling unit, thermal lance and the other oxygen cylinders. A lot of the smaller pieces we ended up tossing right into the river where they would be buried deep in the silt that constantly built up in the last part of the Fraser before it emptied into the Strait of Georgia.

I don't know why, but polluting the river made me feel guiltier than robbing those deposit boxes, similar to how I had felt when I stole the cylinders in the first place. I also ended up throwing our barriers against a junkyard fence.

When we had emptied out the van, Harry headed to our rendezvous site to meet with Bob and Dan. Though we had worn gloves any time we'd been inside the truck, I still used a spray bottle of Dan's chemicals to douse the entire inside of the unit while Harry drove, including the now empty tool boxes, which we would be leaving in the back of the truck. Our meeting spot was in a warehouse parking area off West Kent about a block and a half from the works yard. We made it there without incident.

Harry grasped the scanner from the dash, pulling the power cord out of the socket and grabbed the map. Harry had stayed in his coveralls during our drive to the rendezvous in case we had to stop for any reason. He jumped out of the cab, climbed in the back to change out of his coveralls and boots. When he'd finished changing, we sprayed Dan's solution on his clothing and boots and put everything into double-layered plastic garbage bags.

Dan jumped into the front of the cube van. Using a rag and spray bottle he wiped off the entire driver and passenger areas of the truck. He tore the maps into small pieces and stuffed half of them in the plastic bag. Yet again, he soaked down the contents of the bag. When he had first purchased the scanner, Harry had removed any identifying serial marks or tags, opening up the scanner to make sure there were no identifying marks on the inside as well. We were attempting to leave absolutely no trace of any of us on anything we might have touched. Harry took another plastic bag, put the scanner in it and stomped on it, which broke the plastic unit to pieces. He reopened the bag and Dan threw in the remains of the shredded map, then sprayed the bleach solution on the destroyed scanner and paper, closed it up and put the bags in the rear of the Suburban.

Bob was ready to go. Harry and I jumped into the Suburban with him. Dan drove out the parking area with the van, with the three of us following him back to the works yard parking lot. We dumped one of the bags in a dumpster on Kent Street, then headed to the works yard, stopping on the street, waiting outside the empty parking lot while Dan parked in plain sight, locked up the van and sauntered across the parking lot like he had just got off shift.

As soon as Dan got his ass in the seat, Bob started off before he had closed his door. We had just one more stop to make, to get rid of the last plastic bag with Harry's stuff in it, so we headed out to Marine Drive and headed east, and then headed south across the Knight Street bridge, getting off on Bridgeport to our last dumpster site. This was another location where I had found an easily-accessible dumpster. I directed Bob to a location off Number Five road to a dumpster behind a carpet warehouse.

We had tried to leave nothing to chance. We had tried to take every scenario into consideration while we were in the planning stages. It always seemed to be the smallest of details that was forgotten that led to the capture of any type of thief or bank robber. Over the previous months, I had looked into some famous vault robberies, and what had tipped of the police to the thieves' identities. I felt confident that we had covered all the bases.

The hours I spent driving alone on my sales trips afforded me a lot of time to think of any possible holes in our plan. Each time I had come up with a potential snag, I attempted to come up with a solution. If I couldn't think of one, we would discuss it, then agree on a plan of action.

Bob parked right beside the bin. Harry jumped out to put the last bag in it. The bin was a lot fuller than I would have liked, and Harry ended up having to move bulky items around to bury our garbage bag under them. Satisfied that it wasn't visible from the top, he jumped back in the Suburban.

I knew from my research that this bin would be picked up early on Monday morning so I wasn't worried about how full it was. With a sigh of relief, Harry said. "That's the last of it, now let's get the hell out of here."

The one thing we couldn't control were the random events. As we were ready to leave the warehouse complex, an RCMP patrol car pulled into the driveway. The light bar on the top of the patrol car came flashing on as he pulled abreast of Bob's window, reflecting off the cement walls of the warehouse and filling the interior of the Suburban with an eerie, strobing glow. Any natural colour we had drained away as soon as the patrol car had pulled up beside us, so the only colour that could be seen on our faces was that of the flashing lights

There were muted curses as Bob put the car in park and pressed the remote for his side window. "Everyone just stay calm. I've got this."

There was only one officer in the patrol car. Staying in the patrol car, he lowered his window to talk to Bob. "Evening officer, everything okay?" Bob inquired.

"What are you guys doing around here tonight?"

Very calmly Bob gave him an explanation: "I've just taken a job at the carpet warehouse at the end of the complex. I don't start till the week after next, but wanted to get an idea of how long it would take me to get here from Surrey."

"Takes four of you to figure out your driving time?"

"Oh no, not at all. My friends and I just finished seeing a movie downtown, so I thought I would show them where I would be working and then figure out just how long it might take to get home."

"What movie were you at?" I cringed and held my breath as I heard the cop ask that one.

Without missing a beat Bob replied, "*Above the Law*, with Steven Seagal over at the Dunbar Theatre."

"You been drinking tonight?" came the next question.

"Not unless you consider one of those huge movie drinks drinking. I just might have to make a pit stop before getting home. That might screw up my driving time though."

"Well, if you do have to make a stop or two, it might just help adjust your time frame. There will be a lot more traffic trying to get here in the mornings."

"I thought I would just add twenty minutes to the trip to allow for rush hour."

"Just don't let us catch you guys doing your pit stop on the side of the road. I'd hate to see you arrested for indecent exposure."

"I'll make sure we make any pit stops at a gas station, officer," said Bob.

The more the two of them spoke the more nervous each of us became. Had he called for backup? Was he just stalling till another unit arrived before they got us out of the car and searched it?

I thought I could almost feel the car vibrating from the tension coming out of the back seats where Dan and Harry were sitting.

"Well we've had break-ins in the warehouse district around here so when I saw your vehicle I needed to check you out."

I could feel my whole body tensing again.

"No problem, officer."

"I meant to ask you. What's the name of the carpet place you're going to be working at?"

I almost threw up right there in the front seat when I heard that question.

Again without missing a beat, Bob replied. "Titan Flooring, right down at the back of this complex."

"Okay. Well good luck figuring out your commute time. Hope it works out for you."

"Thanks. I won't have any business cards till I start but if you ever need any flooring come see me. I'll see if I can get you wholesale pricing. Just ask for George Meeks," said Bob using his alias, "I'll be working Saturday shifts as well"

"I just might take you up on that. Have a safe drive home." With his interrogation complete, the officer switched off the flashing lights and waved us off.

Bob put the Suburban in drive and raised the driver window as he drove off. We all let out a collective sigh of relief. Out of the back seat all we heard was "Holy crap."

Bob kept watching the rear-view mirror all the way back to Bridgeport Road. When we made it around the corner he quietly exclaimed, "God damn. That was way too much stress. I've never been that tense assisting with breech births."

"How the fuck did you know it was Titan Flooring back there?"
I asked.

"Fortunately, I was able to see the marquis sign for the complex
through the window of the cop car."

"That was amazing, Bob." Came Harry's comment from the
back seat. "I was sure we were toast."

"I can't believe you offered the guy a discount. That took balls.
I would love to see his face if he goes in there looking for you,"
sputtered Dan as he began to laugh.

"How did you know the Seagal movie was at the Dunbar,"
asked Harry.

"I'll have you all know that I am very well read. I noticed it in
The Province at the office last week, don't know why, it's not like
I thought we'd be going to a movie down here."

Soon we were all caught up in nervous laughter. The more we
talked about what Bob had done, the harder we laughed. "Maybe
we can get Harry to add a dinner theatre to the motel, you can
be the headliner," suggested Dan as we all laughed harder.

Bob was now laughing so hard he had to pull into the parking
lot of a gas station and convenience store. The other three all
got out and ran inside. I decided I should wait in the Suburban
while they headed in—I didn't want to have it stolen while we
were having a piss. Once they were all back, I would head in to
get a coffee and use the facilities, then we'd be on our way.

CHAPTER 36

Driving along the causeway approaching the terminal of the airport at night always made the entire area look so much bigger. There are lights everywhere. The huge Air Canada hangar was wide open, allowing us to see inside the cavernous building, which was big enough to hold two Boeing 737s. The other huge building was the Canadian Airlines hanger, which was larger and could hold a 747 and a 737 side by side. The sodium vapour lights were casting a yellow glow along Grant McConachie Way and we could make out the blue runway lights and amber taxiway lights as we drove.

We pulled Bob's Suburban up to the Domestic Departures area, putting on his hazard lights, while Dan and Harry jumped out to retrieve a pair of carts to haul our bags into the terminal. Bob just stayed in the front while the three of us grabbed the bags out of the back of the Suburban. As we loaded them onto the carts, I was sure they'd all be overweight.

Bob headed off to put his Suburban in the long-term parking area. He would then catch the shuttle to the departure terminal. We pushed the heavily-laden carts into the concourse of the terminal and waited for Bob to return. I would arrange to get Bob back to Vancouver next week to pick up his vehicle.

Harry had arranged all the flights for us. Since starting our caper, this was the first and only time we had used our own names when buying anything. It took Bob almost forty minutes to get back to the terminal building. We still had lots of time to catch the last plane of the evening back to Kelowna. Checking out the departure screens, we learned that everything was on schedule.

Our fight, Canadian Airlines 2314, which would stop in Kelowna before heading further east, was set to take off at ten thirty. "Are you guys ready to head home?" I asked as we headed off to the check-in counter.

Considering it was nine o'clock on a Sunday night, the terminal was bustling. The logos of the various airlines seemed to call out to the travellers to change their mind and fly to wherever that airline would take you to. Dan looked from the signs then said to the three of us, "What if we just took one of these bags, headed over to Cathay Pacific and told them to give us four first class tickets to the best place they fly. We open up the bags, drop a pack of bills on the counter and waited for a reaction."

"I think we might have trouble getting these bags through the luggage x-ray machines for international flights they've been using here since that Air India disaster back in eighty-five, not to mention customs officers at the other end when we get off," replied Bob.

Harry piped up, "That's why I chose domestic. No customs and no x-rays."

We'd known that we might end up with bags that were overweight. Our plan was to pose as sales reps for a door hardware manufacturer, giving us an explanation for the weight of the bags. Our story would be that our display had been damaged in shipment, forcing us to take the sample products to a sales conference in our own luggage.

We had purchased cheap door locks, cut the logos off and attached them onto each of the bags. Hopefully, the counter clerk wouldn't ask about our hardware. Hopefully. In case anyone did inquire about the extra weight we had placed a layer of door lock sets on top of the loot in each of the soft-sided bags, making even our smaller bags overweight. We hadn't bothered with the suitcases because if these were opened, there would be no hiding the loot.

We were the only ones in line when we arrived at the roped off aisles of the airline's counter so we rolled our carts right up. Being a domestic flight, all we needed was our tickets. The agent at the counter confirmed that the flight was on schedule. Removing her portion of the tickets, she handed them back to Harry, "You can head out to the departure lounge anytime. We'll begin boarding at ten to ten. Just put your luggage on the scale right here," she said, pointing between the counters.

Harry noted the attendant's name tag and said, "They're probably all overweight, Amanda."

She watched as Dan struggled to get the first one on the scale. Her eyes opened wide as she watched the scale hit eighty pounds, "Wow. That sure is overweight. I'm going to have to charge you guys for that much extra weight. What the heck have you got in there?"

"Well, we just robbed a bank. All these bags are filled with gold and jewels," said Bob in a deadpan voice.

Three pairs of eyes flew open as wide as saucers.

"Well in that case you can probably afford the extra charges," laughed Amanda.

Bob laughed as well before telling Amanda our cover story as the rest of us relaxed.

"Well, if each of these bags are overweight and you have two extras. I'm going to have to charge twenty-five dollars each for the extra weight, but I'll give you a break on the two extra bags." Amanda used a calculator then looked at Bob and said, "That will be two hundred and fifty dollars, please."

"Sure hope I can add that to the expense account for this trip. Thanks for the break, Amanda," said Bob as he handed her the cash. "I can put those on the conveyor if you like," offered Harry.

"You're really not supposed to, but I think I'll take you up on that offer," said Amanda as she made out the baggage tags, wrapping them around the handles as we set them onto the scales. Dan then proceeded to swing them onto the conveyor, taking a great deal of effort to do so.

Amanda handed Harry all the luggage receipts and reconfirmed our boarding time. Then with a big smile, she told us to enjoy our flight and hardware conference.

We watched as the bags headed down the line toward their rendezvous with the baggage handlers. The bags would travel miles on the conveyor belts, ending up in the basement of the terminal where they would be loaded onto a baggage cart, hooked to a baggage tractor and eventually pulled out of the basement to be loaded onto the plane.

I watched our bags disappear behind the flaps of the conveyor belt, hoping all our bags would arrive with us in Kelowna. It would be hard to explain if one of them ended up in Winnipeg. What if the tags had come off, requiring a baggage handler to look inside the bag to find out where it really belonged?

We headed off to the departure lounge in silence, realizing it was out of our hands until we picked them up. Just as Amanda had promised, the flight was on time and we commenced down the gangway to the plane right on schedule. Harry and Bob had a pair of seats near the front, while Dan and I had two seats one row past the emergency exit. Dan was in the aisle seat, with me in the middle, and no one beside me in the window seat. Not that there would have been much of a view at this time of night.

I was trying to stay calm and cool. My mind, however, was racing, thinking of how I would explain the details of the trip to Trish and the girls. Although it had been years since we entered a tournament, Harry had found a lower mainland tournament taking place at just the right time. That became our excuse to get out of town. Harry had written out a script for us to memorize, with details that had to match to ensure that any time we were together in the future, even minute details could be talked about as if they had really taken place.

During our investment club meetings, we spent time going over the details of the trip. We had quizzed each other about specifics, even making up trivia games about the facts until we knew that the entire curling weekend was permanently etched into our minds as if we had experienced it firsthand.

The attendants were still helping to get people settled into their seats and store carry-on luggage in the overhead compartments. Dan and I were still the only two in our aisle. I removed the in-flight magazine from the pocket of the seat in front of me, the one that's in the same place as the air sickness bag, which I had fortunately never needed to use. I slowly flipped the pages of the magazine without seeing what was on them.

CHAPTER 37

Our bags had taken their circuitous trip along the conveyor belt highway and arrived at the baggage staging area. Amanda had attached a bright orange-and-black tag with a silhouette of two men lifting a heavy load to each of them. There was a spot to fill in the actual weight of the luggage, but Amanda hadn't taken the time to fill those in.

Carl, one of the luggage handlers in the bowels of the terminal took note of the ten bags that had arrived at the end of the beltway as they started their slow journey around a carousel similar to the ones in the arrivals area.

Company policy stated that bags with orange tags required two handlers. They did not want time lost, or the increased Workman's Compensation Board premiums that they would incur if handlers ended up hurting their backs. Like all safety rules, having two handlers worked well in theory, but seldom happened in the real world. As usual, Carl ignored the tags. He pumped himself up, snatched a medium-sized sports bag off the carousel and swung it onto the cart. "Not too bad, I should be able to get all these myself." He reached over, grabbed two smaller bags that had arrived at the same time as the heavy ones. With one in each hand, he tossed them onto the cart, then carried on loading other bags as the orange-tagged ones made another lap of the carousel. When the heavy tagged ones came back around he stopped the carousel.

Carl used both hands to take hold of another of the sports bags. With a grunt, he managed to get it onto the cart. He repeated the process with one of the suitcases. At first it didn't budge. He took a second pull, lifting it off the carousel, but as he tried to swing it onto the cart, the handle separated from the suitcase. The suitcase crashed against the side of the cart. Carl looked at the handle that was still grasped in both of his hands. "Damnit I'm going to catch shit for this. Should have got Ben to help."

He looked down to see what damage had occurred to the suitcase. The case had dropped at an angle, landing on its corner, causing the locks to open, its contents spilling out onto the floor. Carl was dumbfounded. The suitcase was disgorging packs of bills, loose diamonds and small gold ingots like a winning slot machine.

In a state of shock, he watched the contents spread across the floor. "Jesus Christ!" he murmured as he stared at the ingots and diamonds that glistened in the glare of the overhead lights. As the shock dissipated, he went to the front of the baggage tractor and used the radio to call for a supervisor to come to his location immediately. "We have a problem, Ian. I think you might want to get in touch with airport security and the cops."

Ian arrived within minutes. He took a quick look at the pile of loot laying on floor. "Holy shit," was all he could utter.

"My sentiments exactly," said Carl as his supervisor headed to the phone.

Ian put a call in to security, as well as the airport RCMP. It wouldn't take a rocket scientist to figure out that there was a problem with this scene. As Carl and Ian stood looking at the golden loot and cash that had spilled onto the floor, Ian said, "I have never seen anything like this in the twenty years I've been here."

Staff Sergeant Groves was the RCMP watch commander at the airport that evening. When he arrived, he got an explanation from Carl as to what had happened. The airport security guard stood staring at the contents that had spread out on the floor.

"First things first," Groves told Carl and Ian. "We need to make sure that plane stays right where it is. When is it supposed to pull away from the gate?"

Ian checked the schedule. "This one is supposed to pull back from the gate in around twenty minutes."

"This is the last train of carts for that flight. The baggage compartments are still open," said Carl.

"There might be a very small chance that this can be explained, but I doubt it." stated Groves. "Are there any other bags to go with this one?"

Carl pointed to the two with the orange tags on the cart. "There's two on there and the suitcase," he said pointing to the one laying on the floor, "I think I counted another seven with orange tags still on the carousel."

"Let's have a look in the sports bags, shall we?"

Carl took Groves to the cart, showing him the two bags. Everyone gathered around as the Staff Sergeant opened the bag, the first thing he noticed was the sets of door handles. He removed the crude attempt to hide the true contents of the bag, setting the locks to the side, he opened the bag wider, which caused everyone gathered to gasp as he revealed that this one was also stuffed with cash, ingots and bearer bonds.

The security guard let out a low wolf whistle as he looked at the bag full of money. "Ever seen anything like this before, Sergeant?"

"Never!" was all Groves could say.

With years of experience, Groves was good at his job and an excellent manager and delegator. Before he started issuing commands and delegating duties, he got on his portable radio, requesting two more of the terminal officers to meet him in the baggage area. Changing frequencies, he then contacted the Richmond RCMP headquarters. Once he was speaking with the detachment commander, he gave a short, precise accounting of all that had transpired to this point.

With an understanding of the situation, Groves' boss told him he would be sending backup and a tactical unit to the airport. "Make sure that plane stays where it is!" was the commander's final order to Groves.

Carl, Ian and the security guard were still standing and looking at the loot before them.

"This is what is going to happen," Groves stated, bringing the other three out of a trance. "We will leave the cargo ramp in place and continue to load luggage, just in case they're watching out the windows."

Carl and Ian put the suspect bags aside and continued to load the balance of the luggage on the carts. When the other two terminal officers arrived, one was left to stand guard over the bags that had been set off to the side. The security guard was sent to the main entry door of the baggage area so that he could direct the other officers that would soon be arriving. The overhead door would allow tactical units to drive right to where Groves had set up his incident command post. The third officer on scene arranged lowboy carts as a makeshift table.

Groves contacted the passenger agents at the Canadian Airlines counter. "I need to get both customer and luggage manifests for flight 2314. I want them brought down to the baggage area, and I want them here ten minutes ago." When all of this had been arranged, ten minutes remained until the scheduled departure time. Groves then spoke to the airport operations manager and explained the situation. "I want all arriving flights re-directed to gates well away from where flight 2314 is currently attached to the terminal by the jet bridge."

The scheduled departure time was now only minutes away. Groves' next conversation would be to speak directly to the cockpit. He was patched through from his command post, giving the pilot a quick explanation of the situation. "I need you and the crew to ensure that no one gets off that plane. You need to tell the passengers you are waiting for some late arriving passengers."

As he finished speaking with the crew, Amanda arrived with a printout of the passenger list, which also contained the list of checked baggage. Groves showed Amanda the suspect baggage, including the suitcase whose contents were still spread out on the floor. "Do you recognize these bags?"

"Oh my God!" she gasped. "Yes, oh my God, oh my God. There were four guys that I checked in at the counter with those bags. I stuck the heavy tags on them. They all have their company logo on the side there," she said as she pointed to the lock company logo.

"Do you have the seat assignments for the four passengers?" asked Groves.

Amanda looked at the manifest, then told Groves exactly where they should be seated then added. "They checked a total of ten bags."

"That agrees with what we have pulled aside. Thanks for your help, would you be able to positively identify them, and match them up with their luggage?"

"Absolutely!" said Amanda confidently. "These guys joked with me that the bags were so heavy because they had just robbed a bank. They told me the bags were filled with gold and jewels. I certainly didn't take them seriously though. They seemed really nice."

In the cockpit, the captain made the announcement to explain the expected delay.

"Ladies and gentlemen, this is your captain speaking. I'm afraid we will have a slight delay. We are waiting on a few passengers from an international flight who have been delayed. We apologize for the delay and promise we will get you on your way just as soon as possible. Thanks for your patience and understanding."

The Richmond RCMP didn't have a fancy SWAT truck like you see in the movies. They arrived in a total of three patrol cars, followed by the Richmond commander and two more squad cars loaded with another four officers from the detachment.

One of the tactical unit officers that had arrived was Special Constable Ann Archer from the Specialty Response Team. In training drills, she was often used to impersonate a female flight attendant in hostage situations. She was a very attractive woman, and all conversation seemed to stall as she joined the testosterone laden team of men.

Groves was ready to give his situation report as soon as she arrived, and everyone was now gathered around the makeshift table. Ian had brought down a white board as well as an oversize seating plan of the 737 and set them on the carts. After Amanda had left, Ian circled where the four men, who were now considered suspects, were sitting.

Groves cleared his throat and started: "Passenger agents have confirmed the exact location of four suspects," he explained to the group. He pointed to the layout of the plane. "Two should be sitting here, two more here. I have had the pilot tell the passengers that their flight has been briefly delayed. Here's what I have in mind—" He looked at the detachment commander to see if he should continue.

"Go ahead Groves, this is your show," said the inspector.

He explained his plan to the gathered officers. The tactical guys were impressed with the simplicity of it, asking hardly any questions, and those that were asked, Groves was quick to answer. "We're running out of time before these guys start getting antsy. If there are no more questions let's make this happen quickly and safely. Nobody gets hurt tonight." The team headed off to their positions. Groves contacted the pilot again and explained what was about to take place.

"Ladies and gentlemen this is your captain again. It looks like we will be on our way in just a few minutes. Our tardy fellow passengers will be boarding shortly. Their luggage is being loaded as we speak. When everyone is settled, we'll get them to back this bird out, then be on our way. Our new time for arrival in Kelowna will now be 11:40 local time. Once again, we apologize for the delay and thank-you for choosing to fly with us. Flight attendants please prepare for new passengers."

Prior to the last announcement, the Captain had spoken to each of the flight attendants, explaining the situation.

* * *

I just sat reading the paper. Delays were not unusual, especially on puddle jumper feeder flights. The events of the past months were behind us. We had scored more loot than I had imagined in my wildest dreams. Stevie Wonder's hit from sixty-six about everything being alright and out of sight came to mind, and I started to whistle the tune.

"What's that tune?" asked Dan.

"Oh nothing, just thinking about a Stevie Wonder song."

"Uh huh."

Minutes after the captain's announcement, we saw the first of the new passengers boarding the plane. I looked up from the paper, and observed an extremely attractive woman with long, wavy hair making her way down the aisle, "If she looks that good after rushing through customs, I'd like to see her when she was starting fresh," I whispered to Dan. She appeared to be checking for her seat designation on the overhead compartments, then slowed as she got to our aisle.

I pointed to the window seat. "This the one you're looking for?"

"Thanks, but no, I'm back of you."

Right behind the fine-looking lady was a guy that could pass for a linebacker for the Seattle Seahawks. He looked at Dan and me. "Sorry guys, you're going to be stuck with me, not her," he said as he pointed to the woman that had just passed.

"No problem," said Dan. "Sure looks like you could use extra leg room though."

We undid our seat belts which had been around our laps since we sat down on the plane. Standing up we both shuffled into the aisle to let him past. The woman was still standing in the aisle, putting a bag in the overhead compartment.

The big guy ducked down and began to ease past our seats.

As I was standing in the aisle, I looked toward Harry and Bob's seats, seeing the same scenario taking place, except that there were just two big guys up there and no pretty woman. There was one guy putting luggage into the overhead compartment and Harry and Bob were out of their seats letting the other big guy into their window seat. I got a sinking feeling in my stomach. I now knew exactly how Clyde Barrow had felt as he realized they had been set up in the final horrendous scene of *Bonnie and Clyde*. There were no birds flying out from the bushes, but I did take a quick look at Dan then back down the aisle to Bob and Harry.

"Don't do anything stupid," came a woman's voice from behind Dan.

The linebacker getting into his seat pulled a gun out of his jacket and stuck it right against my ribs. I watched the same thing happening with Bob and Harry near the front of the plane. The weapons had come out of nowhere and all four of us now had guns pointed at us.

"Alright, alright. None of us have any weapons. We'll go quietly," Dan muttered.

The four officers did a cursory frisk of each of us. Canadian law is funny: despite having reasonable grounds to detain us they were not ready to place us under arrest. I heard the female officer behind Dan. "All clear, all four in custody." I couldn't see her but presumed she was talking on a radio.

It had gone so smoothly that most of passengers weren't aware of what had transpired. There were no hysterical screams, but I did hear a lot of murmured voices coming from the passengers about what they thought had just taken place.

Groves came onto the plane from the gangway. "It's okay everyone. Everything is under control. Please stay in your seats. We will be escorting these four passengers off the plane then you will all be asked to exit the plane in an orderly fashion. Go to the departure lounge. There will be officers there to take statements from everyone. We will then match everyone with their luggage and then get you back on your way. Thank you for your understanding and patience."

The four officers then escorted us down the aisle and off the plane. I saw the three stripes and crown on the jacket of the officer who had spoken as we were escorted off the plane, identifying him as a staff sergeant, and probably the one in charge of this takedown.

He stood in the aisle between the exit door and cockpit as we were removed from the plane. Passengers had begun to grumble and become boisterous as we exited the plane, all of them complaining about the further delay they would be experiencing.

While the takedown was being prepared, Groves had inspected our other suitcases, substantiating that all of them held huge sums of money, gold, diamonds and stock certificates. The detachment commander had been in touch with all lower mainland police departments, Vancouver, New Westminster, Delta, West Vancouver as well as the outlying areas of Abbotsford, and Port Moody, all of which had their own police departments. He had contacted RCMP Headquarters of E Division, which was responsible for any other areas in the province not handled by their own departments.

By the time we had been removed from the plane, they were aware that the contents of our bags contained the spoils of a robbery of some sort. The only problem was that they had absolutely no idea what had been robbed, or where the suspected robbery had taken place.

While the takedown team had entered the plane, two officers had been positioned on the gangway with assault weapons, and each of the planes emergency exit doors were guarded in case the suspects had tried to get out, using the emergency chutes.

The departure lounge, as well as the gate areas on either side of ours were completely empty. The concourse area had been cordoned off with yellow police tape. We all knew that any attempt to flee would be futile, so we just let ourselves be herded where they wanted us to go. We were whisked away through an employees-only door, leading to a long hallway and ultimately to a stairwell.

The officers were very polite as they escorted us, guiding us with one hand on our upper arms and telling us exactly which way to turn. When we reached the stairwell, they made sure we watched our step as we headed down so that we didn't slip and fall.

At the bottom of the stairs we were led down another hallway which finally connected us with the baggage operations area under the main terminal building. We were escorted right to the area where our bags had ended up. They had all been opened and set up on one of the cargo trailers.

No questions had been asked, and none of us had said a word on our long walk of shame. I accepted the fact that there would be many more of these shameful walks in the months to come.

The officers escorting us were instructed to bring us to the front of the carts, by whom I presumed was the man in charge. I took note of a tall officer. His balding head was framed above his ears with short grey hair. His uniform was still crisp, considering how long he had probably been in it today. I could see the name of J. Hollis on the tag pinned just above his breast pocket. "Have they been searched?" he asked the officers who had escorted us from the plane

"Basic pat down on the plane, sir," replied the female officer behind Dan.

"Well, let's get it done right," ordered the inspector.

"Are we under arrest?" asked Dan.

"You can be if you prefer to be," came the inspector's reply. "We would prefer if we could figure out just what is going on without placing you under arrest at this time."

"If you're not arresting us, can we leave?" came Dan's next question.

"Not until we sort out exactly what is going on."

"So, we are under arrest."

The inspector glared at Dan. "Are you a lawyer, son?"

I could tell his temper was rising but was still surprised at how cheeky Dan was becoming. "No, and I'm not your son either."

That seemed to do it for the inspector. "Alright smart ass, have it your way. You can now all consider yourselves under arrest, under Section 322 of the Criminal Code of Canada, for suspicion of being involved in the theft of the items now in your luggage." He walked right up and stood face to face with Dan and looked into his eyes. "Happy now? Son!"

We still had not been placed in handcuffs. We were each pushed up against the carts in front of us, told to stand still, spread our legs and place our hands, palm down, flat on the carts. We were each asked if we had anything sharp in our pockets.

"No. Nothing. No, Sir. Nothing at all," came our individual replies.

We were all frisked thoroughly. All our pockets were emptied on to the carts. Other than a bit of loose cash, there was nothing in our pockets. Our identification was removed from our wallets. Bob still had close to a thousand dollars in cash in his wallet.

One of the officers took our driver's licenses to a patrol car to put in a request to the Canadian Police Information Centre. CPIC was the national database for all Canadian law enforcement. It would tell the officers if there were any wants or warrants on any of us. We knew they would come up with zilch.

The Canadian constitution required that after being placed under arrest, we had the right to free and immediate council. "Do you wish to call a lawyer?" he asked us.

"We'll consider that option, sir," said Bob.

"You may also apply for free legal assistance through the provincial legal aid program."

Since we had not asked for council and had agreed that we understood our rights according the Canadian Charter of Rights, the inspector made another statement to us.

"I wish to give you the following warning: You must clearly understand that anything said to you previously should not influence you, or make you feel compelled to say anything at this time. Whatever you felt influenced or compelled to say earlier, you are now not obliged to repeat, nor are you obliged to say anything further, but whatever you do say may be given as evidence."

Having done his duty to tell us our rights the inspector looked at us and inquired. "Do you gentlemen understand why you are being detained?"

None of said a word, so he continued, "Do you recognize the bags on the cart before you?"

We all remained mute. Again the inspector continued, "Just to make this easier for everyone, I want you to know that we have confirmed that you were the ones to check this baggage onto your flight."

Bob was the first to speak. Cool as a cucumber, using the quick wit we had all known over the years, he asked, "Well, sir, they do look a little like ours, but I was wondering what you did with the rest of our hardware samples?"

"That the way you boys are going to play this?" he snapped.

The officer came back from the patrol car with our IDs, looked at the inspector, and tilted his head to the side. "Could I speak to you, sir?" They stepped to the side to talk in private but I did manage to hear them. "Sir, I'm afraid there is absolutely nothing in the system on any of them. A speeding ticket here and there but nothing recent."

"Nothing?"

"No, sir. They all came back completely clean."

The inspector turned back to us. "Well boys, I guess we'll have to continue this back at station," he pointed to the officers who had escorted us from the plane. "You four, cuff them and take them back to the detachment. We will get to the bottom of all of this there."

As we were being placed in cuffs, the inspector told the remaining officers exactly how he wanted the evidence handled, assigning officers to bag and tag everything.

We were each being escorted to separate patrol cars by two officers. They placed me in the rear of the cruiser, the same way I had been taught to do when transporting prisoners while with the police reserves. They eased me into the back seat, making sure I didn't hit my head on the door frame. I tried to look around to see the other guys who were being loaded into the cars behind. They closed my door leaving me alone in the back seat, separated from the front seat by metal bars. I sagged against the door and rested my head on the glass. The car bounced and swayed as the officers settled themselves in their seats. The car was started, the flashing lights flipped on, creating a kaleidoscope of colour inside operations area. Then the doors slammed closed.

That's when I finally lost it. I started to yell at the top of my lungs: "You can't do this! We're good guys! You can't tell my kids!"

"Hey! Shut the fuck up. What the hell is the matter with you?"

My head shot up from the spot it had been leaning against so fast it felt like I damn near snapped a vertebra.

"Chris, who the hell are you yelling at?" asked Bob.

The other door in the back of the Suburban closed as Harry settled himself in the back seat. My voice felt raw from yelling. I could count my pulse rate as it pounded through my ears. In the three minutes since they had gone into the convenience store to get coffees and use the facilities I had experienced the most realistic dream of my entire life. I was so frightened by it I started to babble.

"We can't go the airport guys. We have to drive. Everything will go to shit if we go to the airport. Remember in *Platoon,* that Sergeant O'Neill guy starts whining?" I continued. "Well I know just how he felt, and I can tell you, Bob, just like him I got a bad feeling about this, man." I said. My voice shaking with emotion, I gave them a quick synopsis of my dream, "I got a really bad feeling that we ain't gonna even get out of the airport."

"Jesus Christ, Chris!" yelled Dan. "We talked about this three months ago when Harry first suggested the idea of flying home. In the end we all agreed that flying home would be the best option, because as we all know going up the Coquihalla at this time of year can be treacherous as hell, and I sure as hell don't feel like taking the God damn canyon drive at this time of night."

"I know, but I've got such a bad vibe about it, we can't ignore it. How many times have I told you guys about my sixth sense while driving? My dreams are what got us into all this in the first place, and I think you should keep trusting them now,"

"You know when you have that feeling like you've been at a certain place at specific time and we call it déjà vu? Well I've got that feeling right now. Are any of you willing to bet your future on the fact that I'm wrong? Dan you're the big gambler among us. Are you prepared to take the chance that I might be right? I'm no clairvoyant, but I know we can't go the airport."

Harry chimed in, "Yeah. If I remember correctly, you all told me it was the stupidest idea you had ever heard for a getaway, but agreed to it anyway," then he added with a pouty voice, "You guys hurt my feelings real bad, calling me stupid."

It was just what I needed to hear. I broke into a hysterical laughter that must have been contagious, because the four of us were now sitting in Bob's Suburban in the parking lot of a convenience store, with millions of dollars of loot in bags in the rear of the vehicle, and we were laughing so hard the shaking was probably visible from the outside.

I needed to use the can and get myself a coffee, so I jumped out and headed inside. When I returned to the Suburban, they were still having a good laugh at my expense. The laughter slowly subsided as the mood changed.

"Alright," said Dan, his temper and mood surfacing as it had in my dream, "I don't believe in any of that mumbo jumbo shit, but I'm not prepared to spend the best years of my life in some fucking prison," he looked at Bob and continued as he pointed at me. "If this whack job is that convinced we're heading into impending doom, who am I to argue? If we don't head to the airport right now we'll miss the plane anyway. If we're driving, let's get the fuck going."

"What about you Harry," asked Bob. "Up for another drive?"

"What the hell, if we leave right now and the roads are clear, we can still be home before two in the morning," he replied.

Bob started the car and we pulled out of the parking lot. "Chris check the radio stations to see what the weather's going to be like." I settled into the passenger seat, and did just that, finding reports on one of the all-news stations, hearing the Coquihalla Highway was bare and wet all the way to Merritt, which would help us to get home in six and a half hours.

"Trust me guys, you'll live to not regret this decision," I said, and it wasn't long before the only one awake was Bob.

CHAPTER 38

November 2016

"Chris, Chris wake up. We're going to be late." Trish's voice came through a groggy fog as she placed her hand on my back.

Running late already; this was not going to be a very good day. I climbed out of bed, heading directly to the shower and letting the water get to temperature before stepping in. The shower's ceiling-mounted rain head beat down hard and hot. I still usually scrubbed myself down and got out in a matter of minutes. I wasn't like my son-in-law who could empty a sixty-gallon hot water tank in a single shower.

Finally feeling refreshed, I shut off the water, squeegeed off the glass, grabbed a towel off the rack, wrapped myself up, and then shaved while I was still damp from the shower. Trish was dressed by the time I finished wiping the excess cream from my face. I then ran a brush through my ever-thinning hair. Can't complain I guess. At sixty-two, I still had more hair than most of my ancestors had in their late thirties. Vic had stopped trying to pretend years ago, opting to just shave his entire head. At least he had a head shape that allowed him to pull off the bald look. My misshapen head would never be considered a thing of beauty.

Trish was clad in an appropriate black dress, while I put on the best—and only—suit I still owned. At one time, I'd had a least a dozen different outfits for more formal occasions. Now, all my closet contained were a lot of outfits that years ago I thought might fit me one day in the future. Today, it was the pinstripe suit and plain dark tie. The black shoes seemed a bit tight as I laced up, but it's not like we were heading dancing.

Trish had been up early as usual, already finishing her morning latte and breakfast, but because I'd slept in, all I managed was to pour myself a travel mug of coffee as we headed out the door.

"Better not drink too much of that or you'll have to take a pee half way through things," laughed Trish as we jumped in the car and headed off.

We drove in silence. I reached up and touched my smoothly-shaven face. "Remember when I forgot to shave when we were going to your dad's funeral? I had to stop and buy that travel razor and shave right in the parking lot of the funeral home."

"A sad day I don't really like to think about. But it was funny watching you trying to shave in the rear-view mirror."

When we arrived at the funeral location, both Harry and Dan were there waiting for us. We parked the car then went to meet them. I gave them both big hugs, accompanied by comforting pats on the back, all of us commenting how we wished it was under better circumstances. We had all come a long way in how we showed our feelings for each other over the years, going from handshakes to hugs, and even Vic and I shared this greeting with each other when we got together. I often wondered if Dad would have liked the man hugs. Trish gave them both a hug as well. Harry and Dan told Trish that their wives were already inside waiting for her.

There was a constant stream of people arriving now. "Wow, this place is going to be jammed," commented Dan.

"Any more details on exactly what happened?" I asked the two of them.

Harry filled us in on what he knew. We all knew Bob had been in Syria when it happened, following what he felt was his calling, helping at an aid station in Aleppo. Harry said "The Docs without Borders had been told to leave because things were getting worse every day. Most of them had left except Bob, one other doctor and two nurses."

"That sounds like Bob," I said, "always the last to leave."

Harry continued, "The building they had taken shelter in took a direct hit from a Russian tank shell. The building came down on top of them. By the time a rescue team could get to them, they were all dead. So were five or six of the kids who they'd stayed to help."

"When we watch CNN, we never think of stories like that affecting us in our little corner of the world. I heard that before it was blown to pieces, Aleppo had close to the same population as Toronto. I knew he had been in hot spots over the years, but had never seriously considered him dying doing what he loved," I managed to say.

"I tried to tell him things were totally out of control over there when he was home three months ago," Dan said. "I told him that he was no spring chicken, and that he should leave the combat zones to younger doctors. Especially after all the time he had spent in Africa working on the Ebola outbreak."

"Gwen tried her best to talk him out of going over again after they had come home from the Syrian refugee camps," said Harry. "He was only home a matter of days, then off again right into the thick of things. He told Gwen that he wanted her to stay home this time and get ready for a long vacation. He promised this would be his final trip. Then they would retire for good."

"Well he told us twenty-five years ago that this was what he wanted to do. Not many of us get to accomplish all the things we want in life," said Dan

"What's your take on how Gwen's making out? Trish has talked to her—sounds like she's still in denial," I said.

"Pam has helped with a lot of the arrangements. It took five days just to get his body back here," said Harry.

People continued to pass by us as they headed inside. Those we knew stopped and shook our hands. "You're right about this place being packed," said Dan. "He certainly had a lot of friends and colleagues. I understand there are doctors he worked with coming in from around the world," he continued.

I looked up as a news van pulled into the parking area. "Looks like he's getting a little press," said Harry. "I guess it is an international story. 'Volunteer Canadian Doctor Killed in Syria.' Doesn't happen often, thank goodness."

"We better get in there before there's no room left for us," said Harry.

There had been days of local, national and international news coverage since Bob had been killed in Syria. Bob used to call himself agnostic, but recently I think he had needed to pray on many occasions. His service was being held in one of the largest churches in Kelowna.

"Maybe Gwen should have had his service at the arena," said Dan as we headed inside.

We joined our wives in one of the pews near the front of the church. I looked around and wasn't surprised to see that the upper balcony was filled as well. When the last of the seats were filled, there would be close to fifteen hundred people in attendance.

I took hold of Trish's hand, giving it a light squeeze then whispered, "I'll be lucky to fill one of these rows when I go." All that got me in return was a glare.

There were boxes of tissues in the hymnal racks. Trish, Rita and Pam already had handfuls. The church was built in a partial circle. The plan had been that as the congregation got larger they could build another part of the circle and so on. There was a huge screen above the apse, as well as two smaller screens on the sides, giving everyone a view of the proceedings.

Each screen projected a smiling picture of Bob, which must have been taken while he was helping in camps on the far side of the world. Printed below his picture in stark white lettering were the dates on which he been born and died.

The remembrance service began right on time. It wasn't a religious ceremony, but certainly was a celebration of life. The MC had known Bob longer than Harry, Dan or me. He guided us through the ceremony with both laughter and tears, giving pause in all the right places, allowing us to think of the man we had called our friend. There were countless speakers who also brought us to tears or made us laugh out loud at the memories they shared with us. Everyone who spoke agreed that we were all better for having known him, and he would be sorely missed by all those in attendance.

Gwen had asked the three of us to be the final speakers, and we agreed to give our tribute together. Many of those in attendance knew that the four of us had been best friends for years expecting us to have stories to share.

Harry began, "The ushers gave each of you a small box when you came to the service today. If you haven't already done so, we would like you to open it." We heard hundreds of the boxes being opened. There were small gasps and bits of nervous laughter from the crowd.

Dan spoke next. "They might never let us back in this place of worship in the future, but Harry, Chris and I could think of no better way to bid farewell to our good friend, Doctor Bob."

It was now my turn. "Each of you should now be holding a small bottle of Grand Marnier. The four of us loved to share the 'nectar of the gods' as Bob referred to it." There was a complete hush. Then we heard positive whispers from various places around the packed church. Dan had written a script for us to read from. We spoke in unison. "Bob wasn't just a friend. He was a great friend. We considered him our brother. He was there for all of us at various trying times of our lives. We will miss him greatly."

Dan continued speaking alone. "When we would get together, whether in joy or sorrow, we would always make a toast to life.

So, while having a drink in this church might be frowned upon, we think it is just what Bob would have wanted."

We each opened our bottles, pouring a little from each into a glass that Dan had placed on the podium. The three of us each also had a small snifter before us. We poured the remainder of our bottles into our glasses, as the three of us continued, "We invite all of you to join us in a toast to our great friend." We clinked our glasses against the one sitting on the podium.

In unison, we raised our glasses high in the air. "Here's to you, Bob. To life. Your way."

We lowered the glasses of amber liquid to our mouths and drank. "One more time please. Everyone stand, and join us in a salute to Bob, and in the future when you're with friends or when you are alone and having a wee dram, remember to send a toast to our great friend," Dan said.

The sound of hundreds of people standing at once was striking. Dan raised his glass high in the air, as a picture of the four of us from years ago flashed onto the screens. It was a picture of the four of us raising our glasses in a toast during a memorable New Year's Eve party. I recalled the night as though it was yesterday, and seeing it again brought tears to my eyes. Then the close to fifteen hundred people joined in our chant to our friend. "Here's to you Bob. To life. Your way."

As the gathered mass sat down, the three of us returned to our seats. A slide show had been prepared of Bob's life, with hundreds of pictures going all the way back to when he was a small boy. A black and white picture of him sitting on a pony, wearing chaps and a cowboy hat, and a smile that lit up the room, as well as oodles of other old black and white photos from his younger days and colour pictures showing his formative years in school and university. Countless pictures brought laughter and tears from those gathered to remember him.

There were images of him and Gwen, taken on their travels over the years, and finally there was a video montage showing happy, smiling, laughing children from around the world that he and the Doctors Without Borders had befriended. The soundtrack that went along with the pictures was befitting, using many of his favorite songs.

When the slide show was complete there wasn't a dry eye in the church. Trish had been constantly handing me wet tissues that I stuffed into my jacket pockets.

Then as quickly as he had passed, the ceremony was over.

There would not be a graveyard ceremony but everyone in attendance was invited to join Gwen in the hall at the rear of the church for refreshments.

The MC had one more comment: "Before we leave I want to share one more thought with you. Death is more universal than life, everyone dies, but not everyone lives. I think that we can all agree that Bob did in fact live life to the fullest."

The six of us headed to the church hall to join the throng of people. We made our rounds, telling people we knew how it was too bad that we were seeing one another again under sad circumstances. A fact of life as we all grew older.

The hall was filled with fifteen hundred voices all talking at once. There were bouts of hearty laughter as funny stories were told in various corners of the room.

Vic had retired from the police force in 2007 and he and his wife had retired to Kelowna. Having known all my friends for years, he fit into our group seamlessly, with one exception—other than the scripted story we had told our wives, he still knew nothing about our curling weekend in 1988. Because there is no statute of limitations for theft in Canada, we were always cognizant that no matter how long it had been, we could still be charged with the crime we had committed in 1988.

Vic would fill in for one of us when we needed a fourth for golf. While talking after a round one day, he started telling stories about dumb things criminals had done. Our favourite was about four guys trying to head back to Quebec with ten suitcases of marijuana, each one weighing eighty pounds. It was prior to the 9/11 attacks, so domestic flights still didn't have a great deal of security. The smugglers had wrapped the drugs well enough to ensure there were no odours, and had paid all extra weight charges. When the bags were heading up the luggage ramps onto the plane, one of them fell off, splitting open on the apron beside the plane.

"These four guys were arrested while sitting on the plane. I don't know which one of them came up with the brilliant idea put that much contraband in checked airline baggage," he said, "but they all ended up spending years in the pen. Hell, they could have driven that eight hundred pounds of dope across the country and nobody would have been any the wiser."

When he told us the story it was all the rest of us could do not to say "Well, have we got a story to tell you."

The next time we all got together I made sure the other three all appreciated the fact that my little dream, or sixth sense should never have been questioned, reminding them on numerous occasions of the words I said as we left town that night "Trust me guys you'll live not to regret this decision," I had been right, and for the past twenty-nine years for the most part none of us had regretted not taking that plane.

Vic left after an hour, then as the afternoon wore on it was time for us to leave. Trish and I stopped and had one last chat with Gwen before leaving, "If there's anything at all you need our help with, just say the word and we'll get it done." She assured us that everything was under control, making us promise that we would all get together in a week or so when things had settled down. "I need to talk to all of you about how Bob wanted his ashes scattered."

We agreed to be there for her, helping any way we could.

"He really loved you guys, you know that don't you?" she said, bringing both of us to unabashed tears.

Prior to heading home, I caught up with Harry and Dan, arranging to meet later to share a personal final farewell to our great friend.

EPILOGUE

It was just after nine o'clock when we all pulled into the parking lot of a small pub on Findlay Road. Dan and Harry left their cars there and climbed into mine. We then headed north on highway 97 toward Vernon. It was a roundabout way to go, but eventually we arrived at a mini-storage facility that had been around since the mid-eighties. At the access gate I entered a code into a keypad, and it immediately began to retract, allowing us to drive straight to one of the midsized storage lockers.

Harry jumped out and opened the lock for the unit. Once we parked the car, we joined Harry in front of the roll-up door that was raising as we joined him. A foot behind the overhead door was a canvas tarp strung from side to side. Dan scooted to the side of the storage unit, and placed his fingers on the light switch. Harry rolled the door down as we stood between it and the tarp, and as it thumped to a close, Dan switched on the interior light, and we slipped between a slit in the tarp to the interior of the storage locker.

We began renting the locker when we formed our personal investment club. There were four comfortable chairs in the middle of the storage space, with a thirty-six-inch round coffee table nestled in the centre. We'd stocked the room with a selection of liqueurs and red wines, and had a mini fridge to hold, beer pop and white wine.

I removed a sealed bottle of Grand Marnier from one of the shelves. We had originally purchased four bottles of Mumm's Cordon Rouge, when we started our club, sharing the first one the week after the heist when we began to sort through all the goods, with the intention of opening one any time one of us passed away. At the time, we were still in disbelief that we had managed to do what we set out to accomplish months earlier.

We later found out that the Champagne would only last three to five years in the fridge, so we ended up drinking a bottle on the anniversary of the heist for the next three years,

Dan grabbed three tumblers off one of the shelves built around the room, while I uncorked the 'Nectar of the Gods.'

I poured out three glasses of the amber liquid and once again we raised our glasses, and gave our traditional salute to Bob.

Then sitting in the silence we enjoyed our drinks, until I broke the tranquillity of the moment, "I had another nightmare last night," I sighed as I looked up at the other two. "You guys ever have them?"

"I can't remember my dreams at the best of times. Last one I remember was having a big eagle swoop down, sink his talons into my dog, and then fly off with him. Must have chased that bird for blocks. First thing I did that morning was to go check to see if the dog was still there," laughed Harry.

"I've certainly remembered a lot of great dreams," said Dan. "Not exactly ones I can tell Rita about, that's for sure. I've read that there are a lot of people who have trouble figuring out when they wake up whether they had just had a dream or whether they were recalling an actual past event."

"As for you, Harry. I'm still pissed at you every time I wake up from a night like that, realizing it was you who even suggested the idea for us to fly out of town, then I get even more pissed that we all went along with the idea, but as I've said too many times, it really was the best decision of our lives to drive home" I said.

By the time we arrived back in Kelowna after the heist it was one-o-clock in the morning, we unloaded the loot, and left it untouched for over a week. The next morning, the heist had been all over the news. In the following days, we picked up copies of *The Province* and *The Sun*, Vancouver's major daily newspapers. It was probably a stupid thing to do or maybe just vanity, either way, copies of those papers now hung on the walls of our storage locker, like a shrine. If the place had ever caught fire and someone had needed to open up the locker, as they used to say in the old movies, the jig would have been up. It was a scenario that thankfully hadn't come to pass. There were bold headlines, reporting on the heist over the days and weeks that followed.

There were stories about how our heist may have been one of the largest of all time, something that would probably never be proven because a lot of the owners of the deposit boxes might never come forward to claim what was missing.

One of the reports talked about what a mess we had left, and that the value of loot left behind was enormous, possibly in the millions of dollars.

Headlines took over the front pages of the papers for days, in large bold face type about police knee-deep in loot, and how mad the patrons of the vault had been upon discovering their possessions had been stolen from what had been advertised as the safest vaults in the west.

There were stories comparing our heist to the Baker Street robbery in England years earlier, but in that robbery all the suspects had been captured.

One of the storylines that took up vast amounts of print was the speculation that the robbery had been carried out with military planning and precision, concluding, it had to have been the work of master criminals, how it must have taken months or years to plan and execute. That one always brought a smile to our face. "If only they knew," we said on more than one occasion. The police admitted that they had issues with the thousands of fingerprints from the ransacked vaults, because a lot of the vault's clients had no desire to let the police take their prints for elimination purposes and with so many prints in such a public place it might have taken years to identify them all.

It was two weeks after the heist when I saw a headline that stopped me in my tracks. Huge quantity of drugs found in pilfered vaults: This story talked about a stockpile of cocaine being found in one of the large deposit boxes. They had never proved that it had belonged to the holder of that box. There was no story of the millions I had left in what I was sure was Chang's other box. When that was reported, I had to come clean with the guys about what I had found in the four boxes I was sure belonged to Chang.

According to Vic, when Chang heard of the heist, he had been apoplectic, making it known throughout the underworld that he would destroy whoever had been responsible for the break-in at the vaults. He would have known if there was another triad involved, so his attention was focused on other groups of criminals throughout the lower mainland. Informants within the department assured Chang that the police had no clues as to the identity of the thieves. Chang had reached out to contacts across Canada and the US, letting it be known that he was taking this incident very personally, and that the perpetrators would suffer death by one or all of the triad's methods. His retribution would be taken out on family members of those responsible as well.

Vic did tell me that a year after the heist, arrests were finally made, as the police were able get fingerprints off the packages of cocaine found in a deposit box at the vaults. These prints allowed them to build a case against Chang's associates. Other fingerprints found on the packages of drugs confirmed they had been in the possession of the three men who had died during a shootout on the docks. It took months of work by a special task force, but they finally put an air-tight case together which lead to the arrest of Chang and other triad members on dozens of charges. Weapons seized at the time of the arrest allowed them to close certain cold case files, including two of the three men killed at the docks.

I looked at one of the stories that mentioned how one policeman working in the vault,

"thought he had trodden on a piece of rubble – but when he looked, he found a diamond embedded in the sole of his shoe." As I looked at the story it reminded me of the Paul Simon song, "Diamonds on the souls of her shoes," and started to hum the tune.

"I wonder what kind of a ring we could have had made up with the diamond that was stuck in the bottom of that cop's shoe," I asked.

We reminisced about Bob, what he had accomplished, his passions, and his giving nature. We had not been as close once we all began to travel a lot, in some cases not seeing each other for six months at a time. We spoke of how each of us would miss his quick wit and companionship.

"You said when we first got here tonight that you were still pissed at me for ever suggesting flying. Did you know that for years Bob was none too happy with you for not letting him take that gorgeous bracelet and necklace? He finally got over it when that story showed up on the tenth anniversary of the heist with a picture of those pieces of jewelry. It was that article about some of the things we didn't take at the time. After seeing the story, he realized you had been right all along. He never said anything because he knew it would just piss you off, and even though it bugged him he knew it wasn't really worth having a fight about," said Dan.

"He never said a word to me about it, even when it was just the two of us together," I replied.

"That's just the way he was," added Harry.

With our recognition to Bob complete, we locked up and I drove them back to the pub where we said our goodnights and headed off home. Driving home I pondered the events that had taken place since that eventful night. "'All Those Years Ago,' George Harrison 1981," I said, still playing my own personal game of trivia.

For the longest time, we all had been scared shitless every time the doorbell rang, fearing that we might find a cop standing on the other side of the door holding a warrant for our arrest. Our fears increased when we learned that Chang was bent on revenge. Every time one of us encountered people of Chinese decent we would wonder if they were a triad assassin who had tracked us down to kill our entire family.

Over the following months our investment club would meet at the pub then drive to the locker, spending evenings sorting through the items looted from the vault. We had installed shelves in the locker prior to the heist to hold the loot we hoped we would return with.

When we had first sorted our booty, there had been shelves of bearer bonds, stacks of Canadian and American currency, pounds of gold in one section and silver in another. We still had a peanut butter jar with loose diamonds in it. We pegged the final tally of everything we stole at eight point three million, not including the diamonds. We had ended up with a total of thirty-six-hundred Troy ounces of gold, the bearer bonds totaled one point two million, over two million Canadian dollars and three million in US currency. The fifty pounds of silver we ended up with was only worth sixty-four hundred bucks back in 1988.

Bob had used what was left of his depleted slush fund and I had used a hunk of my inheritance from mom and dad to seed our investment club. We began with a forty-thousand-dollar purchase of Royal Bank of Canada Shares in 1989 and by 2000 it was worth over 170,000 dollars, not including the dividends that also went directly into our account. This was small potatoes compared to other investments we ended up making.

Considering all the planning we had put into the robbery itself, we had never given a lot of thought to how we could turn the diamonds and gold into real money. One of the things we hadn't expected was that gold would drop in value to the extent it did. It had fallen from $380 an ounce all the way to $290 by 1998. It wasn't until 2003 that our gold reserve rose above what it was worth when we first stole it.

The problem we faced was that we were not criminals in the true sense of the word, even though we had pulled off an incredible heist, getting away with millions. The exact amount was never determined by the police because a lot of people never came forward with a list of what they had lost.

In the movies, there was always a nefarious person that would give you a certain percentage of what you had stolen for "clean cash", but we didn't have a fence. We had used up the Canadian currency first. Getting rid of the gold had not been as easy as we thought it might have been. I hadn't noticed when we first found the wafers in Mom and Dad's deposit box but most of the pieces of gold we had in our possession had serial numbers and the name of the institution who had issued the ingot engraved on the gold.

I had thought it would be as easy as taking the pieces to the bank and getting cash for them. Most of the banks however would only give cash for pieces that had been originally sold by them. The CIBC bank wouldn't take one from the Royal Bank, and most of them wanted the original certificates that came with the wafers, and we had none of these.

Even though the gold prices didn't get back to the $380 range until 2003, we did slowly start selling some of the pieces around 1995. We had found that we could take up to $10,000 worth of gold at a time to local gold merchants in various cities when we travelled and sell them without too many questions asked. The price was discounted from the spot price of gold at the time, but it was necessary to take what we were offered. By 2003 the spot price was over $400 per ounce.

We had split the gold into four equal shares, leaving it up to each of us to dispose of as we saw fit. I still have four hundred Troy ounces stored in several safe deposit boxes, which in today's market is worth over $600,000 Canadian.

We finally got a value on the diamonds we had sacked. In 1988, we had a quantity of loose diamonds with an estimated value over half a million dollars on the retail market. Harry's friend in the jewellery business revealed that the retail value was in the realm of twelve hundred for a good half-carat diamond and over three thousand dollars for a diamond of one carat in size. He told us that diamond prices were based on the four C's: cut, clarity, colour and carat weight. The street value of the diamonds we had come up with was very rough as none of us were experts. The ones we have left are still worth a lot of money.

We put cash aside to cover the cost of the locker for the foreseeable future. We had now paid over $25,000 in rent for the small locker. Everything else was divided into four equal piles.

We kept our vow not to spend any of the loot for a full five years, and after that we could each do whatever we wanted with our share. We still had to be smart, not doing outlandish things that we couldn't explain. It's not like we could tell everyone we won the lottery. There was too much publicity, making it easy to prove that we really hadn't won a thing. Dan had continued to buy his share of lottery tickets over the years, never winning more than one or two hundred dollars at any one time. One of the things we knew would be a red flag for Revenue Canada was if we all started living beyond our regular lifestyles. Having regular, well-paying jobs allowed us to slowly improve those lifestyles. Going out to dinner at a fancy restaurant once a week was one thing, but ending up with an Aston Martin or thirty-five foot Bayliner in the driveway was another thing entirely.

We thought taking the bearer bonds had been a smart thing to do because they were not registered in a person's name. The problem we discovered was because they had been issued mostly by American companies, various states and the US government, we needed to contact American bond agents. Certain companies who had issued these bonds were no longer in business, so those bonds were now stapled to the wall of the locker. As it was, it took us years to cash in on a variety of the government-issued bonds.

It took time for our American cash to dwindle. Bank regulations for deposits of over ten thousand dollars cash prevented us from taking in a large amount to a bank at any one time.

Each of us had set up accounts at a variety of banks and credit unions throughout the Interior. Each was set up with two of us having access to these accounts, so that if one of us died we would be able to cash out the account. We would then arrange for that money to go to a variety of charities each of us had chosen. The surviving spouse would get the shares of the investment club to do with as they wanted.

We used every legal option to ensure that these basic accounts would not produce any interest. We didn't want the bank sending us a lot of tax slips showing we had earned a lot of interest on these accounts which would prove difficult to explain on our individual tax returns.

We had opened American money accounts in each of these. The people in these banks must have thought we must be either very good or very lucky gamblers. At a variety of times we would go into a different bank, depositing anywhere between five and eight thousand American dollars into our US accounts.

Whenever we travelled to the States, we would take the American cash with us. I had managed to open an account in Orville, Washington. It took extra work to get it set up, but once I did, I could drive across the border south of Osoyoos and deposit US cash in the Wells Fargo Bank there. Dan had opted to open one at a branch of the Bank of America in Las Vegas. He and Rita loved it there, travelling down there at least once every three or four months.

Probably the toughest part of the whole ordeal was finding creative ways to make certain our wives never suspected where we kept coming up with the green stuff that over the years had made all our lives so painless. When a serial killer is apprehended, you hear people asking how the killer could have hidden in plain sight for so many years. The wife or family must have known that there was a problem. Neighbors would comment that the heinous killer next door was just a normal guy, always seemed friendly, appeared to be a great father and doted on his kids. Nobody had died in our caper, but I would testify that we had all become accomplished serial liars.

Anyone asking our wives how we had managed to make all our money would be told what we influenced them to believe, and that was that our little investment club had invested shrewdly and wisely in a variety of the twenty-five most successful companies on the market over the years. We had invested in stocks which were held jointly by our investment club. Microsoft, Cisco, International Gambling Technologies and Home Depot. Some of these stocks had risen by over twenty-three hundred percent.

Trish had been very sceptical when I first told her how I wanted to use a portion of my inheritance to help fund the start-up of our investment club, but in the end, she agreed to let me use some of it to invest in our future. With the money we got when we finally sold Mom and Dad's house, we had been able to pay off our own mortgage, so she had been willing to "gamble" with some of the remainder.

To get the motel completely rebuilt after the fire, Bob had co-signed for a loan because we realized we couldn't just show up with a suitcase full of cash to pay the insurance company for the shortfall. Then, as the Starlite completed its rebuild, which had taken over a year, a major hotel chain had purchased the property. Kelowna's growth, and the charm of the Okanagan had started to explode in the late eighties, and the rebuilt Starlite fit right into the chain's niche. Harry and Pam got back into the housing market, and built a suite in the basement of their house for his mom. After finally getting rid of the albatross that had hung around his neck for years, Harry found a job with one of the emerging tech companies that had opened in Kelowna. He retired from that company as Vice President of Innovation in 2005, after which he and Pam had also ended up doing a lot of travelling.

Dan had been patient, waiting until we cashed in some of the bearer bonds. In January 1993, he finally realized his dream by opening his own state of the art private lab that did testing of polymers, as well as material failure analysis. Dan had patented testing methods to determine the cause of rubber, plastic and coating failures. While he had been waiting for us to cash in the bonds, he had designed some advanced instrumentation and testing equipment. His concept was to use the minimum amount of equipment that would give the maximum amount of information to the customer in the shortest time. In 2004, Dan sold the business off to a world leader in the field. He and Rita had been taking trips to vacation spots around the world ever since.

Bob had done exactly what he said he would do. He spent years prior to the sale of his practice telling everyone that he planned on retiring in five years and that when he did, he would buy a sailboat and spend half his time in the Caribbean. When we finally started to cash out our loot, much to the surprise of everyone he really did sell his practice. Patients and staff members were shocked that he was really doing what he said he was going to do for the past five years. After the sale, he and Gwen had taken trips for months at a time. With the proceeds from the sale of his share of the clinic and practice, he bought a sailboat which he kept moored in the Bahama's. He and Gwen spent months touring the Caribbean, and the eastern seaboard of the US and Mexico.

Deciding it was time to start giving back, he and Gwen joined up with Doctors Without Borders, spending years travelling with them to wherever they were needed, splitting their time away between their home in Kelowna and their boat in the Bahamas. Except for his final trip to Syria, Gwen had always gone along, assisting him wherever disasters would take them.

Bob had been able to sell a considerable number of diamonds on his travels, taking small amounts of them on his trips abroad. During his first trip as a volunteer doctor, we told him to use any money he received for the diamonds to help anywhere he saw fit. We let him use his discretion with the diamonds to do charitable works.

As for Trish and me, I continued to work for the same company I had been with for seventeen years, right up to 1993 when life became interesting. I often wonder if my dream years earlier had been a premonition, because one morning I did get a call from my boss telling me I had to meet with him. At that meeting, I got the spiel about tough economic times and was sent off with a severance package eerily similar to the one in my nightmare so many years before.

For years prior to my layoff, I told Trish how incredible it would be to travel the world, telling her that we should sell the house and home school the girls. Her fear had always been of not having a home to return to. When I got my notice, I assured her we could keep the house. She accepted the fact that we were financially stable thanks to the investments I had made with the inheritance and our investment club. She finally gave in and our family spent the next three years going wherever we wanted, with the girls choosing our first destination by throwing darts at a world map. We met up with Bob and Gwen during one trip, spending a month sailing around the Caribbean with them.

We returned home so the girls could experience the last few years of high school and graduate with their classes. It was a little tough for them both to settle back into the groove of attending a real school, but in the end they agreed it was the best thing they could have done. Trish and I couldn't be prouder of how they turned out, but I wouldn't trade those years of travel for anything. Both girls are successful in their chosen careers, and Trish and I are proud grandparents to a beautiful little six-year-old. Maybe we'll be able to take her to wonderful places soon.

I guess if I don't leave this world in a sudden catastrophe, I'm going to have to tell Trish about our loot, and where it came from. I've thought of doing it many times over the years and I think that the other guys had considered it as well.

One thing that I wondered about from time to time was whether or not we had ended up breaking into the deposit box owned by Mr. and Mrs. Penny. All the other people we stole from had been anonymous. I don't know why, but I had always hoped that we had left their valuables where they had been.

There would be a good payout to Gwen from Bob's share of our investments. When we began the investment club we used an accountant and lawyer to properly incorporate our club, with each of us having an equal number of shares. We used a brokerage company to buy and sell shares in various stocks, and each year our company paid the appropriate taxes on the taxable gains and then paid each of us a dividend to our own personal accounts, which helped to keep our personal taxes lower.

We didn't want to end up like Al Capone. His days as a mob boss in Chicago ended in 1931 when he was convicted to eleven years in prison for tax evasion. We were much happier to be compared with D.B. Cooper, who was a legend that had never been caught. There had been a lot of speculation over the years about who could have pulled off such a successful heist, but no one ever considered it could have been accomplished by four ordinary, average guys.

Dear Reader:

I first read about this incredible heist the week after I moved away from Vancouver in January of 1977. I couldn't believe the headlines at the time. The real thieves *were* captured on a plane at the airport in Vancouver because a luggage handler huffed and puffed and couldn't get a suitcase off the ground. When the suitcase was opened they discovered millions in gold, jewels and cash.

It wasn't until the Monday morning that the vault staff discovered the robbery had taken place and that the thieves had cut through the theoretically impregnable wall of thirty-four inches of concrete and steel encasing the private downtown Vancouver vault.

The idea that these men had pulled off the perfect robbery only to be caught at the airport always made me wonder: If they hadn't tried to fly back east and had driven instead, would they have made a clean getaway? Over the years, I have asked myself time and again, "Why did they decide to take a plane?" One day I hope to get the answer.

Four of the five men involved in this brilliant and daring heist in Vancouver received prison sentences of five to eight years. A fifth member of the gang skipped out on his $50,000 bail, and there was always speculation that the mastermind of the crime ended up getting away with at least a million dollars and that he may have flown to South America on a private jet. For him, maybe crime *did* pay.

The more I thought about it, the more the idea for my story began to take shape. I really don't know if I could have talked three of my law-abiding friends into joining me in the caper I describe in the book. I know some of them would have been tempted, but would they have taken the leap?

How about you? Do you think you could convince your best friends to help you to pull off a world class heist?

ABOUT THE AUTHOR

Don Levers has been making up stories to entertain his daughters and granddaughter for four decades. His first book was based on the legendary lake monster Ogopogo. In 1985 he self-published a children's book, *Ogopogo the Misunderstood Lake Monster*, which has sold over 25,000 copies.

In 1987 Don began work on *Loot for the Taking*, which was inspired by real events. His own life events delayed completing the book. After being caught in a corporate shuffle in the early nineties, he went into business for himself, running it successfully for eighteen years. After selling his business in Victoria and retiring early, he and his wife Deb built their dream house just outside of Edmonton where they now live full time. With the house complete, Don had time to return to his passion of finishing his first full-length novel. He is currently working on his second book, *Terminal Vengeance*, and is confident that this one won't take thirty years to complete.

ACKNOWLEDGEMENTS

I want to thank all the people who helped in the writing of *Loot for the Taking* over the years. I found it truly amazing the things people will share when they find out you are writing a book. Thanks to Mark McGahey for taking on the editing and polishing job and being so detail oriented. Finally, words cannot express my thanks to my wife and family for spending countless hours proofreading the various drafts of the over the years. I couldn't have done it without everyone's help.

CPSIA information can be obtained
at www.ICGtesting.com
Printed in the USA
LVOW03s0713170717
541627LV00001B/1/P